EARTH-BOUND

LAURA POWER

Winter Goose
Publishing

Winter Goose Publishing
2701 Del Paso Road, 130-92
Sacramento, CA 95835

www.wintergoosepublishing.com
Contact Information: info@wintergoosepublishing.com

Earth-Bound

COPYRIGHT © 2014 by Laura Power

ISBN: 978-1-941058-10-7

First Edition, April 2014

Cover Art by Winter Goose Publishing
Typesetting by Odyssey Books

Published in the United States of America

This book is dedicated wholeheartedly to you
for taking a chance on Air-Born

welcome back

The Slimmest of Chances

Shadows slithered uneasily across a low ceiling dripping with gnarled stalactites. A chill crept along Amber's skin as she followed Rraarl through into the next chamber; she hadn't expected the swift-flowing ink-black water or the jagged shadows lancing across the low ceiling. Rraarl was already across the river.

Even as she glanced to him she registered the blur from the water, and as the Vetch's banshee shriek knifed her heart she saw the Gargoyle turn; heard his roar of vengeance; felt the cavern explode into their mortal struggle as the river erupted and Rraarl plunged.

Amber didn't hear the scream that tore from her throat; didn't register the distance she'd crossed before she was scouring the river frantically. Yet she could hear nothing roar but the waters; saw nothing rage but the foam.

He couldn't be gone. He couldn't have survived all those torturous years, only to now—

The flickering figure hovered before Rraarl's eyes as he grappled with the yielding water, a deadweight falling through a sunless sea, the vibrant glitter of the air above fading with all possibility of survival. Memories escaped him like bubbles, sweeping his mind to the far surface while his body failed—the choking pain of nights long past, the chains, the cries, the torch-lit touch in the darkness, the breath of life, the starlight and sunrises warmed by companionship and trust, the mirror, the words, the girl . . .

And then his body jolted to the riverbed and even those thoughts faded into an endless void.

Choking down her panic, Amber raced along the river's course until it broke from the tunnel's dark hold and its surface spilled freely again in the wide, life-giving air. Yet the torrent twisted fast and thick and inescapable, black and suffocating as oil. She stumbled, dazzled by the bright sky of a Realm where the sun should never shine again. From here she could go no further, for the water dropped steep and fierce to ground, sweeping into a writhing torrent that swept beneath the rock to race the rest of the way unseen.

Numbed by her failure, unable to tear her eyes from the spot where the river disappeared with any chance of finding him, Amber's time freefell into a ragged dissociation where the only thing real was the desperate ache of a grief that had yet to take its deepest hold.

En route to Loban, Jasper, in the first instant bewildered and in the next terrified, found Amber at the riverside, screaming Rraarl's name with all the grief of the Realm, about to—

"No!" He lunged for her, catching her shoulders and pulling her back.

"He went under!" She kept struggling as if crazed. "The Vetches; he went after them—I was at the other end of the tunnel, I couldn't reach him and I couldn't stop them—Jasper, I lost him."

"We're not losing you as well!" he shouted over her hoarse pleas, his own voice shaking, clinging to her as she fought him. "You can't save him, Amber—not this time. We can't win against the Vetches. And it nearly killed me last time trying to get him out of open, shallow water, when we could find him, with all three of us helping. Amber, look at me: he protected you in life; don't do anything stupid now. For his sake, listen to reason."

Finally, his words registered, and beneath his steady gaze the wildness in her eyes subsided.

He loosened his grip apologetically, and instantly she shoved him backwards and ran for the edge.

"Amber!" he bellowed, skidding helplessly to the side as he saw her jump, but she had already disappeared amongst the roiling surge.

The lung-crushing cold of the water sobering her instantly, Amber floundered towards the bank, spluttering violently, until tearing fistfuls of clod in her haste she dragged herself from the river's deathly clutches and lay shivering and bone-chilled in the now freezing air, tasting mud and tears against her lips.

"Get up," the Prince commanded, clasping her numbed hands in his and hauling, but his voice had never been softer and he spoke not a word of reprimand.

"Good work," he advised as she unprotestingly let him replace her sodden shirt and cloak with his dry ones, her haunted gaze locked on the churning waters as if she would never be able to turn away. "What's going to happen now is we're going to leave together in twenty minutes and get you somewhere warm, so your next step is to go in and say goodbye. It might give you some measure of peace," he added carefully. *They'll be far away by now, so it's got to be safe*, he added to himself, trying to anchor the reason in reality.

Amber visibly trembled. "I don't want peace. Not when it means giving up hope."

"Then don't say goodbye," Jasper soothed, his voice threatening to betray his emotion. "Don't listen to me. You knew him better. Talk to him as you did. Time pauses for some words. Say what needs to be said. Say what's right."

He let her cling to him for a moment, hoping his body could warm hers as he encircled her sadly in his arms, wishing he could protect her from such hurts of the Realm. Then resignedly he let her go, watching her stumble into the cave as if each faltering step were a certainty displaced by a trauma that he wasn't sure she'd ever successfully renegotiate.

Amber's first thought, when the shadows loomed and his last roar tore through her mind, was to curl up in a corner; just hide and never come out, and then nothing would have, could have, happened. But, forcing the terror of their last shared moments into the furthest places of her thoughts and clutching instead the better memories she had made with him, she found the strength to continue.

And instead of finding herself assailed by flashbacks of the Vetches, she felt Rraarl's touch when she reached to the walls and heard the heavy chink of his footfalls in the echoes of her own, as the darkness seemed now to welcome her into its concealing embrace. She'd had no reason to be afraid of it when he was here, so how could she be now, when it had sheltered him and been something they'd shared? And here in the lightless void he could be waiting at every corner, watching her, guarding her, waiting to be rediscovered.

But the rock was just rock, and the shadows returned to what they had been before him: the recesses of fears. As the refuge of darkness dwindled beneath the unforgiving brightening of the passage, she could no longer hide, raw grief gnawing into her chest, consuming her until she howled and choked and gasped for breath.

Sinking to the ground she sensed herself falling as if a gaping chasm had torn the Realm asunder and she felt the abyss rush past, dragging away everything she knew. In desperation her hands clung to the ice and she felt it bite; felt the hot blood squeeze from her scuffed skin, anchored for a moment in the knowledge she was still here—but the memory of his gaze pierced sharper than the dread fog of her emotions and she cried out in defiance, strengthened by the remembrance of his hands catching her fist and her fingers closing round his.

Clinging to the recollection she withdrew her hands, scraped herself back together, and dragged herself up. Stumbling resolutely on to the last place she had seen Rraarl, Amber stood gazing at the gnarled crags until she saw him in every trace of the cavern ceiling, in every silhouette of rock jutting from the distance.

And through the imaginings something real returned, and she grasped it fiercely to her despite the desperate pain, her throat twisting and her eyes sore and dry, for clearly visible in the half-light the words he'd scratched such a short time ago lay still in the ice; one half of a conversation she'd never finish. As she leant over the precious words to touch them, to feel close to him again, hot tears fell, hissing meltingly into the ice and streaking the words into a meaningless blur. She drew her hand across them in a silent goodbye, her soul curling into a tight ball of misery as shakily she stood.

Treading numbly back to the entrance, blind to the returning light, she dully felt the Prince's hand upon her shoulder as he steered her outside again. The journey back drifted into a detached haze. She remembered following Jasper. She remembered knowing that she had to, despite everything.

Dusk fell heaviest that evening, and as Amber trudged the lonely road to Arkh Loban, heedless of the wonders she had been able to see by Rraarl's side, the winds sang a lament through a darkness now menacing instead of magical that would never again yield his silent presence, through a Realm forever changed, forever colder.

Thinking that she wanted to be left alone, Jasper walked behind, worrying at every step whether it would be worse to lag further or risk getting nearer; until she glanced at a shadow and he was beside her, and at the word she spoke so quietly it sounded like the last scrap of strength escaping on her breath he knew his choice had been right.

"Life's never going to get back to normal, is it?" Her voice shivered, more fragile than the leaves scudding in the fretful breeze.

Jasper stared into the empty darkness. "Not the same version as before, no. But mayhap your task now is to carve out a new 'normal', and sew together a continuation of your life. You will feel better than this again, Amber. You will even feel happiness again. It might be more tremulous, but it will also be even more gratefully grasped and deeply experienced."

As he drew his cloak around her, Loban rose palely shimmering through the desert night to beckon them on towards the loved who were yet living, the sweeping winds bearing beside them the memories of those departed worth living for.

A Fortune of Sorts

"I will not be party to this!" Naya stepped into Nabb's path with her jaw set, the shadows jumping in the swift-falling desert sun as the light sank irretrievably behind the stables. Maybe she couldn't stop him, but she could buy the foal time.

The Authority pushed closer with a sneer. "You?" he spat derisively. "What choice do *you* have?"

"The one you can never take from me." Naya's dark eyes flashed, and it took all her self-control to keep her voice measured. "Despite what you have tried to drill into me, there is nothing binding me here. It is true I have no other job to go to, that I have little savings and no idea where to go—but once I have faced those details, what is left? No more reasons." She locked her gaze with his, no longer trusting herself to speak.

Her manager merely smirked. "Why do you care for the Unicorn?" he asked lightly. "You are a peasant, a servant, and a girl; you will never ride such beasts. The Emperor would not have allowed it, in his infinite wisdom, and neither will I. You will pay for your crime, wench. You will be brought before the high councillor, and all shall hear his judgement of you."

"The words of such a false and twisted impostor deserve no such audience," Naya spat back, unable to keep her voice in check any longer, her hands grasping the pitchfork with such coiled anger that even the Authority dared not, just at this moment, punish her indiscretion with anything stronger than oaths and curses.

"I do not ask you to release me from your service," Naya finished, summoning the last dregs of her failing courage. "I will waste no such courtesy on you." Even as the words tumbled from her lips she could feel her Realm spiralling out of control, and the knowledge that her own reckless hand had set in motion events that would decide her future sent the bile rising to her throat. She could only stand in silent witness to the irrevocably changing course playing out, and focus all her strength on masking her fear until this was over and she could run to Taiko under the cover of darkness and bury her head in his mane.

"You wouldn't dare leave," Nabb dismissed. "You walk from here, you'll lose any semblance of protection granted to you by my patronage."

"Maybe so," Naya countered, composed now, her voice steady with conviction. "Yet I will walk from here a free woman, with no man's noose around my neck. Your 'protection' was neither requested nor required, and my soul will be lighter without it."

"You're safer in here than you'll ever be out there," Nabb cajoled her, for a moment sounding like the man she used to think she knew. "You weren't doing too badly. You'd have a place here for life, if you learned to keep your mouth shut and your head down. It's foolish in such times to wish for more."

"Then foolish I will be!" Naya snapped back indignantly, rapidly losing her grip on her temper.

"Go, then," he mocked, his voice dangerously quiet. "There is good reason why these gates are shut before nightfall. You'll curse the day you decided you no longer valued our security."

He would have dragged her out forcibly but she twisted and ran, nearly falling over her skirts in her haste. The great wooden doors groaned shut for the last time behind her, and she heard the metal bars slam on a Realm she was no longer part of.

And although she had never bought the services they so frequently offered; although she had resisted the incentives of their schemes; although she had risked her life every week to filter their information to Roanen, right now having left terrified her more completely than all the months she had whiled her life away there put together. Yet as the wind moaned its relief across the sand-strewn cobbles of the empty street, lifting the subtle, expansive scent of freedom as only the desert night could, Naya faced the darkness with a gleam in her eye.

Her doubts crumbled beneath the tread of her boots with every step she took as resolutely she pushed the stray strands of hair back from her face, adjusted her bag of meagre possessions slung across her shoulders, and started walking. There was just one more thing she had to do before she could put this accursed place behind her for good.

Hurrying through the chill night, as the scrublands beyond the sand flats spilled in a jubilant moon-blanched welcome before her, Naya broke into a run, feeling for the first time since her fateful decision, amongst the maelstrom of jittering emotions, the thrill of conviction that her choice had been right.

"Taiko!" she called as loudly as she dared, trying to keep her voice as level as possible for his sake despite her churning nerves.

A low whinny shivered through the darkness, chasing back the ghosts in her mind, and impossibly she felt the years fall back until she were a child again, watching him canter towards her with the same pulse of excitement she had known all those nights ago when she rescued him from the Authorities just after starting work at the stables.

The skewbald snorted in recognition, thrusting his whiskered muzzle towards her in his familiar snuffled greeting, and Naya rubbed her hands over his neck to stop them shaking. Taiko, her beloved Taiko— half dray horse, half who-knew-what—her confidante, confessor, and as stalwart a companion as the constraints of her working surrounded by the Authorities would allow. His ears twitched forwards, alert with interest despite the strange hour of her arrival as he watched her through deep liquid eyes much calmer than her own, his breath clouding in the chill of desert night like Genie smoke. To Naya, though, his own presence was just as thrilling an omen.

"Oh, Taiko, you don't know what your mistress has done," she murmured, spilling the thoughts she couldn't voice in front of anyone else. Her throat burned with the effort of not crying, and she cursed the clumsiness her emotions had wrought upon her fingers as she ran her hands across his coat, tugging gently through the coarse mane as she remembered all the times when as a young girl she had sneaked him out under the cover of darkness to the night-cooled paddocks after sheltering him through the blazing daylight hours, and sought solace in telling her dreams to the only listener who would not laugh.

How many times had she promised him that one day they would ride out together with only the sun and moon for their witnesses, far away from the staff who had once abused him, to the very corners of the Realm, free as the Unicorns Roanen said still roamed the hidden places?

Now she was making it happen, and yet she was scared—mortally so, for could she really trust herself to shape the void stretching out before her, slipping irreversibly closer so fast it made her catch her breath and so charged with the unknown that for a second she almost wished she could stay where she was, even though she hated the place, just so things wouldn't change? Could she really risk the doom-mongering voices of days to come proving right and unveiling her before all as an impostor?

You've wanted this all your yesterdays, Naya berated herself fiercely. *You'll want it all your tomorrows, and it hinges on today. Your nightmares haven't broken you, so how can your dreams? These troubles will soon prove but a footnote in a previous chapter: just another obstacle that increased your later triumph.* Naya curved her lips into a shaky smile. *Mayhap not soon, but definitely one day.* She'd believed in those words so much more when she'd been saying them to Seb.

"You have to live your own life," Roanen had told her, when she had questioned him on the hardships of his nomadic existence. "It will not be easy, but it will be your own, and you can ask for and receive no more." *Oh Roanen*, she thought now. *You have more faith in me than I do. What if I can't live up to that?*

"Look, this won't do, will it?" she admonished herself aloud for Taiko's benefit, belatedly realising that she'd have to ride him home bareback, and scrounge new tack from her brother to replace what must now remain where she could no longer return. "I'm only in such a bad mood because this was my own accursed choice, but if I had none, we'd be in a far worse state, wouldn't we? So," she vowed, scratching his jaw affectionately as a smile slid across her face at the recollection of the poem still in her apron pocket that she'd read earlier—mere days ago when such things seemed the only way out, "mayhap there's no knight in shining armour who's going to ride up upon his white horse; and brandish his sword, and smash through the door, and take me away out of there."

Awkwardly without the aid of stirrups and saddle, she swung herself onto Taiko's back, and her grin widened—it was so long since she'd ridden bareback; it spoke of a time much younger and freer. "But I can get my own white horse, I'm done with hesitating; I'm going to jump on that white horse right now, ride like the wind—I can pick the knight up later!"

His snorted breath misted like dragon's smoke in the chill of the desert night as Taiko caught her excitement and reared up, and she whooped and clung to his mane, the Realm's possibilities scattering star-like before her as she urged him into a gallop and they raced across the featureless sands towards the Golden Griffin—Loban's last remaining haunt of heroes.

Night of Shah-Does

The night hung heavily beneath the desert stars. So much was now lost, her mind railed. And yet not everything, her soul whispered: Amber couldn't remember at which point Racxen had found them, nor the moment when Jasper had wordlessly pressed ahead into the darkness, awkward in his helplessness—but as a night splintered into pieces drew around them, the only constant she knew was that Racxen was there. There when words could be said and nothing could be done save for just being there. The hours blurred; she could hardly breathe, let alone talk. And yet he walked beside her. He stayed.

The stars hovered mutely behind a veil of carefully neutral night, as if they could no longer bear to shine fully. Yet shine they did, softly and insistently, whilst beneath their unjudging, unflinching gaze Amber finally released the burden of howling misery and anger and desperation into sobs and yells and bitter, bitter tears. Her Realm crumbled into the gasping rush of breath that could not be regulated; and misery that she feared could not but be sustained, and the gaping desert bore her screams and pleas without question or answer. And the shadow next to her knelt to hold her; a solid anchor against the rushing, drowning plunge of injustice; a container against the terrifying fear of fragmentation as she felt her soul flail and strain against itself, as if her mind were trying to flee from each of its own corners in a desperate attempt at saving even one sliver of itself, and she feared it would succeed in splitting itself into a hundred bleeding shards.

And yet Racxen wrapped his soul around them all and didn't bleed, but held her tighter, and she knew she could piece the fragments back together, and with a dry-lipped, wet-eyed, pressing kiss, attempted it, rocking back on her heels to crouch unaided and pledge it to herself and the sands that were surrounding her. Understanding, he relaxed his hold, shifting to give her space, although his soul squirmed to witness the pain in hers.

She cried until she felt like her heart would be crushed under the pressure; until every last drop of blood would be wrung from it along with her tears.

And yet the desert sands accepted her tears calmly, and swallowed them up so that they were no longer scrunching at her heart and throat and temples, and were instead sustaining the brave, barren-yet-bearing plants striving impossibly through the starving landscape. And so the tears cleansed her soul as a storm cleans the air, and the misery floated out of reach for a while, her soul buoyed temporarily as a cloud newly lightened that has just discharged its intolerable load.

The night settled, or at least drained, into an empty kind of quiet, washed of its tension by the violent passion of the broken tempest. Thus she sat now, exhausted but with a strange sense of tired accomplishment at having come this far midway through the longest night, hunched before the fire Racxen had coaxed into a semblance of life, staring into the sputtering flames to avoid the terrible emptiness of the yawning darkness beyond. The daylight had afforded fleeting distractions, but at night there remained no pretence, nothing to distance her soul from the gaping chasm of loss.

Would she feel more alone if I did not reach out to hold her—or if she were wrapped in my arms only to confront the inevitable: that it would not be enough? Racxen sat quietly next to Amber, thinking automatically of the bargain he had once believed he could never consider for another.

"I'd do it again, you know," he blurted, his heart almost physically hurting as the words spilled out. "If it would transfer your pain to me."

She couldn't answer; too choked, but she squeezed his hand, and her eyes spoke to him.

Racxen growled helplessly in apology. "I know it's only words, I—"

"It's *your* words," she managed shakily in rebuke, clinging to his hand.

"The night changes things," he murmured in response, glancing to the moon, compassion sliding the words out through the choking fear of saying something wrong and making it worse. The gnawing guilt that he could not ease her suffering twisted deeper, but knowing that she would be too scared to sleep for fear of what would visit her unwaking sight, how could he stay silent, no matter how the words tried to squirm into futile wishes and apologies on his tongue?

"I remember a ceremony a few years ago, not dissimilar to your Presentation of the Gems," he disclosed. "The Arraheng initiation into adulthood, marked by a journey made entirely through darkness."

When she looked to him Racxen saw reflected in her reddened eyes not just the desperation to lose herself far away from here in another's story, but also a glimmer of her old curiosity. "I can remember thinking I'd never get through it," he admitted. "When your senses have nothing to latch onto, they have free rein through your mind. The demons flood into you; there is nothing to hold them at bay save for your own resources. At the time it feels as if there can be no respite; that you can do nothing but wait powerless for the light to return.

"But the night does not mean to frighten. If our time were made only of days, we would stumble through life blindly, drowning ourselves in their welcome refuge as best we could with too much to see and hear whilst always fearing we would not be able to handle the alternative. The blessing of daylight hours would become instead a masking superficial glare bringing empty comfort; for it would deny the watcher the triumph of gazing into the darkness to behold the true form of what lies within, instead of the twisted visage framed by the mind's unharnessed thoughts, and learning that it can be met with courage instead of feared as the looming pressure of a growing shadow. It is during the night that your defences build and you grow to trust yourself; to know you have the strength.

"Amber, I wish I could summon a Phoenix out of one of Mugkafb's books to light your path, and bid him stay for as long as you wanted—but you do not need me to fight your battles. You will walk through the darkness and emerge stronger—or rather," he rephrased with an honest shrug, "*you* will think it's a new strength; whereas the rest of us have always seen it, as bright and sure as the lanterns guiding the way across the marshes."

Amber's gaze was calmer now, and the ghost of a smile flickered across her drawn face. "Is that why you've walked all this way with me, when I've been such accursedly bad company, so you could give me strength?"

"No," Racxen shook his head firmly, his voice peaceful despite the wretched mess they were in. "Just to remind you that you already have it."

Life seemed to flow back into her with his words as she lifted her eyes to him. "Anyone who thinks there's no magic left in the Realm," she promised, her voice stronger now as she shifted closer to rest her head against his shoulder, "isn't looking in the right places."

This of all nights could not afford to bring confusion amongst comfort, and so in response he simply found her hand in the darkness, and held it tightly, as he had through so many paths of darkness before. *It is enough to be this for her*, he reminded himself. *Who needs a lover, if friendship can be this?*

"Things can be spoken at night that cannot be by day," he reassured her. "Any Arraheng will tell you so, at least."

Amber managed a watery smile as she scrubbed at her eyes, and dragged a hand over her face. "I just can't stand him not being here. He went through too much to now be—" she gulped a breath, and started again. "Nothing's ever felt more final, and yet it doesn't feel real. I don't think I could cope if it did, but I can't try to block it out, it'd be like denying it happened, denying him—and it's my fault, Racxen, it was because of me he died—"

"Ro," he shushed. "No. It was because of you he lived again. Never forget that. What you did was amazing. And he withstood the Vetches. No one else has lived through that—so do you really think anyone could cause him to do anything he didn't want to do? And if he wanted to, do you really think anyone could stop him?"

"Maybe you're right." Her voice sounded tiny, as if she were trying out the answer.

"You know this," Racxen insisted quietly. "It was written the first time you stumbled lost into that cavern and reached out your hand, and underlined every time you didn't flinch at his touch as so many had, every time he slept through the night without terrors because he knew you were there. Don't fear the memories for the tears they bring now," he added gently, seeing her eyes filling anew. "Love them for the comfort they will bring in the future. I know you grieve now that he died, but Amber you will rejoice forever that he lived. Ash nanto rekko, there's no shame in tears," Racxen murmured as wordlessly she wrapped her arms around him, hiding her face against his shoulder.

Feeling the shudders of the sobs escaping her as she struggled not to cry again he hugged her even tighter. "Brave one, you must rest, even if you cannot sleep. Come—let the darkness shield you," he whispered. "Let the ageless stars bear your burden until morning."

Amber nodded resolutely. "What's Arraheng for 'thank you'?" she asked shyly.

Racxen shrugged with a smile. "You'll never need to know."

With a frustrated half-grin, Amber lay down, wrapped in her cloak now warmed from the fire, and Racxen drew the blanket from his pack over them both, and she lay, cocooned against the Realm, listening to his breathing and holding his hand, until here, at last, the relief of sleep stole over her.

For a long time after, Racxen lay awake, attuned to the hand within his, listening as Amber's breathing mingled with the quiet night noises that had for so long been his only company through the loneliness of early hours spent beneath the stars.

Amber—Racxen woke suddenly, cursing himself for having succumbed to sleep when there was no one else to keep watch. Craning his neck to massage sensation back into it, he felt the Realm sink again as he beheld Amber, wrapped in the innocent sanctuary of dreams. His heart twisted. She was almost smiling, her cares inaccessible.

Dream of him, he willed. *I know it's a different love; I know it's not a threat, but that holds no comfort, for if it meant seeing you happy again, and him gracing these lands impossibly as he should, I would have him live and be your love.*

Racxen let out an exhausted breath as the full weight of the tragedy crushed through the heavy, slumbering darkness now that he could no longer focus on reassuring Amber. *I hope you've found the peace that eluded you for so long*, he told the stars in his mind, picturing the Gargoyle crouched beneath them in a silhouette that had so recently seemed as eternal as the rocky caverns upon which most of the Realm rested. *I wish the road towards it hadn't proven so traumatic, and I hope knowing her eased your pain somewhat. I wish I'd known you better, too. We were born of the same earth; mayhap our spirits still walk under the same stars.*

He let his mind wander through memories of Rraarl in honour of the Gargoyle, before his eyes rested again on Amber curled in the calming embrace of oblivion next to him. At least her sleep could stave off the intrusion of reality for a few more hours.

With an indistinct murmur, she turned over, and opened her eyes.

"Sorry," he breathed. But she wasn't looking at him; she was staring to the failing glow of the fire sunken almost into the cinders. His gaze flew to follow hers, and before their eyes the flames guttered and spilled sparks as the shadows took on shifting forms.

"Racxen, look!" Joy stirred in him to hear the wonder return to her voice as beside him she sat bolt upright, peering into the flickering darkness. "What are they?"

"Allies," he reassured in a hushed whisper, his eyes reflecting in the low light. "Unique allies."

Amidst the smoke lifting from the dying embers, shapes shimmered on the edge of vision, emerging fluid and indistinct against the cloudless night. The friends stared in awe as the shadowy figures surrounding them drifted in and out of vision: now blurring into obscurity with the darkness beyond the fire's glow, now flitting closer.

"They're *deer*," Amber hissed in astonishment, glimpsing the silhouetted antlers of a great stag fleetingly against the inky sky. Flame-mottled eyes flashed from the sleeker profile of a hind.

"Shah-does," Racxen explained, his voice reverent. "And stags. They form from the last sparks and longest shadows of campfires, to show travellers that they are not alone and to keep watch through the darkest reaches of the night over those who are far from home. They exist only in the desert, as far as I know, mayhap because the nights are clearer and deeper here than anywhere else in the Realm. The tribe have told stories of them for as long as I can remember, but I've never seen them with my own eyes."

"How are they even possible?" Amber pressed eagerly.

Watching her squinting into the darkness so intently it was as if she thought she could will them closer, Racxen grinned to see a semblance of her usual self returning. "I guess you were right about the magic."

Amber stared silently at the velvet silhouettes; their eyes glinting reflections of the fire's glow, their movements ethereally graceful, their darkness absolute in strength. She felt herself relax as she watched them dance against the deeper night; living shadow and flame light mingling as one into the suggestion of some old, benign power from the beginning of the Realm as sparks scudded from the fire and spiralled to the air.

They must have fallen asleep, for when Racxen next woke, it was to an eerie, stretched silence, the comforting night noises snuffed out. A braying cry splintered the night with its warning, and as he shook Amber awake and pulled her to her feet the Shah-does were scattering, a familiar guttural roar breaking like thunder.

Adrenalin spliced through exhaustion, shifting the night into focus as they ran for their lives, knowing that just for now it was worth living again; that if only they could get through this they could face together anything that came after

Against the huffing of her breath and the pulsing in her ears Amber thought she heard something thud behind her, but when she spun round the rushing sand kicked up behind her clouded her vision. "*Racxen?*"

The Arraheng fell heavily to his knees, the sands spinning with the night. "I'm right behind you," he managed before the pain took him, sending him clawing at his leg in agony as the venom's effects coursed like fire through his system. "Keep . . . running."

Charged with relief at his voice, she raced on.

Racxen slumped gasping to the ground as his whole body spasmed, his eyes rolling skyward unseeingly, every scrap of draining energy fixed on wheezing air through his strangled throat into his frozen, shrunken lungs; if he stopped focusing on it, he didn't know if his body could take over. His thoughts started to flit away from him, and he fumbled for the moonshaft, feverishly trying to find it and wrap it around his wrist, to fight—but too late he registered that it was all just a pathetic, insubstantial thought; he couldn't find it, couldn't pick it up, couldn't even move any more; couldn't do anything but wait alone with the life-stealing pain and the soul-crushing knowledge that it would end soon with the monster upon him.

"Don't . . . look . . . back . . ." His last words sinking on his tongue as unconsciousness enveloped him in its shroud, the last sight he registered was Amber in the distance, running away from danger and running away from him.

Knowing he wasn't far behind spurred her on, the night blurring into a deliria of exhaustion until Amber skidded on the sand, all further thought drowned in the echoes of the aquiline screech ripping the sky overhead with a challenge as ancient and far-reaching as the desert and sending the monster fleeing whining across the plains.

A rush of wind tugged through her hair, pressing in her ears as she ducked instinctively to stare up at the shadow blocking out the moon with its passing. The air pulsed with the heavy slap of wing-beats, and she glimpsed spur-clawed haunches kick out beneath a pale, scale-armoured belly as the phantasm rose, great leathered membranes stretched taut framed in startling lunar relief.

As the vision faded, the eldritch cry lingering amongst the stars, Amber stared until her eyes watered, conflicting emotions flooding within her. Dragons. There were still Dragons: as old as the Realm itself, the length of three Zyfang and fiercer and wiser than a whole pack of Wolfren together. Yet now the only one she'd ever seen was flying away into the wastelands—it was leaving.

"Did you *see* that?" she blurted eagerly. There wasn't an animal in the Realm Racxen didn't understand; he'd make sense of it all.

The silence crept up on her more chillingly than a stalking Venom-spitter. "Racxen?" Hysteria squeaked into her voice as she spun round, scanning the empty sands.

"*Racxen!*" Even as she registered the prone figure slumped there unmoving and broken in the embodiment of her worst nightmare she was running to him, falling to her knees beside him, reaching instinctively to tug her Gem from its cord. *Oh please,* she begged. *Say something, scream even—anything other than this deathly silence; you didn't trek through all this darkness not to live to see the sunrise.*

Panic seized anew as her fingers clutched air: she'd already used the Gem up on Mugkafb. She felt Racxen's pockets—no soulroot left either. *There's nothing you can do!* The words flitted shrilly in her mind, threatening to paralyse her as she struggled to grapple her mind around an alternative.

The broken yowl of the returning Venom-spitter shivered through the night, and Amber started violently, dragging her mind back from the recesses of primal fear. She pressed her fingers into Racxen's neck, but what if the racing pulse she felt was just her own, thundering in fear?

What would Sarin do? She forced herself to stop, crouch mouth to ear and hold still, watching for painfully dragging seconds until mercifully she saw his chest rise slightly.

Raising silent thanks, a sudden thought struck her, and she tied her sash around his swollen, purpling thigh in a tourniquet. Then, panicking that it might do more harm than good, she loosened it a bit. But now it wouldn't do any good at all, would it?

You don't have time for this! she screamed at herself. *You have to move him!* But then the poison would spread faster, wouldn't it? Yet the monsters couldn't be far, and she didn't have an antidote—she could have cried aloud at her own inadequacy and the unfairness of it all, if only she'd had the accursed time.

Groaning weakly through the returning onslaught of pain as he slid back into consciousness, Racxen's eyes flickered onto her and then away; he probably didn't even know she was there as she sobbed in relief. "I . . . fell," he gasped, his voice alien and guttural, ragged with the effort of talking. "I can't stand—"

His bellow of pain tore into her soul, and as his claws gouged into the mud she drew his hand from the rent earth and took it tight and safe into her own, her touch a life-link through the pain.

"You don't need to," she hissed back, trying to keep him talking as she worked out how she could do this without hurting him further. "If you fall down, I'll drag you up. If you can't stand, I'll hold you steady. If you can't walk, I'll carry you," she promised, choking on the futility of her words. "Curse it all, Racxen, I'm not leaving you in the dirt."

Racxen brought his claws up ineffectually as a shadow fell.

"Come *on!*" it said, and he felt his arm pulled over its shoulder until he was dragged to his feet, leaning heavily against the curiously solid illusion.

"Amber . . ." he protested, his vision momentarily clearing. "No, the monsters—you must go further . . ."

Staggering under his weight as she lurched into the first faltering step, Amber locked her eyes onto Racxen's. "You got me this far."

Teetering at the edge of the abyss, with only her gaze to stop him falling, his eyes sank into hers as if she could block out the pain and make things right, needing her to save him now as he'd saved her before, so many more times than he'd ever know.

Amber clung to him, willing herself to be strong enough for both of them. "We're going for help," she promised fiercely, with as much conviction as she could muster. The words knotted in her throat as grimly she took another step, her progress excruciatingly slow with Racxen a dead load at her shoulder.

Panic bubbled overwhelmingly as her clinging gaze fell upon nothing but lingering shadows rising from the far edge of darkness. "Keep going," she gasped, almost to herself as she stumbled on with his weight nearly suffocating her, no way of knowing if he could hear her. *Just be okay*, she implored him. *Please, just be okay.*

A bellowing groan forced from him in a shuddering window to his agony, and Amber nearly fell, unable to see through her tears. She'd never felt so helpless in her whole life, yet what else could she do for him but continue?

"Nearly there," she managed, hating herself for the fact that for all she knew it could be a complete lie.

Yet as she lifted her tearstained face to the horizon, refusing to give up hope, a possibility floated tremulously, for she recognised now the curve of those shadows: they were the cliffs. To reach them would be to reach the sea—and the Knights and Maidens.

"Racxen, you see them?" she urged. "We're going to make it!"

"Ash fensho rak hanar . . ." Racxen gasped, clinging to her hand so tightly that his claws dug in. Barely registering the pain amongst the adrenaline, she hoped he'd never let go—that those hands would never fall limply away. "Engo en nekksag . . ."

A coldness gripped Amber; hearing him slip back into his native tongue was too much like holding him in her arms when he'd crashed through into the clearing, close to death, when he'd lost all hope of life. It was happening again.

"Engo ro fash," she urged him. "Racxen! Hold on; just a little while longer." Helplessness washed over her. *They never taught us any of this!* she couldn't help fretting, nearing hysterics. *I can declare I'm under the protection of the King and tell you to keep back; that was all the wretched teachers thought we'd need . . .* In her head, she cursed herself savagely. "When we get back," she pledged. "I'm learning your entire language; I'm never leaving anything so important to another day again. You've no idea the things I want to ask you; the things I want to tell you—"

She almost choked on her own words then, a disbelieving grin splitting her face despite his terrifying silence, despite the weight-seized cramps wracking her limbs, despite the exhaustion trembling through to weaken her body until surely they would both fall—for with her next faltering step, instead of sinking into sand, her foot rose onto scrubland. "Racxen!" It came out more as a gasp than a shout. "We're nearly there! Hold *on*."

No reply came now, not even in Arraheng; and her hand had to grip his wrist as tightly as his claws had once held hers. "Stay with me!" she begged aloud. "You've felt alone for so much of your life, but you never have to again. I'm not leaving you, Racxen; I'm here, for all the good its ever done you—you're not getting rid of me that easily, and you know Mugkafb'd kill me if anything happened to you—oh Racxen, it's going to get so much better than this, but it won't without you."

Gulping a shuddering breath, she choked back her tears. "Curse it all, Racxen, I *love* you, and not just like a friend, like that and so much more; and you've got to be there so I can prove it; I've been too much of a coward to do so yet and I won't be again, I promise."

She fell into shallow gasps, unable to keep talking. "Or," she managed shakily, the truth quivering into her words more painfully than the burning air dragging through her lungs, "you've got to be there to tell me not to be such an accursed fool and go and live a happy life with someone normal who isn't going to drag you into danger every twenty minutes and who doesn't ramble on for hours when she doesn't even know you can hear her. Racxen, if I could do one of those bargains that plague your memory; whether the price for you living were facing the Goblin King or never seeing you again, it'd still be the fastest trade in the Realm."

She broke off, no longer able to do anything but breathe and step, breathe and step, until he shifted and she felt her grip slipping. She froze. She couldn't drop him, couldn't let go—but how much longer could she hold on, with no strength left but that of will?

Dull, rolling eyes, their fire burning low, locked onto her as froth bubbled between swollen lips and Racxen spluttered weakly. "Good . . . bye . . . Am—"

"No! We're almost there! Don't say it!" she panicked. "You can't go if you don't say it!" The words slipped out from years ago, even as the older her knew savagely of their futility. She wanted to collapse next to him and wait for rescue, but as she cast desperately into the distance, trusting no answering call to come save for the desolate keening of the wind, she knew the only way she'd let herself fall would be down dead beside him.

She just had to get him to the cliffs; then it would all be okay. *But it still wouldn't be over, would it?* the truth dug at her cruelly like a knife. *You'd still have to follow the streams; it'd still be so far to go.*

"Not *too* far, though," she retorted grimly, staggering on.

"Darkness . . ." Racxen's voice escaped suddenly in a pleading whisper; and although the sound was dangerously weak her heart soared with an elation to conquer all else, for that one barely-word proved that he had regained consciousness—that he could live—*would live,* she promised. *Will live.*

"This is nothing," she retorted, grinning through her tears. "Shadows've never stopped you before. You were the one who taught me that a way could be found through the longest night. And you just wait till you see the sunrise. I'll walk with you through any darkness," she vowed, "like you walked with me through my doubts and pain. And I promise you, when this is over—" Her voice nearly broke with emotion, but she made herself finish, as if voicing it would force it to come true for him. "When this is over," she gasped, screaming futilely in her head for her body to obey her as she nearly fell again. "When this is over, we're going to walk together in sunlight again."

Knowing from the exhausted shudders coursing through her body that the next step she took would be her last, in the only act of defiance she had yet strength to muster, she fixed her lips in a grimacing smile and lifted her head to stare to the horizon—and it was then that she heard the first, faint song of the rushing sea.

Sea Folk, A Centaur, and Sanctuary

New energy spurring her steps, as Amber staggered towards the cliffs and the rush of the waves grew louder she saw glittering flashes amongst the surf that could not have been just moonlight surging on broken water.

Clear above the roar of the sea there swelled sweet, strong voices, and as she stared out to the ocean Amber saw lanterns dotting from the waves, their lights flooding out across the distance shining true and far to reveal her way as the Maidens clinging to the rocks in defiance against the rushing winds reached high above the spray. Towards the shore swam a Knight of the Sea, barely visible amidst the roiling crests but wild and free; a light was in his ocean-grey eyes, and he flung his voice against the strength of the storm, his words soaring clear above the gale to lead the Folk in song:

> *"This night will pass as all nights must*
> *The storm shall soon be gone*
> *Till then a light shines over the water*
> *We call you on! We call you on!"*

By their guiding light Amber saw with lifting heart the path towards the forest illuminated, and suddenly she heard hoof-beats like a knight from a tale of old charging to the rescue.

"Amber!" Han galloped towards her, his hair streaming in the wind. "I've been trying to find you all night; I heard the Maidens' song—it was awful, like a lament; as if someone—"

Seeing Racxen slumped against her, he broke off, lifting him from her grasp with practised care. "Engo ro fash! Eshek negon ka, hashella sogor kensha fash," he urged in Arraheng, for the Centaur knew the tongues of many, from the time when the Elves dwelled still in the forest and the trees were young and whispered to all.

"I was trying to get him to the Glade Pool," Amber explained, wheezing air back into her lungs now that his weight had gone.

"You did so rightly, and bravely," Han reassured her. "Our choices are but there or Moonstruck Lake—and the latter is no destination for a night like this: there stir stranger creatures than Sea Folk in the furthest reaches of its waters. Gather your breath and follow closely, for our friend needs you more than he ever shall me, and the night is not yet through. Come!" He broke into a canter from standing, Racxen limp in his arms and bouncing with the rocking gait like a dead thing.

Ducking hastily under reaching branches along a path she'd never taken, Amber was soon left with only the tattoo of the Centaur's hoof-beats to follow. *Please be in time,* she entreated silently, wondering if these trees still held the listening spirits of the ages. *Please let him be in time.*

Hearing the song of the waterfall, Han slowed to a smooth trot, further lights glittering on the water to guide him in as the darkness softened and the trees parted into a moonlit glade.

"There now, Darkseeker; we're here," he soothed to the limp bundle in his arms as he strode into the centre of the pool, the water deep enough to rise above his withers. "You have been to this place of safety before, and there is nothing to fear."

Holding the senseless Arraheng securely in his strong arms, he lowered him so that all but his face was submerged, allowing the warmth of the healing waters to lap over his stricken body. The Centaur didn't allow himself to doubt that this would work. Couldn't allow himself to.

"Sisters and sons of the sea, come now to our aid," he sang in the old language, his ringing voice shivering through the leaves brushing the water, and even as the words floated away into the sky the water was lightening, wordless choruses of healing rising from the depths as four Maidens surrounded him.

"Racxen!" Amber hadn't meant to cry out when she saw him, but this was too much.

As she stumbled down the bank into the water and nearly fell, a pale form broke the surface and the Knight from earlier took her wrist in his fish-cold hand to steady her, just before Han reached her, his equine form awkward in the water.

"Rest now," the Centaur urged, reaching an arm around her reassuringly as he kept vigil. "You've done all you can. I don't know how you got him here; you've got the strength of a mule."

"Just the stubbornness," Amber managed in embarrassment, her voice shaking as she leant against him thankfully. Han's ragged coat was soaked, and steam rose from his flanks in the darkness. "What do we do now?" she asked, relieved that the Centaur was here to take over.

"We stay," Han assured her calmly. "Because, right now, that's all there is. So we will stay, all night if that is how long it takes, and when he's ready we will take him home."

Amber nodded fervently, emotion knotting in her throat and rendering her speechless.

Han nudged her understandingly as she stared towards the Sea Folk and their charge. *How can I help*: he could read it in every fibre of her being. "Better than anyone," he counselled. "Go to him, and at first light, I'll carry him home."

"Thank you," she whispered. No further words felt necessary, for with the strange intuition of his equine cousins, the Centaur seemed to understand beyond speaking.

The night passed in a strange blur: of droning, hypnotic song, of holding Racxen's hand and cooling his fevered brow, and of standing anxious and impotent as the Sea Folk worked their magic.

"Oh, Racxen," she murmured, holding him there in the water. How could she tell him how she felt? Maybe it was better that she didn't. When Ruby had been with Sardonyx, it had all been her constantly explaining where she was going; saying that no, just because she talked with Tanzan sometimes didn't mean she fancied him; knocking on Amber's door stressed in the middle of the night because—

She shook her head. *It wouldn't be like that with us*, she promised, both to herself and to him. Her mind went back to sharing the blanket that night, remembering how he'd held her when there had been no words; how his presence had helped when she'd thought that nothing possibly could; how she'd woken in cold midnight beneath a far lonely sky and yet, nestled at his side, instead of feeling scared as she usually did, had in contrast experienced a warmth and belonging and oneness that she'd never known she'd missed before.

She kept the memory tucked close to her heart, a balm against the terrible hurts of the Realm. It couldn't lessen her trials or shield her from them, but its gift was far more valuable, for it made her feel that just maybe she could get through them. Racxen believed in her, but more than that, when she was with him she could believe in herself. Unlike Rraarl, he didn't treat her like some fragile creature needing protection—but neither, unlike when she was with Jasper, did she have to spend all her energy pretending to be braver than she felt just to avoid losing face; for when she couldn't cope, instead of lowering his opinion, he respected her just as much, accepted her just as fully, and told her she was strong even when she felt at her weakest.

Sure, Ruby had kissed Sardonyx; done things Amber would probably never do—but had Ruby ever held someone in her arms and known she'd give her life for him, whether she was more than a friend to him or not? If Ruby's version were real love, she'd take this over it any day.

"I'd rather share this with you," she whispered, "than anything else in the arms of another." Who needed, she told herself firmly, anything physical, when you felt like this without even having touched?

She flinched as a murmur of pain escaped him, and all other thoughts flitted away, irrelevant, until finally, through the night's delirium and pain, the sweetest sound of all pierced the darkness as he spoke, a shadow visibly lifting from him.

"The Griffin . . ." he murmured hazily, slowly taking in his surroundings and trying to piece back together the night he'd lost. "We had to meet the others . . ."

"I will," she shushed. "I'll tell you everything we find out. Han's going to take you home; you need to rest."

Racxen shook his head blearily. "*You* carried me—*you* need to rest."

Amber grinned and glanced light-headedly to the brightening sky, loving the fact he was strong enough again to be arguing with her. "It's dawn already. I'll be back before you know it." Her voice shook slightly as she said it, but with the first golden hues spilling out between the pink-streaked clouds, she had to admit it was as though a certain grace had returned to the Realm. She knew she could do this. With him safe, she could do anything.

Last Hope

"Dewthorn elixir, when you have a moment."

Busying herself with the drink, Naya sighed, suppressing a worried smile. This was risking it, but he would insist on perpetuating the delusion. "You have news, sir?"

"Always, my lady," he proclaimed, with a drunkenly dramatic wave of the hand. "Unicorns—they exist . . ."

"You're overdoing it," she hissed scoldingly, but her heart danced. He'd seen the foal then, she translated, it was safe.

Jade returned with new glasses, startling her so much the drink sloshed onto the bar. "My lord, you have had too much ale, of course there are no more Unicorns," Naya answered lightly for her benefit, mopping briskly with her sleeve with only the briefest glances towards him. "There are no more white horses even; not in this town—here they are all just grey."

Roanen smiled. "Then you have not seen them at night, my lady," he murmured. "Beneath the moonlight, they all turn to silver."

So there were sightings last night, Naya interpreted rapidly. *It's working.* Stalling her smile, she looked up again, but the Nomad was gone.

"Weirdo," offered Jade helpfully in a bored tone, looking up from cleaning the glasses. "Just ignore him, everyone else does."

Naya stifled a grin. *Just as well . . .*

At the table nearest the bar, Jasper's heart sank as Amber trudged through the door. He didn't have the heart to berate her for her lateness as he usually would, and instead wordlessly pushed out a chair for her. What would be the point of saying anything? What was left to be spoken, when nothing at all could help?

"Racxen got hurt," Amber explained heavily, slumping down thankfully beside the Prince as exhaustion seized now that she could finally allow herself to stop. Everything was happening so fast, she wasn't sure she knew what to feel anymore. "He's okay now; he's with Han, but it was a long night. I'm sorry, I should have got a message to you; I didn't think of calling my Dartwing."

Jasper dug at a knot in the table with his fingernail. "This quest is exacting a lot of its participants," he muttered uncomfortably. "I seem to be the only one left unscathed, and that cannot be right."

"Don't talk nonsense," Amber dismissed, lifting her gaze in solidarity.

"Difficult habit to break." The Prince slid her a glass of nectar. With tired dignity, he raised a toast. "To Rraarl: in friendship, honour, memory, and love."

Biting her lip to stem the tears, Amber echoed his words, and with a last silent goodbye, she drank. The cloying sweetness clung bitter on her tongue as memories rose. "You're a good man," Amber conceded, when she could trust her voice to hold. "I don't say that enough."

"I shouldn't feel the need to hear it from you," Jasper acknowledged grumpily, but his voice was lighter now. "We cannot allow the Gargoyle's sacrifice to have been for nothing," he proposed decisively. "Our quest was Rraarl's also, and he would not have us falter on his account. His tragic loss proved something—that the Vetches have regained the power to break free from their stone prison. We must find a way of binding them again. Even though they cannot be killed."

Glancing distractedly away to contemplate their next move, Amber realised that the sympathetic-eyed tavern maid was watching as if she wanted to say something.

Feeling her enquiring gaze, the girl approached. "Begging your pardon for listening, sir, ma'am," Naya started. "But there's a man who believes that's not quite so."

"Roanen?" Jasper blurted, eyeing the patron before them in undisguised surprise. With his cloak richly patterned in symbols only visible when the light fell a certain way and austerely shaven head, he cut an unusual figure. He seemed at once remarkably plain, and yet there was an air of the chameleonic about him: if someone had asked Jasper what he could tell of the man, he would have been able to reveal neither his age, nor his eye colour, nor his profession. To make matters stranger it appeared to the Prince, as he glanced across the crowded room, as if the other customers could not—or chose not to—see the personage before them. Yet this was the individual, apparently, from whom his mother had learned the Dragontongue in the desert years before he had been born.

"The very same." The Wanderer nodded courteously. "I can see you've inherited the Queen's talent for finding trouble. I hope you have the same skill in getting out of it." His eyes darted appraisingly over the companions, his evaluation veiled as the tavern girl spoke quickly to him.

"Well, this is a fortuitous meeting," he murmured with interest once Naya had left, his fingers tattooing the table softly as he continued to watch each of them for a moment, as if judging the extent to which he should speak.

Amber examined his face in turn. She couldn't work out whether he put her more in mind of a monk or a soldier. His manner displayed solemnity and benevolence in equal degree, and his every action appeared similarly measured, as if each possible interpretation had been pre-considered—although his affection for Naya glimmered in the smallest touch and glance. She wondered fleetingly what he had deduced of herself.

"With regret I must caution that your sorrows are not over," Roanen murmured, his voice whisper-quiet but clear. "A three-pronged attack lies before you, and your company will be divided many times, ere your unity prevails. An evermore twisting path lies before your feet: you will lose much, yet when day finally breaks you will stand stronger."

"You know our business remarkably well," Jasper grumped. "Such a strategist might well choose not to ally himself with us, if our purpose were so laughably transparent."

Roanen chuckled, unperturbed, his eyes somehow constantly looking beyond his audience. "Peace, my young warrior. It would be a lessened land indeed if only the oldest, strongest, and wisest sought to save their fellows. In the spirit of aiding you as well as I can, I shall ask you a single question. Do you believe," he toyed, "in magic?"

"By my soul!" the Prince exclaimed, forgetting himself for a moment. "You are intent on wasting our time, if you are really suggesting that—"

"Ah, will you not humour an old man?" Roanen replied calmly. "What I am merely reminding you of is that the origin of this issue harks from an ancient time. Mayhap things were not so dissimilar then—but they were *perceived* differently."

Jasper shrugged awkwardly. "Even were it so, magic would still be just a perception."

Roanen grinned. "Ah—but that could be the greatest illusion of all."

Jasper dropped his gaze to glance smugly at Amber—and looked back to find the man had vanished. *Actually* vanished.

The realisation stunned Amber out her despair and she gawped silently at the empty air, as bewildered as the Prince.

"If you can find me, you will have proved yourselves worthy of my information."

Jasper studied Amber suspiciously. "Did you say—"

Amber rolled her eyes, the trace of a grin curling on her lips. "Yeah, 'cause *that* would make sense."

With a conceding shrug, the Prince gestured helplessly. "I guess we couldn't complain with someone of such skill at our side."

Amber returned his gaze innocently. "But he still is, can't you see him too?" She stifled a laugh as Jasper flicked the foam off his drink at her, and darted after him.

"Caves!" Amber promised emphatically as she overtook Jasper, skirting the outbuildings of Loban as she headed into the desert, relieved to finally know the answer to one of these riddles. "It's got to be the caves, 'cause we were talking about the Vetches getting banished and they were held in stone—"

"Very good!" the Nomad's voice pronounced, and a second later it was as if he'd been there the whole time, resting casually against the rock where seconds ago had leaned only the sun's rays.

"Are you *actually* doing that?" Jasper challenged, staring at him intently as if to uncover invisible wires.

"Ah, let an old man keep some secrets," Roanen dismissed lightly, clapping the Prince on his shoulder. "Now," he began. "Let us talk more freely. Your assumption is that the Vetches cannot be killed, am I right?"

"It is more than a theory, sir, it is irrefutable given the evidence." The Prince was not about to back down.

The Nomad smiled disarmingly. "One could say that about magic, and yet to you it is merely a belief. Let us use this to our advantage, and consider mindfully the seeming incontrovertibility of the evidence."

"If you say so," Jasper assented, feeling less and less sure of himself.

"The Vetches have been *held* before," Roanen continued. "Therefore we can logically deduce, if we so wish, that they are not invincible—

and we know the means to hold them has, in the past, been *magic*."

Jasper passed a hand through his hair. "Granted," he conceded uncomfortably. "Although, given the current climate—"

"Ah, so our chances are improved already!" Roanen declared, ignoring the Prince's misgivings. "Be of heart, my friends. Now . . ." he rubbed his hands, warming to the theme. "Cast your minds back to the time of magic. Allow the possibility into your mind; let things be for now the symbols they once were. Answer everything on instinct and trust that it will be proven right."

They nodded, cautious and eager by turn.

Roanen snapped his fingers. "What is the only thing that can conquer darkness?"

"Light," Amber answered automatically, before she could realise just how stupid it sounded.

Roanen nodded approvingly. "Follow that thought to its logical conclusion."

"But we're talking about the *ultimate* darkness," Jasper protested, hastening to catch up. "Such a light as to conquer that—even putting aside rational disbelief in its existence—could never be natural, so where, then, could it be found in this age? The only masters who could capture magic and bend it to their will were the Sorcerers, and—" the Prince broke off at the dead-end, "the Emperor banished all of them."

Roanen's eyes betrayed his amusement. "All of *them*, yes," the Nomad acquiesced wryly.

Amber stared at him, the memory of a tale Queen Pearl had once documented stirring; about a band of renegade sorcerers of such gentleness and morality that the force which broke like the waves of an ocean to destroy half the nation in the wrong hands softened and supported and rose to sing like a life-bringing stream through the arid reaches of a ravaged land under their guidance. A disbelieving grin spread across her face. "You're a *Magician?*"

"Aye, near enough," Roanen confirmed, the lines of his weathered face crinkling into a smile. "A Magician, or an Enchanter—or a teller of tales! Listen, for there is one you need to hear, ere we reach our destination. A Magician would rather allow themselves to die than perform a curse upon a living being whether human or other, and so it is with Sorcery that this tale is concerned. Why will become apparent, for it is dark indeed. Do you know much of Griffins?"

"*Griffins?*" Jasper echoed, realising in annoyance that this would all be a lot quicker if Mugkafb were here. "But they were little more than glorified watchdogs, weren't they? And they died. Right?" He shook his head, chagrined. "Do I know nothing of my own Realm?"

"If you'd think of it as other than *yours*, young sir, perhaps you might," Roanen noted dryly. "In any case, much of the old knowledge has been systematically quashed by the Authorities, so do not be too quick to despair. The Griffins were treated, as you so eloquently opined, like the Emperor's watchdogs—captured to guard the treasure he horded so jealously. That tyrant's cruelty knew no bounds, and the day came when the Griffins managed to break free from their chains and attempted to mount an airborne escape. But after years of mistreatment and malnourishment their wings were pitifully weak, and they were easily brought to ground by a volley of arrows and dragged into the dungeon vaults to await their punishment."

Disgust dripped from the Nomad's tongue. "What the Emperor could not conquer he sought to twist to his own ends. Legends have their basis in magic; they're so drenched in it that not even the Authorities can remove the traces—think of the Phoenix, that revered symbol of light internal and fire unburning, kindling the possibility of rebirth and freedom in so many hearts. The Emperor's depraved mind reworked from that undying legend a tool of savagery, framing for the Griffins the worst punishment he could devise to prevent any future escape attempts. Such a curse was wrought upon those noble beasts that if they were ever to beat their wings again, an unnatural fire brighter and fiercer than any seen in the Realm before or hence would ignite amongst their fur and feathers."

"And logic tells that such a fire would kill and consume a being instantly," Jasper noted, subdued. "So we are no further forward, sorcery or none."

"But—" the ending had shocked her, yet Amber kept her eyes trained hopefully on the Nomad. "This story has spoken only of sorcery—earlier you mentioned magic."

Roanen's eyes grew distant. "You must remember that this tale is not yet over. Our question still remains."

Jasper's lip curled. "What, whether we believe in magic?"

"I was going to say in possibilities," the Nomad corrected, his voice hypnotic.

"I'd humour any fool if it gave me a fighting chance of saving my people," Jasper shot back unromantically, with equal fervour.

To Amber's surprise, the man laughed softly. "Well, then. Mayhap there's someone you should meet. Follow!"

Roanen didn't stop until they had inched through what felt like miles of meandering darkness, with only a faint red glow emanating from the Magician's left hand after carefully whispered words to help them find their way.

"Slaygerin, the remaining Griffin, is no longer accustomed to light," he explained in response to the Prince's suspicious glance, his voice low. "The darkness is his refuge, and by using infrared we may trespass into his domain with the least impact for, like many beasts, he cannot perceive it. Make no mistake, though—he will have sensed our approach when first we entered the tunnels, and will be waiting for us."

As the Magician knelt to wrestle a rusted monster of a key into an ancient lock, Amber shivered. The reddish tint from Roanen's hands, despite the light it gave, spread a hostile air through the shadowed passages, and an unearthly noise kept echoing unsettlingly from behind the door: not quite the growl of a sand lion, nor the shriek of a desert hawk, but an eerie combination of both. "Are we in Dread Mountain?" she whispered. Somehow it'd help to have a location as an anchor to the outside world.

"Part of it," he murmured calmly, concentrating on the lock. "Many of these tunnels were used as crypts by the Emperor. Fear not, we shall go no further than the next chamber—the dungeon—and I shall bring you both out unharmed."

"Hang on, just Slaygerin?" Jasper stalled uncomfortably. The incongruence of the cries had shredded his nerves. "I thought you said there were three Griffins imprisoned down here?"

"There were." Roanen's tone was matter of fact. "Initially."

"I see," the Prince managed faintly against the nausea folding in his stomach.

"You cannot judge him by human standards," the Nomad rebuked mildly. "It was before I found him; before I could feed and attempt to help him. I wish I could have been sooner and saved them, but the laws of time are irrefutable even for a Magician. The bars are strong; you will be safe. However, you are under no obligation to continue, and if you wish, we will turn back immediately."

When neither Jasper nor Amber moved to retreat, Roanen nodded, the light in his hand flaring as he drew back the heavy door.

Amidst the sudden clanking of chains Amber bit her lip fiercely and Jasper fought back a shout as the Griffin stalked, terrifyingly leonine, towards them through the darkness; rangy muscle rippling across the gaunt frame, talons clicking on rock with each elastic stride, the red-tint illumination lending an even more frightening slant to the surreal beast. Through the rusting bars of the dungeon cell they glimpsed char-streaked golden feathers intermingled with tawny hide hanging ragged across the great shoulders; could see the matted patches of fur crusted with blood and plucked feathers where the Griffin had savaged his own coat with that monstrous hooked beak. The massive paws shifted in the ghost of a kneading motion against the rock as the lamp eyes locked on the newcomers to burn with a madness both frantic and despairing.

Consuming wrath seeped sweat-like from the prisoner; Amber could feel it curling towards her. Suddenly those bars didn't look so strong. Yet she couldn't let herself look away. *All he's ever done is try to escape a tyrant*, she reminded herself. *That, and learn what human hands can beget*—

Seeing the look of pity cross her face Jasper reached out to Amber, unable to put doing something stupid past her. Avoiding the glare of its drowning eyes, he struggled to remain objective as he let his glance dart over the Griffin. *Why would the Nomad insist on bringing us here, when our only hope is impossible?* Watching the wretched creature, he couldn't help questioning why Roanen hadn't ended its suffering long ago.

He's a Magician, the Prince admonished himself. *He looks beyond the obvious.* Jasper breathed against his impatience, and forced his own gaze to settle. *And he's probably not bound by the 'possible'.* Scanning Slaygerin's emaciated body more carefully, something caught Jasper's eye amongst the bedraggled neck ruff—something that glinted, other than the chain—and his initial astonishment fell away to a dreadful realisation.

With Jasper steadfastly refusing to so much as look at her Amber guilt-ily yielded to silence, hating herself for proving incapable of helping her friend but unable to find the words to reach him through the rising tension when she had no idea what had changed, as Roanen guided them through the long passage back to sunlight.

At the cavern mouth, she stared back into the darkness behind them, unable to get the intensity of the vision out of her head. "You think there's hope for him, don't you?" she asked the Nomad impulsively. "In his eyes, there was something . . ." She shrugged inadequately, grappling for the word.

Roanen looked at her directly, as if taking her measure. "I have attended Slaygerin for many seasons now, and still he draws my hopes and dashes them in equal measure," he cautioned. "That he has the potential for something *else* is beyond doubt. Whether he is capable of becoming something *more* remains to be seen."

His voice shimmered in the air, close to her ear. "Our capacity for hope determines our persistence long after all else is gone," the Magician advised softly. "Do not relinquish it, however dark the night may feel."

His words squeezed into Amber's soul, and she had to blink quickly as she bowed her head in thanks. "You ready, Jasper?"

The Prince hesitated. "You go home," he ordered distractedly, more brusquely than he'd meant to. "There's one more thing to do here."

Unconvinced she watched him, her eyes reading the shadow of his fear. "But I don't understand."

A frisson of warmth crept back into Jasper's dry voice. "Amber, you very rarely do."

Her scathing glance in response mellowed more quickly than usual, and for a moment he panicked that she had guessed what he was about to do; but just this once she must have decided not to argue, for instead she said something quickly to Roanen and trudged off into the desert.

Watching her leave, Jasper sighed heavily, the sinking burden of the inevitable worming into his heart. She hadn't seen the key, then.

"You each have your own path to take, as much as they may intertwine, ere the quest ends," Roanen advised. "You doubt your courage too much."

Jasper stared helplessly at the Magician, awash with the impossibility of the road revealing itself before his feet. "What would Mother think?" he muttered wryly.

Roanen smiled as he turned to stride back into the desert. "You might be surprised."

Desert Trial

As the adrenalin of the Griffin encounter faded into creeping loneliness, Amber trekked on, keeping her eyes fixed on the parched, crusting ground.

Jasper would have flown off, so he'd probably be two-thirds of the way there already. To make things worse, he was probably skin-breathing by now instead of merely lung-breathing; a necessary phenomenon when the faster speeds were achieved to avoid gagging and suffocation against the wind. The rumour that such a technique—realised at the pinnacle of a flight—rendered one enveloped in an almost spiritual experience of ecstasy, together with the certain knowledge that she could no longer ever approach let alone hope to experience it, constricted her throat and stifled her own breathing.

Nothing lay ahead save for shifting sands and dying vegetation sprawled in pitiful clumps beneath the mocking sun, and as she traipsed further and further into the desert all her certainties began to waver. With everything so far having proven in vain, could they really trust that their goal lay now any closer than it had in the beginning? There was evidently no help to be found from having seen Slaygerin, and the elation of the night before dimmed into a far, treasured memory replaced by pressing guilt. Racxen had been hurt so deeply, again and again, Rraarl had made the ultimate sacrifice; how else could this end, save for in blood and tears and—

It's the desert talking. She shook her head angrily. *Just put one foot in front of the other until you've come far enough to hear your own voice again. Keep going. For all of them.*

To distract herself, she watched the sand-spiders scuttling erratically beside her across the cracked earth, the last scrubs of dry grass scrunching brittle beneath her feet.

The hardest battle, the Genie's voice slipped back to her amongst the rhythm of their infinitesimal footsteps, perforating the insidious shadows swamping her mind, *is the one fought alone and in silence against that which feels it cannot be changed. It is when you feel weakest that you must fight hardest, and it is when you feel you no longer can that you must most ardently continue. You know the stories—you know how it is, and how you can make it be . . .*

The words tugged back through her memory, and shielding her eyes with a hand Amber lifted her gaze, squinting fiercely. Her head throbbing at each step, she licked her parched lips as she steeled her courage.

She thought of the spiders, fleetingly marvelling at how anything so small could survive out here. *If they can,* she admonished herself sternly, unfurling her sash and winding it round across her head, letting out a breath as she knotted it thankfully. At least now it didn't quite feel like her hair scalp was on fire.

Now, she planned, hoping it would feel more secure if she actually formed the words. *Once you've crossed the desert, you'll find the others. Let them in; let them help, and get back to aiding them. And preferably pull it together before Jasper sees you like this.*

Yet as she stared out through bloodshot, heat-stung eyes over the barren lands stretching endlessly in every direction, Amber fervently wished that it had been him she'd seen, feeling a dart of fear lodge as she glimpsed a dark figure on the horizon, its gait unmistakeable between the sparse, jutting rocks. Shimmering indistinctly in the heat haze hovering at the edge of vision, it was quickly growing larger—and closer.

Amidst the stifling temperature, a chill grew within her. It wasn't as if there was anywhere to hide. And who else would venture so far into the desert, save for a solitary Goblin? Everything that Racxen had told her flooded weakeningly into her mind. The loners—the Pedlars—were the most volatile and dangerous, ostracised even from their own hordes.

Amber's first thought was relief that Racxen wasn't here to have to face this. Her second, shivering guiltily into her, was that this left her pathetically vulnerable.

Okay, she deduced, trying to coerce her stricken mind into rational thought. *If you must be seen, be seen to be fearless.*

She strode on, trying to veer away from the figure without abandoning her course. Yet the Goblin refused to deviate: no matter how much she twisted and turned, every time Amber looked up the shadow was right there, advancing directly into her path. The realisation sent knives into her.

She swallowed with difficulty, her desiccated throat scratching painfully. *He'll be carrying liquids.* Her own water pouch flapped ever more hollowly against her thigh. But even as thirsty and far from civilisation as she was, Amber knew she couldn't allow herself to contemplate it; everything depended on keeping the Pedlar at a safe distance. Yet as she stumbled on, her energy sapping away into the draining sands, she knew he would eventually reach her—she knew it, and she kept going.

It was past noontide, judging by the crispness of his shadow as it fell across her path, when the inevitable finally caught up with her.

Slowly, she lifted bloodshot eyes, refusing to speak. Her vision shuddered in the searing heat, but seeing the Pedlar standing there viscerally close, the days of luckless hunting glittering in his eyes, made her question why she had ever denounced her life. It was hers, the good and the bad, and she wasn't about to relinquish it to any Goblin.

"Taste the wares, missy." His voice cracked hungrily, his gaze as merciless as the sun's. Phials of unknown potions hung from a faded strap of some hapless animal's skin across his chest.

Amber kept walking. *Don't answer, don't look, don't—*

"So much pain for one so young," he tried more softly. "Who could ask you to bear it? And what if you could turn it back—who could ask you not to? They do not know . . ."

She shivered at the silken growl of his voice. *Goblin words are honey laced with poison. Remember it!*

"Such a shame that stone must sink . . ." The Pedlar's eyes burned with a strange fire as he beckoned her closer. What harm could there be in just one step?

"Leave me—you'll get nothing!" she countered angrily, trying to find the spider to keep her eyes on. *One step is one too close!*

The awkwardness of his gait vanishing, the Goblin nipped suddenly in front of her, reaching a wizened hand towards her face. "Your eyes are dead. They will burn again."

She flinched back and shoved his hand away, those eyes flashing fire. "I'm not buying."

"Oh, but lady, I'm merely giving," the Goblin urged, easily keeping up with her. "These phials can give you anything, remember. Everything."

Too despairing now to check her instincts, her intuition numbed by a cacophony of raw emotions, Amber's guard slipped. "Not what I seek—" She clamped her tongue abruptly, furious with herself against a rising bubble of fear. She'd said too much already, and she knew it.

The Goblin pounced. "Oh, really?" His voice lowered, dangerously soothing. "And what might that be, missy?"

"Something to make the pain go away." The words slid out from somewhere gnawn through with grief deep inside, lulled by the false concern before she could stop them, desperate to be heard and comforted, even if by him. "Some magic elixir, or something." She could have howled in shame hearing herself, and prickling tears threatened to witness that she couldn't prove herself stronger. *No excuses! Keep fighting!* She clenched her jaw shut.

"Magic elixir, Fairy-girl?" The Pedlar sneered, his gaze locking predatorily onto her. He dropped his voice to a gravely whisper so alluringly quiet that Amber had to consciously stop herself from moving closer to hear.

"The best I can do . . ." His ink-dark tongue flicked almost imperceptibly along cracked, narrow teeth as he reached into the folds of his tattered jerkin to lift from a faded skin bag a scratched glass phial of liquid. "Is *this*." His thin lips parted, and she heard him swallow dryly, his eyes never moving from her face.

Amber stared at the vessel transfixed, drawn as a Dartwing to a lantern. It looked so harmless: clear, like water. She couldn't tear her eyes away. "Poison." The statement settled flatly, devoid of judgement or rancour, in the air between them.

The Goblin didn't deny it. He was standing next to her as carefully motionless as a newly emerged Vetch, the desire catching audibly on his breath as he waited for her to drink. In his own way, she found some part of her reasoning, he needed her; he cared.

Her hand went out. She was so very thirsty, and it would so good to dull the pain.

Her fingers closed around the bottle, her mind noting as if entranced how the glass felt surprisingly cool in the heat. She glanced, woolheaded, to the Goblin. He wouldn't sell her poison, not really, would he? That happened to other people, didn't it? This was a test; that was all. She'd show him she wasn't scared. She'd prove it to everyone. It wouldn't matter that she couldn't fly. She wouldn't feel like just a silly winglet for the rest of her life, never to be whole again. Her world shrank into those seconds.

The hardest fight is silent, she remembered the Genie whisper, and she wrestled with her fogged mind, reaching for memories of things painfully far from here that now seemed too long ago to bear. Voices floated ephemeral and unconquerable: those of Racxen, Han, the Genie, the Prince; and fleeting technicolour moments pierced the grey: searching for fireflies on Mid-Recö night with her parents before the Sea Battle turned the stars to ash, Finsbury at the breaking of this nightmare leaping high to save a stranger, Ruby choosing her over the clique, Racxen crashing through the night to warn a people who would persecute him, the Sea Folk surging to the shore to bring them strength, the light blazing into Rraarl's eyes at her first touch—they all rushed into one affirming moment to which she knew she had to add.

Tearing her gaze from the phial, she dragged her eyes back to the Pedlar until she was staring him squarely in the face. In the midst of the desert, everything hushed slow and real, the seconds lengthening as they gathered in clarity. The Fairy's hand opened slowly, strength building on the triumph of each smallest movement until the bottle fell released, smashing on the rock-studded ground into a myriad of shattered pieces, the contained poison bursting harmlessly to sink beneath the sands forever with an acrid hiss.

"I don't play with Goblins," Amber snarled, striding away into the wilderness on a path he could not follow as the Pedlar scrabbled in vain at the damp sands. *Even at my weakest, I'm stronger than you.*

As she pushed on alone again, clouds gathered as if out of nowhere until the droplets fell in their thousands and she stood amongst them gasping, the rain spattering down until it seemed to be sluicing right into her core, deep down where she had locked everything away. Amongst the thundering falls she cried and cried, as the cleansing deluge washed everything away—not gone, but moved and dealt with just enough for her to gasp again and lift her head and walk on renewed across steaming sands.

Ever On

Purpose drummed with every footstep as Amber cast her eyes across the sweep of rippling trees, the intricate crest of a purpling cloud and the new glint of the tiny stars dotting onto the horizon, refusing to let herself slow as she recognised the sights of home. She couldn't afford to let herself question how it would feel once the swiftly gathering darkness had fallen absolute. If she could just get herself through the next short while, that would be a start.

Scanning her surroundings for something brighter to fill her mind with, her gaze settled in relief upon the Genie as wisps of cloud coalesced into his familiar form and he floated down beside her. There was nothing he could say, of course; there were wishes that could never be granted. Yet he was there, and right now his insubstantial presence bestowed an entirely solid reassurance as they completed the rest of her journey together.

For all her bravely meant intentions, she reached her door too soon. Her hand lingered over the lock as she stalled without meaning to, and taking note the Genie flowed from the keyhole, his expression all sorrowful, attentive eyes.

Amber smiled gratefully. "I'll be okay once I'm in," she promised, trying to believe it. "My nights were always alone before. It'd mean a lot if you were able to come back tomorrow morning, though? I think I'm dealing with it, and then I realise I've forgotten the reasons I have to get up."

The Genie bobbed swiftly. "Rely on it. If you've already gone out—no, don't look at me like that, life is all around you and it wants to sweep you onwards with all its little normalities and surprises—then rest assured the winds of the Realm will carry me to you wherever you are."

On her breath of thanks the Genie drifted back, left with his thoughts as the door clicked shut behind the Fairy. As his eyes grew to soft pools of compassion the worry in his gaze tangled with trust in her future, hope that she would in time open herself to its possibilities, and faith that she had the courage to do so.

Three hours later Amber was still staring sleeplessly at the ceiling, alone with her thoughts and the night, her mind incessantly repeating things that she hadn't been able to tell Rraarl as she tried to lock in the moments she had spent with him, scared that in time even those few brief precious memories might slip away against her will and leave her.

Pangs like fear or adrenalin but stronger clutched painfully at her heart with each fleeting remembrance and refused to weaken even as she gasped against their power. She hoped bleakly that they wouldn't kill her, because they certainly didn't feel like they'd ever lessen.

Not only his death itself but also the manner of it; the sense of horror and interruption, hollowed her soul, until there was only the sense of injustice and the sense that it could not truly be over so violently and abruptly—and if so, then was there not something left that could still be done about it?

Carefully, Amber made herself lift her eyes to the window and the serene nightscape beyond. Rraarl had fiercely tried to protect her from stumbling onto the path that had haunted his steps; and surely she owed it to him to demonstrate towards her own beleaguered mind the same compassion she'd always tried to show him he had deserved, no matter how ashamed he was of his demons?

Grappling with fears and questions that squirmed into inexpressible forms as they scuffled with her internal defences, Amber forced herself to acknowledge that mayhap she would have to trust that she could learn to cope with, instead of merely hope to get rid of, these feelings. Perhaps if she could make peace with them, they would lose their power. She imagined the Genie's equable and inescapable gaze encompassing her struggle; containing benevolently even that which she could herself barely accept writhed panicked and unchecked within her mind. Easing her breath into a steadier rise and fall, she felt the battering tide ebb.

Even so, now that the Gargoyle wasn't there, she didn't know if she could ever sleep again. Her mind replayed the nights, both travelling and having returned, when he had watched over her, and she had slept. If she closed her eyes and lost herself in the memories she could almost feel him there, silently watching over her, never wavering; the deepest of silhouettes to stave off the shadows that threatened her mind.

Against all things, the respite of sleep stole over her, and with it the solace of dreams where she saw him again.

That morning Amber woke early, although bland swathes of cloud muted the sun and the weak rays piercing the window lent but a pale wash to the waterlogged landscape. She lay staring up at the cracks in the ceiling for a moment, their veined stone drawing her to memories of his skin, wishing she could return to the oblivion of sleep snatched fitfully last night.

Yet the murky predawn light nestled in beside her like a blanket, and through the smothering grey outside pierced a dawnful of birds, warbling and fluting and trilling their tidings of comfort, and bidding her rise and greet a new day.

Heeding their hopeful message, carefully, meticulously, she turned her attention to the steps now in front of her; to the things she needed to make sure she did for the others. How could she allow herself to succumb to feeling soul-dead when Rraarl had taught her that spirit could endure through anything? What a travesty would it be to the memory of the greatest survivor of all if she were to place now any less value on her life than he always had? She owed it to him to keep going; he would have demanded it of her.

And what about Racxen, Mugkafb, all her friends? Cocooning herself like this, wishing futilely that the thundercloud of danger gathering overhead would fade like a wisp of a nightmare instead of breaking over the Realm, would only prevent her from completing with her friends the preparations that were their only hope in standing against the evils yet to come. To falter now would be to forsake all that had passed, the wondrous as well as the despairing.

Sitting up, Amber let her eyes skim her room, tracing the vestiges of a life she wasn't sure would wait for her much longer, like a half-sloughed skin she didn't know if she was supposed to be returning to or shedding. Her ribbon poi draped over the dresser—when would the Realm feel light enough for her to wield them again? The unstrung longbow poking out of the wardrobe—how long ago had she taken that course with Tanzan? Ruby's friendship bracelets from years ago—why did she still keep them in the jewellery box she'd made as a winglet containing precious little else?

Amber allowed herself the ghost of a smile. Maybe this particular skin would stretch to fit until she was ready to decide. Everything might have changed, but there'd be better times, and more memories. She had made the kind of friends she'd never thought she'd find; struggled through things she'd never had cause before to believe she could survive. It all had to count: she had so much to fight for. Without thinking about it, she reached over and felt for one of the charm-bands, and tied it around her wrist. It was almost as hard to do one-handed as she remembered, and she grinned self-consciously.

Flinging back the covers resolutely, she swung out of bed, her toes curling protestingly into the cold rug beside her bed as she flicked the lamp on, feeling the fragile warmth bloom beneath her fingers. The normality of the actions soothed her; anchoring her in a reality that however hard, was at least for now secure and present. *Time can't heal, but maybe it can distance. Either way it won't wait. Let life sweep you on.*

Pulling her still-warm duvet up around her shoulders, Amber padded over to the window, staring out at the drizzling rain. *See, at least you're not out in that.* She thought of Han amongst the trees, and hoped the weather didn't bode too ill for the Centaur and that he'd found somewhere dry to wait it out. At least the swamps would be deeper, which should make the caves more inaccessible and the passageways safer. Hopefully that would mean Racxen could relax a bit.

And what would he tell you? Amber admonished herself. *"Troubles aren't so oppressive when they're not confined by four walls."* Get up. Get out.

Decisively slinging the duvet back onto the bed and bracing against the chill water as she washed, Amber wriggled into the first clothes she could pull from the closet and grabbed her travel-cloak from the hook on her door. Shoving a couple of nectar sticks into her pocket, she hesitated over the waterleaf nestling in the sink; it hadn't really osmosised enough yet and was looking pretty wrinkled, but it would have to do until she had time to pick some fresh ones. Raising her hood against the rain, she ducked out into the flooded pre-dawn, resolving to find Han.

Amber pushed through the deluge unheedingly, finding herself veering from the trees' shelter to let the rain drive against her, the tiny arrows tattooing into her skin and numbing the magnitude of pain in her heart. She allowed the incessant needles; she deserved their retribution, for he had joined her at the cave because she'd asked him to, and he had paid with his life.

Yet the forest stretched its arms above her quietly, coaxing her back along knotted paths unravelling into familiarity, until beneath the sheltering leaves the rain eased, slipping instead of stabbing, and she grinned to find she was as mud-smeared as when Racxen had first greeted her.

"Han?" Amber called, grimacing against the slaver of wet leaves as she pushed through the touch of another dripping branch, her eyes squinting protectively against the driving rain until she could barely see where she was going, but no longer doubting he'd be here.

"You have better friends than the rain," a deep voice greeted her, his usual exuberance tempered in consideration as he ducked beneath the branches, approaching without reservation to enfold her in his arms.

Amber returned his hug gratefully, enveloped in the comforting scent of woodland and stables even as she noted in concern that the Centaur's long hair hung in thick tangles plastered wetly to his skin and that his flanks were soaked dark. "Couldn't you have waited out the storm?"

Han smiled with reassuring ease. "And waste good seasons before it passes? No, far better to dance beneath the clouds."

Amber grinned back, the Centaur's optimism infectious. "And here was I thinking the weather might have dampened your spirits."

Han's footsteps echoed as soothingly as a steady heartbeat as they walked on through the forest together. "I'm glad indeed to see you," he promised warmly. "You're amongst friends, Amber, and if you hadn't sought us out we'd have come to find you. Don't berate yourself for not knowing all the answers at a time like this; every step moves you forward and you're doing well."

Amber nodded thankfully, breathing more easily now. She wasn't the only one to have lost Rraarl, nor was she the only one hurting, and she needed to make sure she was there for her friends as much as they had been for her. "I'm going to find Racxen," she decided as they reached the edge of the forest. She wasn't sure how she could actually help him, but she had to try. "He's been through so much and after everything last night—I hope it didn't bring it all back, you know? I want to make sure he's okay."

"Excellent idea," Han agreed, in the brightest voice she had heard for what seemed like a lifetime. "He's probably gone back to the marshlands with Mugkafb; he came to your window, but didn't want to wake you as he imagined it had taken you most of the night to fall asleep. No, don't worry," he insisted firmly at Amber's dismayed exclamation, "I'm certain he'll be glad to have judged right and to see you today instead. This weather should be doing their spirits a Realm of good— the waterways must be swollen to bursting by now."

Amber nodded contemplatively. She wondered fleetingly whether they'd rather be left alone, but then she remembered how dearly it had touched her to realise that Han had been waiting, in case she'd needed him, in the wetter, closer woodland instead of having taken better refuge in the deeper forest that would have taken her a day to reach.

"Thanks, Han." She hugged the Centaur swiftly, bade him find cover, and strode forth again with a lighter heart.

The tempest had worsened intolerably by the time Amber, squinting through the battering downpour, saw at last from the slope of the grasslands the marsh-flats heralding the outskirts of Arraterr slide into view across the sodden horizon, their surfaces shimmering with the pummelling rain. The trees above erupted in a hissing dervish as the raging wind tore through their leaves, the drenched fields beyond rippling silver as the grass bowed before the majesty of the storm.

Soaked through, Amber skittered across the squelching ground, buoyed by the anticipation of reaching her friends. Exhausted as she was, and with her vision tricked into a false security by the veiling downpour and faltering marsh-light, it took her several uneven steps to realise the missing segment in the landscape. Where were the Arraheng?

Sheltering her eyes with her hands, she scrunched her face to squint against the driving rain, fighting back the panic thrashing inside her. The marshes lay empty, devoid of signs of life. Maybe the weather was too bad even for them, Amber tried to tell herself. Maybe she should give that call, like Mugkafb had done when they'd first met.

But even as she was forming the thought, the storm-laden sky splintered with another cry: a desolate, wavering scream that arched into unnatural silence and rooted her, stunned, to the sodden ground. *What could—*

Then she saw. Saw, despite distance blurring them into faceless forms, the terrified Arraheng spill out from hiding, at first staggered and straggling, but gaining in numbers and momentum to stream together into a frantic exodus as the unearthly sundering cry flung out again.

Fear closed her throat as Racxen's words flooded back to her, recounting the times the Venom-spitters had rampaged through their encampment. It was happening again, and they were fleeing to the caves.

She knew, deep down, that there was no way she could help them, but she found herself running towards them to try, and suddenly they were all around her, almost stampeding. Shouts reared; words she didn't understand thrown in her face as several Arraheng around her tried to direct their panicking kin to safety. Awash with their fear, Amber struggled to keep her focus amongst the massing crowd until through the confusion of yells and commands she heard—

"Racxen?"

Instantly she froze to orientate herself, hope bubbling as with shining eyes she scanned the crowd for him, the rain filling her sight like tears. Yet her gaze stalled over the speaker, as an adjacent figure—destined or desiring to be a tribal elder judging by his painted skin— shook his head with grave finality. Amber's entire Realm narrowed into his answer, as numbly she watched him push his companion forward and they merged into the storm as the whole tribe ran on.

"Racxen! *Racxen!*" Her eyes no longer registered the fleeing multitudes as she spun round disorientated, desperate to catch just a glimpse of him. But even the obscuring rain sheets sluicing through the wavering marsh light, grey as despair, couldn't be hiding him. She'd know his loose, steady gait anywhere; would recognise his footsteps as intimately as she knew her own heartbeat.

An Arraheng woman nearly crashed into her, reaching out her claws urgently to the Fairy, pleading with her in a language she didn't understand to run for safety. Amber shook her off, gesturing wildly for her to follow the others, and turned to run against the flowing crowd.

Racxen, where are you? The reverberations of the marsh evacuation still pounding through her, Amber turned at the hilltop, desperate for its height as she scanned frantically to no avail as the final scattered members of the tribe caught up with their clan and disappeared into the landscape.

An agony of futile options flitting dismissed across her racing mind, Amber fought against despair. She didn't know how to call the Zyfang and it was too far to go back for a Bicorn. Fierce tears of helplessness squeezed into her eyes. Oh, to fly to him!

Wait—who said she couldn't? A final possibility glinted: one first opened to her the very night she had thought she'd lost the gift forever. Alien, and undone, and warned against, but . . .

Heart and hope burning in her chest with the urgency of what she must now attempt, Amber raced towards the Fountain.

The Fountain

The silence of the chamber scattered into slapping footsteps as Amber burst into the Fountain basin, heaving with overexertion and skidding abruptly on the smooth rock in a belated attempt to stop, for wreathed in the mists of the chamber stood an old woman as still as marble, her long flat grey hair skimming a draping floor-length gown shimmering the colour of fish-scales. Soaked and shivering and finally still, the savage coldness of the stone beneath Amber's feet felt almost life-sapping, and yet she could not help but for the shortest moment lose herself in her surroundings and stare, for here around her soared both bitterness and beauty, in a transcendently warning promise proving what could not only be suffered, but also survived.

Stern of gaze and stiff of bearing, the Water Nymph watched the Fairy impassively through eyes both gaunt and deep, lending Amber the sudden impression that before her waited one who had seen the ages of the Realm unfold and been unable to forget any of it, good or ill.

"Please, ma'am," Amber gasped wretchedly, gathering her manners with a quick bow. "My friends are in mortal trouble and I need to rescue them; I can't fly so I need to use the Fountain."

She looked up; the Nymph hadn't moved and instead was staring at her emptily.

The echoes of her voice scattered, through a chamber as hollow as a broken promise. Amber's heart slumped. Why would the Nymph believe her, after a lifetime of losing faith?

"*Please*, my lady." Amber struggled not to shout. "I wouldn't be disturbing you if it wasn't life and death." She let her glance travel the height of the Fountain in trepidation as the impossibility of actually reaching the bubbles hit her, now that—*a thousand curses!*—she couldn't fly. Her gaze fell on an uncanny darkness twisting far above as if clinging to a rupture in the cragged basin wall, and she couldn't look away.

"That," warned the Nymph in her first acknowledgment of the Fairy's presence, her voice unexpectedly harsh as her glance stabbed the lofty shadow, "is not a way you would wish to traverse, and nor will I allow it before being certain that you will be able to handle it."

Amber tore her gaze from the gaping fissure to turn back to the Nymph in anguish. "But I don't have time!" She hadn't meant to sound so whiny, but there was too much at stake to be wasting minutes like this.

The Nymph's gaze remained unyielding, and she eyed the Fairy dispassionately. "You will make time, if you do not wish it to be your last, child. You have no idea what you are doing."

Amber stared at her in disbelief. "I still have to do it," she protested. "My friends are going to die."

"It will destroy you."

"I won't let it!"

The Nymph regarded her objectively—a small Fairy wracked with such emotion that it was tearing her apart. "Your statement, however brave, contradicts the evidence."

"I don't care!" Amber pleaded, not knowing what else to say. Her voice echoed rashly around the ancient chamber.

"I do, however," the woman admonished sharply. "As will you, one day, should you be fortunate to live that long."

The Nymph neither blinked nor moved as Amber stumbled over what was in her heart. "Fine: maybe I can't take it. You understand why I have to do it though, right? I bet you've done things to help others and then had to pay the price yourself, and at least this way I'll have done *something*. If this is to be my price for helping them, I would gladly pay it tenfold."

The Nymph waited a crisp moment. "Do not presume to tell me how I feel, let alone how this works," she reprimanded frostily.

Amber bit her lip, chastened, and taking a breath against her frustration she nodded carefully. "I'm sorry."

The Nymph afforded the Fairy a barely perceptible incline of her head. "So, child," her voice echoed coldly. "Why have you come to the Fountain?" Bitterness crept into her tone. "To seek pain? Guilt?" She looked away suddenly. "For they will find you here, no matter your initial intentions."

Amber tried to speak proudly, although her voice sounded as weak as a flickering candle in the chamber before such a powerful figure. "I do not seek them, my lady. Yet neither will I shy from them if my actions can ease the burdens of my friends."

"Ah, yes," the woman acknowledged dryly, her voice cutting like ice. "Many have spoken thus, but where are they now? The time for heroes, they say, is over, and yet there is always one young fool who thinks they know better and chooses not to listen." Her gaze roamed the shadows curling in the gloom as if sweeping back a veil drawn long ago across the past.

"They come, thinking they can change things, and when they fail I witness, distanced through the bubbles, their final breaths, and I hear them curse the day I let them pass as the day I sent them to their deaths."

Amber felt herself shrink away with the dying echoes of her voice. "I'm so sorry," she whispered, against the futility of the words.

The Nymph shook her head dismissively, although her eyes no longer bore the same fierceness as before. "It is for your own good that I warn you against this endeavour. I have gazed into the darkness, found where it can lead. I know a little of the price demanded even just to slow its progress."

Amber swallowed, awareness of what must have happened all those years ago blooming fiercely in her chest. "I know, Lady Zaralathaar," she whispered, recalling the name of the Sea Maiden Princess, next in line to the throne and famed for her ethereal beauty, who was never found after the Sea Battle.

The Nymph regarded the Fairy closely, as if seeing her for the first time.

"You fought back against it all and brought hope through your own sacrifice, for not only did you bind the Vetches to rock, trapping them insentient in the bowels of the Realm, but you did so knowing that this act would drain your power and result in you ageing and dying at the usual rate instead of achieving the near-immortality of your birth-race."

Tears glistened in the Water Nymph's eyes, which she made no move to attend to.

Amber bowed deeply. "My lady, you are a queen to our Realm, whether it's recognised or not. We owe you everything."

"You know that it was ultimately for nothing." The old Princess's voice was no more than a whisper when she finally spoke. "My years have nearly ended and what power I still hold is waning fast. You know that is why the Vetches are coming back."

"If it had not been for you," Amber contradicted ardently, "the Realm would have long since sunk into darkness and there would be no light left to fight for now."

The Nymph's response was barely audible. "You cannot prove that good can actually conquer evil, child."

"Maybe not," Amber admitted. "But I'm human enough that I can still believe it."

"So I see." The Nymph's voice softened almost imperceptibly. "Yet I can give you no substantiation to ease this trial."

Amber struggled for what to say next. "I can't use magic," she acknowledged. "I can't win battles, I can't kill monsters, and I can't save lands. What I'm proposing might not prove significant at the end, and it's not going to be easy, or heard of, or talked about, or admired—but it is something I can do and you cannot turn me from my path, however ill-advised or inconsequential you view it to be."

For once, the Nymph did not contradict her. "Do not judge me too harshly," the woman entreated quietly instead. "I have been jaded by what I have been forced to observe. I have lost my faith in others: in the fidelity of their intentions, in the capacity of their endurance, and in the wisdom of their belief that strength of heart and goodness of soul are enough to carry someone who should never have died that way out alive." She touched the Fairy's cheek briefly, her wizened fingers cold as an underground stream. "I do not want you to go the same way." The chamber faded into a potent silence, absolute save for the slow *drip, drip, drip* from a stalactite somewhere in the darkness.

"You neither can nor will be blamed," Amber tentatively offered at last. "Perhaps you will see my last breath, so far away you cannot do anything about it, and I probably will think of you who enabled the journey that ended thus. But it will not be to remember you as the one who risked a life being lost, but rather as the one who chanced a life being saved."

Within the Nymph's eyes grew a heavy sadness. "Brave words are easily bandied. You cannot promise anything at the point the storm breaks."

Amber's throat squeezed hotly, so tight that she could barely swallow. Maybe the Nymph was right; that there was nothing she could do, that this was all beyond her and that she was foolish to think she could even attempt to challenge it. Maybe one day she'd even start listening to her. But for now she kept quiet until she felt surer of herself, and returned the Nymph's gaze steadily as she gathered her courage. "I can't promise that I'll succeed," Amber acknowledged. "I can only vow that if I fail, it will not be through lack of trying."

"Very well," Zaralathaar acquiesced in fate-laden tones. "I have tried to warn you, even if you will not listen. Yet your argument, although naïve, is powerful nonetheless, and I will do as you ask for the simple reason that you believe now as I once did. For your courage, and the selflessness of your quest, I will grant you but once this gift." She beckoned to the Fairy. "Close your eyes."

Amber did so, hearing a clap of hands and, to her astonishment, the scrunch of stone grating over rock.

"Open your eyes. Come." The Nymph held out her hand, tutting with impatience as Amber stared awestruck at the carved opening, newly revealed by the Nymph's words, leading up into the rock-face. "Do not stand there gawping, child; you must have known I still hold a semblance of power over rock of all things, but my magic is not strong enough all these years to sustain this shift for long. Follow me, and swiftly."

Stumbling her apologies, Amber clasped the Princess's chill hand and they strode together into the crevasse, their footsteps echoing through the darkening passageway until the cold light of the chamber sank, vanquished amidst the cloying black depths within the crag.

The initial far-off sea-rumblings grew thunderously overhead as they advanced, until the chink of light above them reached into an exit and the Nymph stepped out onto a rocky platform, her hair streaming as if caught in cliff-top winds. Scrambling after her, Amber squinted against the glaring blue-white light and gagged in shock as the chamber erupted with the resounding crash and heave of roiling water far below and the buffeting winds teased her balance. It felt as though the Realm itself had been torn open; the safety of darkness and enclosure ripped away into the most blinding of lights, the most incomprehensible expanses of cavernous space. In the face of it her own flame shivered and quailed—and then billowed, reflected in the clarity of ice. The way suddenly felt open again.

Inching as close to the edge of the precipice as she dared, Amber struggled to take in the scene. So much closer now than when she had first glimpsed it from the Bicorn, the noise of the churning maelstrom was almost deafening and the amount of froth and foam flung high amidst the battling green-blue currents bore testament to the terrifying forces raging beneath.

From her current position on the ledge—a rim seemingly running the circumference of the Fountain itself, stretching in width at least two lengths of Amber should she choose to lie down and wriggle towards the edge for a better view of all that rushed and pounded below—she judged that they must have reached the halfway point of the structure.

A cold unworldly light flooded forth, swirling to the distant sky in serene contrast to the conflicting tides forming a thrashing circular pseudo-sea below whence jutting rocks protruded as if from a snaggle-toothed maw. Between these two aspects, spiralling the full majestic height of the cavern, gargantuan bubbles glistened wetly in the darkness, drifting past in stately orbit and humming as their own power sparked against the elements warring beneath and beyond.

The Nymph gestured resignedly. "Each one reflects a scene in real-time. If you jump into a bubble's depiction, you will be transported to that situation, wherever it is in the Realm." She turned abruptly, her expression as she did so missed by the Fairy still staring captivated as the orbs swept past.

Zaralathaar's dress dragged quietly over the floor as she stepped back. "The choice you make in the Fountain is one you must live with alone," she warned. "And so alone you must make it."

Unable to tear her eyes away, Amber barely heard her. As the bubbles neared each one grew until it dwarfed her, drawing her gaze until she lost all sensation of standing safely at the side and the scene within the shimmering globe became her entire Realm. Screams, shouts, whimpers; cry upon horrifying cry forced into her until she was drowning in them, the images shivering across the glistening surface slipping oil-like beneath her skin to lodge cankerous and eternal inside her soul.

Appalled, she flinched away, but the Nymph's bony fingers clamped round her wrist like a vice. "*Watch*," she insisted, in an almost Vetch-like hiss. "The others have their part; you have yours. *This* is why you must not fail."

Paralysed by remorse, Amber forced herself to do as she knew she must. Yet the implications of what she had just seen firsthand had until now been only the vaguest of assumptions as yet incomprehensible, distanced by a naïve trust that the other bubbles would hold normal situations, or at worst ones that still weren't that bad; things that she could pledge to help later when the greatest danger had passed and she'd found Racxen. But now the truly Realm-wide extent of the catastrophe wormed into her, sending Amber's whole body seizing with a churning sickness of guilt, her hands flying subconsciously to her head as her mind raced into a desperate whirlwind until she felt like her own thoughts were tearing her apart. She could only choose one bubble—so what about all the cries for help she couldn't answer?

She sank to her knees and howled, her body wracked with sobs, consumed by grief and anger and helplessness. She couldn't do this. She just couldn't. Not choose one and consign the others to such misery and suffering. She couldn't forsake those poor souls; all clamouring for someone to help them, all believing no one could, all unaware that she stood here with the power to race in—to *try*.

She couldn't close her ears to the screams of those fleeing possession-less as their homes were trampled by rampaging Venom-spitters; couldn't shut her eyes against the gaunt stare of the starving child slumped in a field the monsters had ravaged, his skeletal fingers reaching in vain for someone, anyone; couldn't turn away and leave those cries unanswered when they were each so close that she could jump in; explode into their Realm and make everything okay.

Movement rustled in the gloaming behind her and a cold hand fell lightly upon her shoulder.

Amber's eyes flashed up, her sight flooded and unfocused from unending tears. "How can you ask this of me?" she begged.

"If you remember, I made no such demand. This is entirely of your choosing," the Water Nymph reminded cold-eyed, the smallest pang of sympathy flickering across her pale, drained face as she beheld the stricken Fairy.

"Yet I am sorry." Her clear grey eyes softened for a moment, and her voice rose like a brook soothing the way over a jagged course. "It is a wretched decision that befalls you, but it is how we make and live with such choices that shapes who we are. Anyone could come here at any time, and choose one bubble. Yet how many, do you think, actually make the journey, knowing how it must end? Child, there will always be those you cannot save. Don't let it stop you from helping those you can."

"But who am I to choose?" Amber whispered brokenly. "How could I live with myself if—"

"That is your problem; it scarcely compares to the magnitude of theirs," the Nymph reminded impatiently, her voice returning to its usual harshness. "If you persist in thinking like that it will kill you. In the end the choice is simple: save one and forsake the rest, or allow your guilt to paralyse you to the extent that you cannot elect one over any other—meaning you will end up choosing none—and so forsake them all."

Amber nodded grimly. Whilst her Realm shuddered and fell away around her, she scraped her conviction back together, pressed her hands against the gritty, damp-slicked rock, and heaved herself shakily off the floor.

"I'll come back," she blurted fiercely. "I'll use the Fountain again. I'll save them all. No matter how long it takes, I'll—"

"No you will not!" the Nymph admonished vehemently, her voice shaking with the potency of the thrashing waves beneath. "I will refuse you with all the power I still hold. It was a mistake to allow you even once. It is for your own good, although the tides alone know why I still care. Move," she advised briskly as the Fairy stared at her in mute anguish. "Your time runs short."

Amber tore her eyes away resolutely. *I will come back*, she promised herself. She had to believe it, or else she couldn't do it—or worse would have to contend with the possibility of the alternative, and then what would that make her?

She blinked constantly as her steps quickened; she couldn't afford to let tears blur her vision now as she forced herself to scan bubble after bubble of harrowing scene. *Anything like this or worse could be happening to Racxen.* Yet her eyes welled uncontrollably and she could barely discern the curve of the ledge now, her footsteps lurching evermore unsteadily as her glance strayed to the worst of the scenes, her progress slowing as her gaze lingered in growing horror until she stumbled, sickened and disorientated by the unending scenes of terror and the relentless speed at which they assailed her. Doggedly she continued, forcing herself to check each one carefully even as she knew they would haunt her for seasons of nights to come.

As she peered into the darkest bubble, the orb of night swelled into a labyrinthine vista of rocks biting through a storm-ravaged sky, punctuated by the familiar blur of Racxen's gait as he pelted through, the hulking shadows of Venom-spitters looming behind him.

Amber's previous uncertainty balled itself into grim determination. Tensing herself in readiness as the bubble drifted closer, with a desperate cry sliding out unchecked, she leapt.

Instinctively, she shut her eyes against the translucent wall and the damp, tingling sensation that washed over her as if she'd jumped into a storm cloud. Something wobbled beneath her feet, yielding as she stumbled yet not letting her fall, and as her eyes snapped open again she glimpsed the oily, iridescent shimmer of the bubble wall stretching to enclose her, trapping her inside.

Now what? Restricted to a claustrophobically distorted view of the outside Realm through the bubble's convex film, Amber narrowed her immediate attention onto keeping as still as she could to avoid the risk of plunging a limb through the flimsy wall. It shivered, sickeningly fragile, its flowing patterns glistening with pearlescent hues as the bubble continued its orbit. As she sat down clumsily to await her descent, the floor wobbled precariously like the bouncy castle at Ruby's party when they'd been winglets—how far away those times felt now. Yet through the knotted nerves of anticipation she felt exultation rush: she was actually inside—it had worked. She'd reach Racxen.

Fear invaded anew as the bubble lurched and sent her sprawling, her hands plunging into the wall membrane and stretching it hideously. For several fraught moments she could discern only the *wau-aum* boom of the Fountain reverberating through the diaphanous surface, as if her ears were filled with water. Although the curved walls shifted her surroundings unnaturally, she could have sworn the little she could recognise hadn't looked this distant a minute ago. A new chill of fear shivered through her as she glimpsed the cavernous shadow below gaping wider like a wound being pulled apart, and she pressed herself pitifully against the membrane as she felt the bubble detach itself from the circuit and float unstoppably towards the core.

She tried to look back to the platform, but she was too far away to even catch sight of the Nymph now, the insidious pull towards the centre as inescapable as the insatiable darkness sucking beneath.

The air around her clung charged and oppressive as if heralding thunder; shimmering with weird hues, expectation hanging so heavily that Amber wouldn't have been surprised to have seen sparks crackle across the glistening orb. Anticipation shivering through the dark, she couldn't stop her mind from flicking back to take refuge in safer fears: at the Mid-Recö night fairground with Tanzan, gripping the bar at the top of the roller coaster as it teetered at the summit. *Ride it out*, she ordered herself, against the wash of icy terror roiling in her chest, so close to controlling her. *This is for Racxen.*

The bubble started to spin, like a nightmarish version of those twirl-ing goblet rides she'd loved as a winglet, sending her sprawling into the insubstantial membrane that was her only barrier between the raging tumult hundreds of feet below, stretching it eye-wateringly thin. Spi-ralling faster and faster in an ever-tightening orbit, the entire bubble buzzed with wind-rush, distending and crushing with the pressure of its acceleration until, pushed flat by the force of its speed, Amber gagged and spluttered against the film pressing around her face. Insubstantial fear stripped away into primal, breath-or-death terror as she struggled for just one more mouthful of air.

Clamping her eyes shut against the rushing wall of darkness, she felt the bile-lifting lurch of weightlessness; all breath sucked out of her as her stomach jumped to her throat, and in the next instant her Realm split with a deafening *crack* as the bubble slammed through the maelstrom, plunging and bucked through the water like a sea serpent of old. She felt the cloying film reshaping itself spherically around her and she gulped mechanically, sucking down air as the waves battered against her prison.

All thoughts fled as the night exploded, sending her sprawling back-wards off-guard as the bubble sprang cork-like from the raging surface, shooting upwards and blurring her Realm into stars and thunder until with the now familiar gut-churning lurch of gravity she plummeted once more, the walls buckling skin-like against her even as the speed of her descent peeled the layers away.

"Mugkafb, you have to run!" Racxen demanded as he crouched together with his brother behind the rock, listening to the monsters advancing unswervingly towards their precarious hiding-place. "They know where I am and they won't let me go—but you're small enough that they haven't seen you yet."

Watching the blood seep through Racxen's claws as his brother clutched at his leg, Mugkafb spat as many curses as he could remember. "But you need me—"

"I need you safe!" Racxen hissed in anguish. "I need you out of here; I need you to live. At the slightest next distraction you have to run."

Rocky terrain loomed out of the night too fast for Amber to scream as the bubble burst jarringly against the ground, disgorging her amongst a scattering of slimy sac-remnants.

The thud sent the monsters' slavering heads swinging round.

"Now!" Racxen breathed before he could see what the distraction had been, pushing Mugkafb forward while the Venom-spitters' attention was engaged.

Mugkafb threw himself from the cover of the rocks and shot away down the hillside, racing towards the forest. No time to glance back and check if he was being followed, he powered every scrap of his energy into running towards the swaying branches beckoning him to their shelter. This was his chance at being a hero. Everyone was depending on him, and he ran as he never had before; jumping over roots and ducking under boughs, the wind screaming anxiously through the trees to hurry him on as he barraged through the undergrowth, running, running, running; as he heard the night behind him shatter with a roar.

"Amber?" Racxen blurted, rooted in astonishment as he saw her, slicked in the glinting sheen of the bubble sac slipping to the ground, scramble to her feet while the monsters bellowed their promise of vengeance to the fleeing form of their smallest prey.

Amber looked on in mute horror as the monsters turned and pounded towards the distracted Arraheng, determined not to let their remaining meal escape.

Do something! her mind screamed at her. *You came here to rescue him, not make things worse!*

As she cast around wildly for anything she could use as a weapon, amidst a scuffle from the rock behind her something crawled out, unmistakeable in the moonlight beneath her desperate gaze: a red-eyed Gantorna. A deathly chill gripped her, but flooded with a dizzying wash of adrenalin her trembling hand snaked out to seize the death-rattling tail, barely missing the stinger. Elated at her sliver of luck she leapt out from behind the rocks, waving the Gantorna aloft. "*Hey!*"

The Venom-spitters snarled warily and turned, averting their fatal attention from Racxen.

As they kept their eyes on the livid bundle squirming in her grasp, it was all Amber could do to keep her grip as the Gantorna writhed in anger, its tale shaking out a furious death-rattle and its deadly poison-dart unsheathed for all to see.

Heads low, tongues slipping warily from between curved yellowed fangs, the monsters hung back, their warning growls uncertain.

Fuelled by their hesitation, Amber thrust the arthropod forward and advanced, bellowing what she'd do to them if they touched her friend.

The closest Venom-spitter tensed into a crouch and, as she saw its muscles bunch to spring, in panic she feinted throwing the Gantorna.

The monster yelped and loped off, its companion overtaking in selfish haste and the pair bounded fluidly away, the wind carrying their howls of displeasure to the mountain as they abandoned the prone body they had moments ago guarded so jealously.

Sensing they had left, Racxen shifted and moaned, opening his eyes. Delirious with relief, Amber's grip relaxed slightly as she ran to him.

"Throw it!" Racxen yelled hysterically, even as the Gantorna squirmed and freed itself just enough to whip round and plunge the cruel barb into her wrist.

Amber choked and gasped, clutching at her wrist as her whole arm started to burn savagely, the pain blooming into her chest to crush her lungs. She tried to cry out, but her desiccated tongue filled her mouth and her jaw seized numbly. As if from above, she pictured herself toppling forward, unable to stop her own fall.

The Gantorna sprang away, its dart ripping through her skin, the poison fully discharged.

"Amber!" Racxen reached her just as she crumpled to the floor. Falling to his knees in the dirt beside her, his own searing wound forgotten, he grabbed her other hand, feverishly trying to get a response and remember what the healers said about poison. Keep the affected part lower than her heart? Keep her still and summon help? But what was the use; he knew the only outcome for a Gantorna sting.

No. No matter that they said it would kill in minutes, it wouldn't. Wouldn't if he followed their advice; wouldn't if he kept her calm. This was Amber. There had to have been someone who had survived it before, and she'd simply be the next. It couldn't have been fully grown; it couldn't have released all its poison.

Arduously, he hauled her onto the slope of the mountain base, leaving her wrist drooping, hoping that would do for protection and elevation. The effort left him seeing blotches and he crumpled beside her.

Reaching instinctively for the remaining soulroot, devastation crumbled into his heart as he realised he'd lost it somewhere along their route as they'd fled. And Amber had used up her Gem on Mugkafb. Racxen fell back, cursing in every language he knew.

A rending scream drowned his words as white-hot agony spilled across her like scalding oil. Maybe the mountain had fallen her—maybe that was why an icy touch was creeping through her veins against the burning in her chest . . . her mind rambled on, dislocated from time. Or maybe she was turning into stone . . . that must be it, for there was music now, close by; maybe someone was here to take her to the other side . . .

"You walked with me through such lonely darkness
Through the nights of my worst fears and pain
I'll walk you through yours; I'll never leave you
And someday we'll walk in sunlight again."

His hands stroking her hair trembling violently as he sang a melody half-remembered through the blur of that night wrapped in her arms in the Glade Pool, Racxen's words began to slur as his wounds refused to stop bleeding. His vision shuddered and he fell back, the tide of unconsciousness threatening to drag him into its unconquerable depths. Groaning with the effort he wriggled closer to Amber, finding her unaffected hand.

"This'll fade to memory; you'll wake to sunlight soon," he gasped, entwining his claws with her fingers. Her body lay limp; she gave no discernable response at all now as he waited with her for whatever was to come. He knew he couldn't stop it, but he could make sure that she didn't meet it alone in this forsaken hellscape.

Yelling himself hoarse, Racxen barraged the unheeding stars with reasons and promises and fears until his failing cries fell dashed against the rocks and their echoes surrendered to the wind. His eyes swam with tears until the sky blurred into a meaningless void as he refused to lower his eyes.

"Where are you, Mugkafb?" he pleaded weakly to the night.

Mugkafb's Moment

Far away now, Mugkafb hadn't stopped running. Those interminable hours of agony on the hillside endured by Racxen and Amber had in reality been only so many footfalls pounding the earth for the young Arraheng before, his pulse roaring in his ears and shuddering his vision, he charged into the Fairy Ring gasping almost to the point of retching. "Racxen, Amber, Venom-spitters!" he managed. "The hillside!"

Alarm flashing across his face, Morgan was already running towards him, Bright Shadow summoned and alighting on the grass. Sweeping Mugkafb up before him, the King sprang to the Bicorn's back. Grasping her wiry mane with one hand and wrapping his other arm steadyingly around the young Arraheng, the King urged Bright Shadow into the air with a wild cry and the Herd Leader leapt forward willingly, pounding the sky along an unseen trail.

Mugkafb had no time to register the wonder of his first flight. The wind streamed into his watering eyes as he forced them open, scanning the blurred landscape flashing past below for any sign of life.

"Hold tight!" Leaning in close around him as the Bicorn raced tirelessly through the night, the King urged Bright Shadow on to greater speeds until her pace seemed to Mugkafb almost supernatural.

From the dimensionless black spilled the lighter silhouette of a boulder-strewn, moon-blanched hillside, and at a word from Morgan the Bicorn slowed, descending along her invisible path.

Their speed almost stealing his voice, the King shouted back: "Are we close?"

"I can't tell!" Mugkafb gulped helplessly as the wind whipped against his face. "No—wait!" His voice shrilled urgently, memories resurfacing as he glimpsed the rock formations. "There!"

Far below, his failing vision trained with a last effort on the sky as he scoured the night almost blindly now, Racxen felt more than glimpsed the glimmer swooping nearer through the endless depths and he yelled and whooped and hollered and cried until . . .

Sighting the bodies slumped in the clearing, the Bicorn plummeted so fast Mugkafb gagged.

"Sorry," the King gasped as Bright Shadow skidded amongst a billow of loose stones. A chillingly familiar scream tore into their ears and Morgan threw himself from the Bicorn, Mugkafb racing after him.

His words jumbling with emotion and exhaustion as they reached him, Racxen spilled his account.

Morgan's heart froze in his chest as his gaze rested on the small body lying supine and silent next to him. Snapping his Gem from its cord, the King struck the teardrop stone against the nearest rock, kneeling to swiftly powder the fragments into the girl's discolouring wound.

"Can you hear me, Amber? Look at me."

Her eyelids flickered slightly as he shook her shoulders, but her vision of him swam against the darkness and her head lolled back senseless against the ground.

Mugkafb flitted powerlessly between his brother and poor Amber whose hand Racxen was clinging to as if it was the only thing keeping him from passing out, before hovering anxiously to watch the Fairy King who was their only hope of saving her. "It's not working!" he choked, unable to keep silent as his eyes brimmed with tears. Why was there never anything *he* could do when everyone was suffering?

Morgan's face tightened in dread. "She's further gone than I thought," he muttered, dragging loose his sash and shoving it into Mugkafb's hands. "I need water." He laid a restraining hand on Racxen as the tracker struggled to rise. "No son, you're badly injured yourself; we're getting you to the rec hall." His voice brooked no argument. "Soak that, Mugkafb. Run!"

"That's the sound of help returning," Racxen promised Amber, wiping her clammy brow as his brother raced back from a puddle-hollow with the sash dripping. Squeezing it over the remaining powder, Morgan stirred the fallen droplets into a paste.

Mugkafb hovered with the sash. "Should I get more water? Can't we make her drink it faster?"

"No," the King's voice lay heavy with sorrow as he scraped together the last remnants of the mixture. "She'd choke on water, all we can do is give this—" he broke off to concentrate as he dabbed the concoction between her gum and cheek.

"Now we get her to your healers?" Racxen cut in, the words slow on his tongue.

Morgan shook his head. "First we must be patient—we can't move her until we know the Gem has begun to work, or the poison will keep spreading. For the next few minutes, we must wait and watch—and hope."

The scratch of Gantorna legs skittered over her burning skin as through a feverish haze Venom-spitters and Goblins merged in the shadows before Amber's eyes and began to speak to her in some dreamt up language she'd never heard. Worms pushed towards her lips, and as a bitter taste flooded her mouth she clamped her teeth weakly against them.

The sluggish bite-reflex split the King's face in a grin of relief. "She's still with us." He wiped his hands with a sigh and stroked her brow, his voice dropping as he whispered: "That's the full dose. All we can do now is hope the tincture infuses fast enough."

Amber spluttered as the taste invaded her senses, turning the air in her lungs to spiced fire.

"Amber, stay calm."

More noise from the shadows flooded into her drifting mind and she thought for a moment she heard the King's commanding voice splice through the fear, but the darkness loomed again and she knew she must have imagined it. Claws pressed coolly now against her clammy skin, but whether those of her friends or the monsters she hadn't the capacity left to either tell or care.

She felt herself lifting until her body was floating, suspended in empty air. Maybe she was dying. The vaguest impression of the sky seemed to spin out of focus overhead, and yet there was a rhythm to her motion. To her now-distant mind it felt almost familiar.

Then even that faded into nothing.

Enigma

Amber heard birdsong: clear, and close, and real. Her hands touched starched linen. Everywhere smelled of a particular kind of clean. A downy pillow had crept under her head. There was no pain save for dull aching, apart from when she tried to swallow her throat felt weird and she couldn't place why.

Memories of last night reared abruptly, slamming full-force into her consciousness until she cried aloud, twisting the bedclothes in her panic as she flinched from something no longer there to fight.

The wave broke, and her surroundings registered again. *It's over*, she practised telling herself. Time had passed, although she couldn't tell whether in hours or days. Soft light infused through the curtain, bathing her room in a gentle orange glow. Everything was calm. *Engo ro fash.*

A smart tap rattled the door, and Amber rolled over carefully, grimacing at needing to think through the manoeuvre she'd previously taken for granted.

"Morning!" A jovial round face and quick dark eyes joined the stridently cheerful greeting as the Matron bustled into the room. "It's Amber, isn't it? You had a lucky escape; we don't get much call for that antidote." She smiled reassuringly as she gave a brisk update. "You were very weak when you got here so we gave you fluids intravenously, and you were on a ventilator overnight so your throat might be a trifle sore from the tube. You're well on the mend now; we just need to keep you here a wee bit longer in case you get a touch of serum sickness from the antivenin. Last thing we want is you getting feverish again and even more fatigued."

"Thanks," Amber croaked huskily, awed.

Sarin smiled warmly. "It all came together, lass. You just concentrate on getting better."

Amber's vision blurred as she watched the Matron busy about from the corner of her eye. "I don't know if I could do what you do," she admitted, voice full of admiration and worry.

Looking up from folding a blanket, Sarin shook her head. "Nonsense, missy," she admonished confidently. "I've been doing this since I was just past your age. Given the same time, so could you." She shook a finger with mock severity. "But no worrying about any apprenticeships, you hear me? Your recovery—that's your job for now. I'll check up on you in half an hour; if you need anything before, use your button."

Amber nodded yieldingly, letting her head sink back into the welcoming pillow of silence.

Scritch-scratch . . . Scritch-scratch . . .

Amber woke from a fitful doze to the noise, twisting round gingerly to find Racxen crouched on the window frame trying to be silent. "You're better quick," she murmured thankfully, confused.

The Arraheng grinned apologetically. "You've been out for a while. I didn't mean to wake you; the door's quieter but I went through the swamps to reassure Mugkafb after the transfusion, so Sarin wouldn't let me back in. How are you feeling?"

"Right now? Really good," she admitted as she returned his grin, realising with a flush of embarrassment that the truth of the statement owed more than it strictly should to finding him here to wake up to.

Racxen dropped back beneath the window as hasty footsteps echoed towards the room and the strains of a particularly fraught voice rang through the hall.

"Your Highness! I must protest! This is well before visiting time!"

Amber grinned as she saw the indomitable Sarin Thornswen striding down the corridor, hot on the tail of an embarrassed Prince Jasper. Complaining vehemently that his business was of utmost importance and clutching bundles of parchment to his chest, Jasper nonetheless at the Matron's scathing glance kicked off his muddied boots and stumbled into the overshoes she thrust in his direction. Flapping down the hall in them, the Prince swept towards Amber's room with as much dignity as he could still muster.

"You're awake," he exclaimed in relief, rolling his eyes at the retreating form of the Matron as he shuffled inside. "I'm sorry, I was . . . otherwise engaged earlier, I honestly couldn't tell you exactly where, but I've been waiting out there with these and that Nurse's been having a right go at me, I don't think they're sanitary enough for her."

He let the scrolls slide to the floor and unfurled them. "I didn't want to wake you, but this is important."

Amber's eyes closed as a wave of nausea rolled. "Sorry you had to wait."

The Prince glanced at her, genuinely surprised. "Don't be; I've had time to look over these maps." His eyes glittered in rare excitement. "We won't stay long, you need to rest but—you'll like this—there are some intriguing discrepancies between the vault and castle map records. Luckily, our young Arraheng friend has an eye for the old legends."

"Hi!" Mugkafb snuck out from behind the door and darted to her bedside. "You'll feel better if you eat something—I brought you some nectar sticks. I ate one, but these two are yours."

Amber grinned her thanks to the boy, breaking him off another half of one. Rubbing her eyes groggily, she tried to make sense of the

Prince's remark. "But why would they be different?" she mumbled, her mouth full of nectar.

"Unfortunately, the castle records are pretty recent; they're all 'Authorised' to a degree and, for some reason, the Emperor's cronies edited out certain tunnels through the rock—a different section in each map." A distant look came over Jasper's eyes as if he were trying to peer through forgotten shelves of memory to delve for what he sought.

"It's not a clear indication, but it's an enticing one. Racxen, you need to hear this too," he admitted with a longsuffering sigh as Amber's eyes strayed to the window.

As the Arraheng climbed in quietly, Jasper continued: "At first glance, each discrepancy looks like an innocuous mistake; a blip in the middle of nowhere. Yet they correspond consecutively to gaps on a much older map."

Mugkafb, fidgeting restlessly, broke in: "This one from the library vaults at Arkh Loban—" the Prince hastily unfurled a discoloured parchment almost flaking with age, "is too old to have the seal of Authority. Hold it up with the others and it joins all the missing sections—you can trace a tunnel through the rock right to the centre of Dread Mountain."

"Although the way is completely sealed," Jasper cautioned. "It both starts and ends miles into the rock. I said it was intriguing," he added defensively. "I never promised it'd be useful."

"They named Dread Mountain so when the Nymph imprisoned the Vetches there, right?" Amber checked, stumbling over her words slightly. "So why did the Goblins take Mugkafb there?"

"Because the Nymph's getting older and losing her power, the Vetches are awakening and they're driving the Venom-spitters out of their caves into Arraterr's path, and so now Thanatos and his Goblins are trying to control the Venom-spitters for their own ends to help them take back Loban," Mugkafb summarised confidently. "Keep up, Amber!"

"The Vetches although stirring have not yet gathered strength sufficient to break free from the confines of the mountains, so the Venom-spitters are being forced out into the open—and into contact with Thanatos. It is plausible that the Goblins are attempting to manipulate the Venom-spitters by appeasing or bribing them with sacrifices," Jasper suggested, with the grace to look distinctly queasy. "Such behaviour indicates the presence of an alpha—a possibility rendered even more shocking when one considers that the only weakness of the Venom-spitters at present is their selfishness and the lawlessness of their packs.

"Mugkafb was going on about having heard of a 'Samire', a breeding individual responsible for the entire subsequent population, and what if that individual's role evolved? If the descendents were to become organised under a single leader, who could hope to stand against them? The very fact that we were led once again to the mountain in chasing Mugkafb demonstrates that such an alpha—it is no great leap to presume it is the Samire—is no longer frightened of the Vetches but is residing somewhere along those endless subterranean twists and knots. Those tunnels have been cursed by Snakelocks, as well as blessed by the Nymph, and with the Vetches newly reanimated and the Enchantress weakening with every passing day, who knows what foul craft the mountain and its denizens are now awash with?"

"There has to be some kind of connection to the Fountain," Amber realised. "At first glance it seems to exist in a time and place entirely its own—but I think that must be an illusion affected by the Water Nymph's enchantments. It was created to maintain a watch over the Vetches, after all—so it has to correlate with the mountain in some way."

"I should have recognised as much," Racxen agreed, his gleaming dark eyes already darting in anticipation towards the exit. "I'd better go scout for information."

"You'd *better*," the Prince glowered, "actually listen for once and leave the heroics to me. You lost a significant amount of blood not long ago and if you go and collapse I'll have that wretched Nurse to answer to."

Jasper's retort flowed unheeded over Amber, her mind churning over his earlier revelation. Something floated at the edge of conscious thought through the meds-induced haze. Something as important as it was out of reach.

Racxen winced as Amber absent-mindedly leant on her still-swollen hand and yelped. "We'll tell you everything we find," he promised her.

Keeping her hand out of the way, Amber rolled carefully out of bed with a grunt and tested her legs. "You won't have to. I'll be right there with you."

"Oh, I'm sorry, are you next in line to the throne?" Jasper warned indignantly, scrabbling for any semblance of authority he could yet muster. "Lie back down before you fall out of bed or something equally ridiculous."

He jumped violently at the sound of a door swishing open further along the corridor. "Or, for the love of pity, at least before Sarin comes back. Look," he suggested more seriously in appeasement as he stowed the scrolls on the bedside cabinet, "what would be really useful is if when you feel better you could take another look at these maps; see if you can glean anything from them that might help."

Amber relented blearily, knowing she was no use in this state. The ceiling wobbled when she lay back down as the others left and, despite promising herself that she would stay awake until they got back, she fell into strange dreams almost immediately; flashes of the night repeating through her mind in random variations as she struggled to accept it was over.

Against the flooding fear that she would be drowned in the fragmented maelstrom of fickle half-memories and fevered imaginings, a rock in her mind arose. Except it was no longer a rock; her fear now subsiding as awareness seeped through of a solid, silent presence emanating strength, and Amber found herself leaning against Rraarl's shoulder once more, letting his power wash through into her, lending her courage for the times ahead.

I was so scared that they'd killed you.

YET I STAND BEFORE YOU ONCE AGAIN.

I feel like you're going to disappear.

YOU WERE NEVER AFRAID OF LOOKING AT ME. DO SO AGAIN NOW; DO NOT FEAR.

Rraarl, I'm so sorry.

WHAT FOR? I AM HERE. ALL IS WELL. SLEEP.

Okay. I can't remember why I thought otherwise. I must have got confused. Or it was a dream.

OR, PERHAPS, IT IS THIS THAT IS JUST A DREAM, his fingers traced in a gentle reminder, sorrow and frustration weighting his hand.

There is no such thing as "just a dream," she promised, a strange sense of serenity blooming even as reality flickered and intruded, and she awoke to a new dawn with the memory of his face carved afresh in her mind, and a weight that was not unwelcome at her shoulder.

A Princely Task

"I know what I have to do, but I need you to help me," the Prince implored, as the Genie hovered solemnly. "I need to seem more in their eyes."

The Genie watched him for a stretched minute, and then gave a passable shrug considering his incorporeal nature. "Destiny is too important to be left to mere chance," he acquiesced. "So, just this once. Temporarily, mind. This transformation will last only until sundown two days hence."

The Prince grinned in abject relief. "Your worth is beyond measure; I will make sure you are rewarded thusly."

"Mm, we'll see. You just worry about your side of the bargain, for there is a catch, as is the wont with these things. Now, let's see, do we have a—hmm, turn out your pockets."

Frowning in confusion, Jasper did so.

"Ah-ha!" exclaimed the Genie triumphantly, pointing an insubstantial finger. "I thought so! You can chuck the other stuff, but keep that piece of mirror. *Very* magical artefact—we can use that, all right. The enchantment will be sealed when you look into the shard, for along the broken edge of a mirror magic is drawn. However—" here Jasper froze, paling, "until the enchantment has run its course you must not risk looking into an unbroken mirror, for that would undo the magic. Simple really—clear?"

Jasper nodded earnestly. "I shall not fail."

The Genie nodded approvingly. "No, I expect you shan't. Get ready."

Jasper bowed his head in anticipation as the Genie inhaled a great breath and swelled to the size of a cloud. The next instant his eyes were shut for him by the wind-rush gusting over him, whipping through his hair and billowing at his clothing as the Genie exhaled.

Trusting, Jasper opened his eyes and stared eagerly into the shard. A grin of astonishment split his face as he beheld his reflection shining back at him as if renewed. The man in the mirror bore a light in his eyes, as if he could conquer all evil and save the whole Realm.

Excitement flushing through him for the first time in weeks, the Prince spun round to thank the Genie—and met with empty air.

Watching him press on exultant, the spectral form reappeared, unseen. "Mm-hm," the Genie confirmed with quiet satisfaction to the desert morning. "I am that good."

You've put this off long enough, Jasper admonished himself as he pushed further into the desert. As he reached the square of Arkh Loban to find it eerily empty save for the shadows of Authority stalking towards him from the distance, he found himself fretting that he might have even now left it too late.

Retreating to the ruins on the outskirts of the town to reconsider his plan, spinning round as a shadow touched his own the Prince found himself gazing into warmth-flecked eyes above a gold-trimmed black veil.

"Yenna?" he hissed in surprise. It felt an age since he'd last seen her like this.

"The Authorities suspect an uprising," the Wolf Sister explained in an undertone. "And we have more immediate battles to concern ourselves with. Don't feel too sorry for me," she warned archly. "In this guise, I can continue my work, unchecked and unchallenged, and stride right into the belly of the beast, while you're still floundering with the guards."

Jasper grimaced. "But you—"

"We don't have time," she reminded him swiftly. "Did you come about the Blade? Jasper, by the Moon I would tell you if I knew, but in–"

"No, not the Blade. Not yet. But I need the key, and I can't remember the route that accursed Magician took us when he showed us where Slaygerin is held."

Yenna started violently. "The *Griffin?*" Her eyes sank still and sad. "Then I have failed him, for I believed all of his kind to be dead."

"Roanen cares for him as best he can," Jasper reassured her. "I think he kept his presence secret for fear of what the Authorities might do if they knew the truth. And Slaygerin has a role yet to play in this sorry mess, for the key," he lowered his voice instinctively, "hangs from a link of his collar-chain."

Yenna watched him carefully, absorbing the information more calmly than anyone else he knew would have, Jasper found himself noting with a mixture of relief and dread. Yet still he could read the question in her eyes.

"I don't know," he whispered emptily, at a loss. "How can this possibly end well? If the Nomad could have managed it he would have done so years ago; the key must bear some sort of curse preventing him from touching it. And as Roanen dares not risk drawing back those bars after seasons of attention, I wouldn't like to contemplate my chances with that half-crazed brute."

Yenna's hands brushed his shoulders in a quiet grip of courage, and those once-dancing eyes now held a solemn sadness. "What we attempt for our people."

Jasper released a steadying breath as he looked to her, and saw in the Wolf Sister's eyes not just her solidarity and allegiance, but also the loss she endured every time she changed form; the toll it repeatedly took on her, and the blazing fervour in her heart driving her on regardless to attempt it yet again in the face of all things. "You're the only one who understands," he murmured.

"To the dungeons, then," she promised, stepping back and casting a cautionary glance to their surroundings. "Let us share the path awhile."

Jasper felt his resolve shrink inside his heart as the darkness loomed. "From here I must go alone," he declared severely, trying to make his voice hold firm in case the Wolf Sister was going to try to talk him out of it like everyone else.

Yenna's lips twitched into a smile beneath the veil. "As must I," she countered airily. But she hesitated before turning to leave. "Jasper, I learned long ago that it's safe in the shadows, but it's no place to live. I refuse to do you the disservice of suggesting you turn back now."

Caught off-guard by the emotion in her voice the Prince tried to craft a suitable answer, but by the time he'd found the words she really was going. Steeling himself with a sigh for what would no doubt lie ahead, Jasper couldn't shake the miserable fear that her faith in him was about to be proven woefully misplaced.

His eyes adjusting far too slowly to the darkness for his liking as he blundered anxiously through tunnel after wretched tunnel, Jasper nearly yelled aloud as from the endless black he glimpsed a silent figure slipping forward.

Recognising him as Roanen did nothing to ease the Prince's frayed nerves. "Come to gloat?" he blurted, furious at the speed his heart was still hammering. "Sorry," he added immediately. "That was uncouth, blame the fact I'm terrified. It's just, I know in my heart that this is impossible, and yet I cannot let myself allow it to be."

"No," the Nomad agreed matter-of-factly, ignoring the Prince's transgression. "You cannot."

"Helpful lot, you Magicians," Jasper retorted bad-temperedly. "I don't even know where to start."

"And yet you have," the other man noted, infuriatingly calm.

Jasper glared back venomously, in no mood for riddles.

"You were saying you believed it impossible, and yet you came despite this," Roanen prompted.

"No choice," Jasper acquiesced grudgingly. "It's for more than just me, and someone's got to."

"And what power holds a curse against words such as those?" cried the Magician in approval, his voice holding an ancient authority as between his hands the air began to glow.

"I lost sleep over that!" Jasper huffed dazedly, staring at the key now nestled in his hand as if it might suddenly disappear in a puff of smoke. "If I'd have known it would end up being that easy—"

"Easy?" Roanen considered the Prince's judgement with a shrug. "It was looking dangerously close to remaining impossible, until you risked to trust yourself. The curse of a sorcerer clings to a Magician with all the draining strength of an opposing magnet, but *you*, Jasper Tigerseye, it cannot hinder."

Still stunned, the Prince felt the germ of a plan forming. "Time to plead another favour," he grinned, charging out towards the light again.

"Please; I don't have anyone else to ask." Breathless from the exertion of flight, Jasper had to cling to the gritty contours of the wall for support as he stumbled into the Fountain chamber and addressed the Water Nymph.

"The First Blade," he gasped. "I've got the key, but I need to know where to use it. Legend says the Blade struck such fear into the heart of the Goblin King that he had it locked into the deepest bowels of the Realm where none could unearth it again."

"Is there no end to your kind's stupidity?" As her voice boomed exasperated through the cavern, Jasper suddenly panicked that Zaral-athaar would turn him into a toad or something worse for his imperti-nence. But instead an odd expression passed across the Nymph's face. "You would be wise to examine such legends more closely. Mayhap you would uncover the reason for his actions."

"I don't care for examining the motivations of tyrants," the Prince assured her curtly. I don't need the reason, I just need the sword."

"You stretch beyond your reach, boy," the Nymph countered, her eyes glittering coldly. "Lofty ideals float from that highborn tongue, yet you can promise nothing."

Shoulders sagging from both exhaustion and the enormity of the truth confronting him, Jasper drew himself up to look squarely into those clear, cold eyes. "I can't convince you to believe in me," he acknowledged. "But I *must* ask you to help me."

Bruised, winded, and shivering with cold and uncertainty as the bubble burst wetly to fling him near insensible into complete darkness, Jasper stared up in a mixture of relief and trepidation as he beheld the First Blade, gripped in the fist of a fully armoured statue.

As the Prince stepped forward gingerly, coughing amidst the dust-motes swirling through the long-undisturbed stale air as light filtered near-ineffectually through from somewhere too unreachable to discern. An subconscious warning twisted in his gut, spilling half-remembered superstitions against the disturbing of such deathly stillness, and yet he couldn't help thinking that the sword and its inhuman guardian looked, well, normal. Ancient, certainly, and his scholar's education was useless in deciphering the runes tracing the blade, but . . .

As his fingers tentatively closed around the hilt, horror seared into him, and he had to force himself to cling grimly on as his vision shud-dered into nightmare, beholding the blade first dripping with innocent blood, then transforming its lengths into stiffened severed limbs until, terror-stricken, he felt it turn finally towards his own heart.

Squeezing his eyes shut with the last dregs of his self-control, he dragged forth the sword, striking out for the statue with a bellowing cry.

The helmet clattered to the floor. Heart hammering, the Prince froze instinctively in fear of retribution. None came. "Hah!" he yelled in triumph to the shadows, unable to trust his own vision but still breathing, still standing, and still holding the sword. "You'll have to do worse than—"

And then the pain took him, and he crumpled senseless to the floor.

Connections

Her eyes staring wide as they flitted over the ceiling and walls, Amber tried to ignore the way the now-familiar objects of the rec hall looked menacingly skewed against so many shadows and glanced at the clock again. Seventeen minutes past two in the morning, seemingly an hour after it had said ten past.

She pushed her blanket off fractiously. It slithered into an unceremonious heap on the floor. *Stop thrashing and do something useful*, she berated herself. *Look at the map again.*

Wincing as she pushed herself into sitting, she stared absentmindedly at the moonlight shafting through the window between the chinks in her curtains. It fell on the corner of the newest map rolled tightly on her dresser, illuminating it in ethereal silver light. Gingerly leaning across, trying not to twist too much as Sarin had warned, she curled her fingers around the scrolls and spread them across her lap.

Squinting in the low light, Amber shuffled fruitlessly through the parchments chronologically until she was left staring blearily at the newest map: the one commissioned after the end of the Sea Battle. What had Jasper said—that by putting the maps together you could draw a tunnel through the rock almost to the centre of Dread Mountain?

Amber traced the invisible line to no avail, feeling her gaze drawn instead to the newly added Fountain. In the darkness, the structure seemed to float apart from the page, shimmering a memory into in her mind: of standing on the basin ledge with the Nymph, staring up at a fissure high above in the rock—and of being warned against its access even though, according to every map and her own observations from the Bicorn, the Fountain hung completely separate and apart from the mountain.

Amber traced the route again, backwards: starting from within the mountain, an impossible option racing now in her mind. The Fountain was the domain of the Nymph: the Realm's oldest remaining magic wielder. What if the Fountain chamber still held the last vestiges of magic? If its solitary floating status *were* just an illusion? Having wrought the nets of power and bound the Vetches, Zaralathaar must have fled the mountain and escaped to the Fountain somehow . . . What if, through magic, she had traversed the two as one? And what if there was just enough magic left for it to be possible for someone to do it again?

With frightening clarity, the Nymph's words pierced her speculation. "That's what she warned me against," Amber breathed to the night. "It was the path she took all those years ago. She wouldn't have warned me if it couldn't still be done."

Speaking it aloud illuminated the connections, and a perilous idea rose fleetingly into a hideous kind of sense even as it conjured a shockingly final portent of doom. *There's no other way*, the cankerous truth squirmed towards her heart, against the inadvisable elation that at least there was finally a plan. *It has to be you.*

Everyone else's lives are in danger, she argued with herself as the flood of fear threatened to drown her. The King and Jasper would risk their lives on the battlefield, Yenna in the ruins of Arkh Loban, Racxen—her fate would be no worse than that awaiting her friends, so how could she shy from it when they stood firm?

That's easy to say when it's not yet upon you, the part of her mind she had managed so far to batten down reared savagely to insist. *You've as good as gone to pieces every time something difficult has happened so far.*

Amber sucked down a breath. *No,* she countered grimly. *I didn't run. I stayed. I tried. Those are my friends, these are my lands, and this is my decision. Although I cannot fight, my risk will be just as great. And as I cannot fight, it will be no loss to them if I do this instead.*

Conviction moulding her decision into solid form, Amber found herself attuned to every aspect of the room: appreciating anew the comfort woven into the fabrics cradling her and the reassurance etched into the well-trodden floor as she waited, alone with her terrors, for her friends to return. Her friends who, as of yet, had no idea the folly of what she was about to suggest; who would come up with a hundred reasons why she couldn't put herself through it; who would feel so hurt and responsible for having to through no fault of their own leave it to her to complete such a trial.

Guilt gnawed into her soul, the minutes stretching into an eternity she wished she could yet still delay as all too soon she heard her friends' footsteps pad down the hall. A lump sprang to her throat to notice as their faces bobbed to the door that their expressions were so reassuring, so normal, as if trying to convince her that nothing bad would come to pass. Her heart quavered to see how brave they were being for her. She hoped desperately she could return their courtesy.

She smiled shakily as they slipped into the room.

"You can tell us, Amber," Racxen's voice was full of concern.

Curses. She wasn't hiding it well enough. But her beleaguered heart filled to know that he cared.

"It's okay," Jasper tried. "We said we'd come back and tell you everything. The Nymph, of all people, was helpful; she called the tunnel through Dread Mountain the 'Way of Ice and Fire', although she wouldn't say why."

"About that," Amber interrupted miserably, unable to keep it in any longer. She let her eyes rest on each of them in turn, storing away the last moment they would spend in unburdened ignorance of what she was about to suggest. "There's something I've realised," she started, painfully awkward, her throat scratching over the words. Her hands shook even now as she reached for the map to illustrate her point. What would she be like when the time came, she couldn't help questioning miserably, if she couldn't even get through this?

"What, about the 'one becoming many' thing?" Jasper pre-empted with forced cheerfulness. "Racxen told me. It was quite a relief; I hadn't been able to find a single reference to it in all my research and the only logical conclusion I met with was that you must have made it up just to be difficult."

In her distraction, Amber twisted the map ever more tightly. "I really want to be able to tell you that that's all it is. But hear me out, before you try to dismiss what I have to say."

Faces taut with anxiety, her friends nodded mutely.

"We know so far that we have three sets of monsters to fight," Amber began, light-headed at the impossibility of it all. "And that each type is manipulating the movements of the others to their own ends. So we have to pretty much defeat them at the same time, right? But," she added hastily before they could contradict her, "at least they each have different strongholds. The Goblins must be flushed out of Loban. The Vetches—I don't know how anyone can kill them, but we can't let that stop us. As for the Venom-spitters . . ." She breathed shakily, scraping her confidence together. "As it was to Dread Mountain, where Snake-locks's Lair used to be and whence the Vetches drove forth the Venom-spitters, that the Goblins took Mugkafb, Dread Mountain must be the lair of the Samire leader. For the same reason, we know the Samire can be lured out—by prey."

Almost gagging on the words, Amber had to gulp down air before she could continue. "We know too, of course, that the Nymph imprisoned the Vetches in Dread Mountain, and that she afterwards escaped somehow to the Fountain basin. She must have accomplished this with magic—for at the Fountain basin I saw, unwittingly at the time, the exit of what had to have been that same tunnel—she was adamant of its danger. So, if the prey were to catch its attention and run, the Samire would be led through the Way of Ice and Fire right to the pinnacle of the Fountain, and if I—I mean the prey—were to jump from the edge the Samire would jump too. And it would fall to its death while I should—I mean would—be caught in a bubble, and . . ." She swallowed dryly, catching her breath. "That would be it."

Four masks of horror stared back at her in utter silence.

"And it has to be me," Amber finished, before the others could recover themselves. "You can't go," she forestalled Jasper, "because we can't risk losing our Prince. And it has to be a Fairy," she added no less firmly as she met Racxen's stricken gaze, "because the bubbles can barely even hold someone light enough to fly, with the hollow bone structure and everything; even a child," she warned Mugkafb who had just stepped forward pleadingly, "would be too heavy."

As the echoes of her words died away, she found she could no longer look her friends in the eye. "It's the best plan we've got." Her frantic heartbeat measured the resulting silence.

"No it's not; it's the only one we've got and there's a difference. It's yours, for a start!" Jasper gestured wildly. "Amber, out of all our people! You can't even fly! Can't you do something to help that doesn't involve destroying yourself?"

"Oh, so when you risk your life it's noble and praiseworthy, but when I do it's ill-considered self-ruin? Surprisingly enough, Jasper, my actions are independent of your agenda." She stared at him stonily, her soul curling protectively against his words.

The Prince turned for reinforcements. "Racxen, tell her how foolish she's being."

The Arraheng shook his head, eyes pained. "I don't judge those who walk a path I would fear to tread."

"You won't be saying that when she's gone and killed herself!" Jasper spat back vengefully. "Amber, sorry, I didn't mean it like that."

She glared at him mutely, the silence weighing into each of them as the gravity of the situation pressed inescapably. "Stop trying to take responsibility for everything," she admonished at length by way of forgiveness. "It's not like you're the King."

"Savage fates, I've got to tell my father!" Jasper blurted in realisation, momentarily seized by even greater dread.

Amber managed the tiniest smile. "We all must make our plans."

"We shall tell our people at first light," the Prince advised at last, his face set. "I will begin preparations in Fairymead."

Racxen nodded, ruffling Mugkafb's hair sadly. "We'll alert Arraterr; start the evacuation to the caves. We'll be the first hit. Once the vulnerable are safe the rest will join the fight, some at the castle to help stave off the Venom-spitters, the rest in Loban to drive out the Goblins."

Pausing by Amber's bed, he knelt to envelop her in a fierce embrace and she closed her eyes as she felt his breath shudder by her ear, willing the memory of him being so close to keep her as safe in the future as his presence had thus far.

The scent of marshlands and mystery, darkness and sanctuary, swirled and spoke in the sacred space between them, touching the sources of her courage and drawing forth her own bravery.

"I'll come back, I promise," she whispered. She nearly dared add "for you", but Mugkafb pushed his way through to wrap his arms round her neck and she returned his hug instead, trying to laugh and reassure him that all this couldn't possibly stay as bad as it was increasingly proving itself to be.

No words left to say, the trio nodded unspoken messages and uncomfortably withdrew.

Last to the door, Jasper turned back, returning to the girl's bedside to lean down and hug her awkwardly. "I'm terribly sorry it's come to this."

Amber barely trusted herself to speak. "I should think up these schemes more often if it gets me this kind of affection," she joked shakily.

Jasper sighed unevenly. "I'd kiss even you if it meant you'd let us find another way," he retorted.

Amber gave a snort of laughter despite herself. "You'd rather I get killed by Ruby instead?"

The Prince's resolve quaked, and he had to smile, tight-lipped and without speaking, in case he fell apart in front of her. "Yes, well," he managed finally. "You get some sleep." He turned away quickly and left, pushing the door closed without a further word.

Alone with the dark pressing in around her, Amber shook her head angrily. *No. You are not going to just lie here and feel miserable. Think of the others.*

Resolutely hitting the pillow into shape—then cursing herself as her arm lanced with pain—she reached across to open the curtain slightly and let the outside Realm spill in with the moonlight.

As its soothing hues washed over her she lay back, gazing over the night-silvered fields that still stood as removed and enduring as ever, and the next thing she knew, morning was glaring inescapably through the window.

Omens

Across the glimmering expanse of moon-blanched sand a shadowed figure approached, sleepless despite the reaches of the night.

"Sister," Blythe breached the subject cautiously. "The pack is restless. There has been word amongst our brethren of Dragon sightings."

Staring out untiringly into the vast darkness, Yenna retied her bandana. "They have been seen by the pack?"

"No," he admitted. "But they hear rumours. Would it not be auspicious to use these to our advantage; to put about the suggestion of a portent to raise morale before we march?"

Yenna shook her head. "You have compassionate intent, my Brother, but we need no such omens. It is better for the pack to know that our victory will be of our own making, not merely foretold by the position of the stars. If we wait for the traditional full moon to make our advance, we will be forever in submission to one circumstance or other. We know in our hearts this is necessary—we need no other compass to steer our course."

Blythe nodded. "I will give word that the pack assembles tomorrow at midnight."

"Midnight?" Yenna barked. "When the Goblins have the cover of darkness for their cowardice? No—" she stabbed the tip of her scimitar into the sand, "we shall begin our onslaught in the predawn hours, when they've had a night of anticipation to shred their nerves, and continue into the blistering heat of noon."

He slapped her heartily on the back. "So it shall be."

Silencing him with a glance, Yenna froze, scenting the air as the wind gusted. "The Goblins spread their menace already." Her voice melded into a troubled snarl as she shared a laden glance with her tawny-haired, hard-eyed companion. "Our fate is approaching. Gather our brethren, Blythe, for I run for the town tonight, and when I return it shall be to war. Before first light, we storm the ruins."

"Be on your guard, Yenna," Blythe warned. "It is an ill moon that rises this hour."

Unable to deny the truth of his words, the Wolf Sister growled her defiance to the sky and sprang away into the darkness.

Beneath the same moon, his mind drifting to the prospect of a hot meal and some time with his own horses after a decent day's work, the air heavy with the delicious smoky tang of the forge, Seb cradled the filly's hoof and worried at the stone with his pick, releasing her leg with a companionable slap on the withers as a sliver of flint pinged satisfyingly onto the cobbles of the yard.

His last charge for the evening thus attended to, the smith returned to the anvil, steel-flung sparks chinking into the velvet Arkhan darkness once more beneath his hammer-strokes. The contrapuntal rhythms of the clanging tools settled the night into hypnotic familiarity until, above the comforting rumble of the furnace, yells and shouts and snatches of confusion arched on the howling winds outside.

Stowing the hammer pre-emptively in his chair, Seb spun through to the doorway in time to see two stable hands run past, oblivious to him in their haste. The panicked whinny of a horse shrilled through the now-deserted street.

It took seconds for the blacksmith to register the stinging cold of the bitter desert winds as he investigated. Wiping the forge-grime from his face with the back of a hand, his eyes still smarted from the smoke as he wheeled out over the lonely cobbles. At first he thought the queer bobbing lights were lanterns shaken in the wind, until they shifted into mortal focus: lamp-eyes, dozens of them, shifting through the darkness, stalking the streets in a parody of the Wolfren packs that defended the town. *Goblins.*

Seb's first thoughts were of relief: the children would be safely home and Naya had elected this night of all times to trek into the desert to bring Roanen news. But the next instant arcs of fire flew as Goblin-whips severed the composure of the town and he saw, too far away to prevent it, men fall with legs broken and clothes ablaze, their thin piercing cries shattering the night as they rolled desperately to save themselves.

Adrenalin spurted through Seb as he gripped the wheel rims. The Goblins were letting the men run: their mission had to lie elsewhere. *The ruins!* Realisation cuffed him round the face. *Thanatos must have summoned them.* Someone had to warn Fairymead. Someone had to deliver the weapons.

Too late, he realised the wind had changed direction, and his heart sputtered in his chest as he felt the Goblins' dagger-eyes lift straight towards him, the mob shifting into hunting formation.

Seb spun to the road, powering frantically against the drag of the cobbles. He knew this route. Could roll it faster than most folk could run.

Yet the Goblins' speed stung of blood-debt bargains, and they tailed him faster than he'd dared think possible. He ducked his head down, racing blindly on as the Goblins' whips lashed impotently around him, incapable of bringing him down as they cracked and slithered harmlessly from the frame of his chair. As the mob's screams of rage melded with the hysteric wind, Seb thrust until his arms burned.

The shouts of the horde closing in as exhaustion threatened to overtake him, the blacksmith glimpsed the ceremonial stairs of the Travellers' Pass, signifying the boundary of Loban.

No time for the long way—careening over the edge of the stairs, Seb could do nothing but cling on grimly as his chair ricocheted uncontrollably down the steps.

Striking the ground violently, he spun the wheels hard, thundering along the dusty road home. Throwing a piercing whistle as he rounded the gateway, glimpsing the two greys cantering obediently through from the paddock Seb forced himself to stop and think for a handful of seconds. He had maybe five, ten minutes before the Goblins reached him. How many of the weapons batches had he packed onto the cart this morning?

Loosing the slipknot and letting the back edge crash down to serve as a ramp, he saw despairingly that it was less than half.

Whistling the horses into their drilled positions, Seb began laboriously bundling the swords together and swinging the bags onto the cart, his shoulders cramping with the effort. Throwing a feverish glance back to the road, he knew the Goblins could only be seconds away. Sweating like he'd spent a week at the forge, he started on the shields, each batch agonisingly cumbersome to load as fighting against exhaustion he wheeled them onto the cart.

With the last lot stacked and his muscles screaming, Seb knew it all hinged on the next couple of minutes. Shunting down the ramp, he spun to the tack room, dragging out the harnesses. With adrenalin coursing through him he fumbled through the tasks he could usually do with his eyes shut as the horses fretted and flinched, catching the scent of the advancing Goblins on the wind, and it took all of the smith's ingenuity to calm them, feeling the last possible moments slipping helplessly as he finally managed to hitch the pair to the cart even as the road clattered with the horde's pursuit.

As the Goblins stormed the driveway, cackling and shrieking their vengeance, Seb thrust frantically up the cart ramp, dragging it up with the rope and lashing it expertly. Spinning to the fore he flung out the reins with a wild cry, feeling the horses' terror flood through him as if it were his own as the Goblin-stench filled their flaring nostrils and their instinctual panic reared, threatening to send them bolting and frenzied to the doom of their driver.

But Seb wasn't thought the most skilful blacksmith in the Realm for nothing, and as the voice of the master they knew and trusted splintered through the mob's uproar the horses leaped galvanised into action, racing for the road so fast that the Goblins were forced to dive aside.

Speeding breakneck through the night, Seb had barely recovered his breath before the cart was skidding to a halt outside the castle, and the King himself was running to him as the horses snorted and pawed impatiently.

"Change of plan," the blacksmith gasped, tugging free the rope to let the ramp fall and throwing the first pack down to Morgan.

All Down to This

You've got to just say it, and then you won't be able to get out of it, Amber ordered herself, fear cramping her chest in recognition of the inevitable at the sight of so many soldiers gathered already. *Everything will unfold as it must.*

"Amber?" Racxen ducked through the hastily summoned crowd towards her, and gathered her hand safely in his.

She couldn't look at him, but if he didn't let go she might just find the strength to go through with this.

"You asked me how you could thank me for saving your life the other day," he reminded her hoarsely. "Stay silent for the next ten minutes and all debts are off."

Amber's reply died on her lips, stolen by the expectant hush rippling through the masses. As she scanned the waiting assembly, her resolve trembled anew. It seemed so cruel that a short while ago the council had convened for the Presentation of the Gems, and now—

"Three irrevocably entwined elements combine to threaten the Realm we hold dear," King Morgan proclaimed in summary to his audience, as Magnus and Pendril continued systematically inspecting the consignment of weapons behind him. "The Arraheng lands lie in the path of the Venom-spitters even before Fairymead, and so our initial priority must be to evacuate their tribes to the swamp-tunnels."

"Once the evacuation has been mobilised the rest of us will return,"

Racxen interjected. A handful of snide comments flickered around him, but he was looking only to Amber and she felt an impossible pain bloom in her chest knowing that she must walk a separate path instead of being able to stand with him through this.

Nodding solemn gratitude, Morgan continued: "The Ring will hold Fairymead's evacuees. Those remaining to fight will take arms against the Venom-spitters to both aid the Arraheng and protect our own land."

"And I'll take the Way of Ice and Fire," Amber blurted, shocked to hear her own voice and realising with a shudder how sickeningly final she'd made it sound now. "I'll lure the Samire out of its lair. It'll chase me and then I'll jump off into the Fountain and it'll fall to its death."

"You think it's only the Venom-spitter that will?" Jasper couldn't help snapping into the silence.

Amber turned her tired gaze pleadingly to him. "We've been through this. What choice do we have? None can take my place in this, although I thank from the deepest place in my heart those who wish they could." Her gaze rested on Tanzan, his face creasing in bewilderment as his normally darting eyes filled with grave recognition.

"We know only Fairies can use the Fountain bubbles without falling through," she apologised next with her eyes on Racxen. The sight of him fighting himself silently, grimfaced in his struggle not to oppose her on this, twisted into her heart, and her resolve shivered further.

Gulping a steadying breath, she turned back to the others. "You all have other ways to help. You're warriors, or healers, or parents, or riders, or traders—" her voice threatened to crack now, but she strove to keep it light. "And I'm not," she finished simply.

"But—"

"Jasper, I've never listened to you before, and I don't plan on starting now!" Oh, curses, she wished she could apologise to him for saying that; but it was too hard just to keep the tears out of her eyes, and didn't he know if he gave her any other option she'd never be able to go through with this?

"The worth of our peoples has never been hierarchical," King Morgan advised gravely. "All citizens of this land, and its allies," he nodded courteously to the Arraheng, ensuring the gesture was clear enough to be noted by the scattering of dissenters who had begun muttering amongst themselves, "are assured of our protection, to the extent that we have yet breath in our bodies to provide it. There are things that cannot be asked of others, Amber."

A chill itched along her spine; somehow hearing the King use her name brought home how sickeningly real this was all becoming. "No, Sire." She had to clear her throat to get the words out. "But they can be offered."

Giving her a *this isn't over* look, Morgan turned to the Wolf Sister. "What is to be the Wolfren's position?"

Yenna's voice rang out stridently. "The Palace Ruins."

Jasper stared. For some reason, he'd taken it as a given that she'd be part of the defences at Fairymead.

"*Our* primary concern must be Thanatos," she explained decisively. "His reign will end where it began. The Goblin King's involvement has tipped this situation into much more than the usual monster-clan onslaught; he is the one driving the Venom-spitters, so to stem the problem at the source we must stop him.

"Long have the Goblins abused our tolerance, insidiously suffocating our lands and liberties—and having bent the Venom-spitters to their will and seen the Realm besieged by the Vetches, they know they are in the best ever position to overthrow the last remnants of freedom and take our city once and for all. Thanatos's weakness was ever his grandiosity, and with these new allies and circumstances he believes himself untouchable—now is our chance to draw him from the shadows, and vanquish him upon the plains."

Howling whoops of agreement broke from the Wolfren section of the audience.

"Thus it shall be," Morgan intoned, the words heavy on his tongue as he looked out over the assembly—so young, so unprepared. Half hadn't lived through the Sea Battle, nor known first-hand the casualties it had taken, whilst during the years of peace since the veterans had been afforded little opportunity outside training to retain their skills. The Wolfren might well prove unparalleled fighters, but at what price to their humanity?

He drew a well-practised, outwardly calm breath. *There is no more uncertainty now*, he told himself; had to tell himself, for if there were how could he stride out to battle, much less expect others to follow? *There remains only that which must be done, and the cost that must be borne.* Stepping down, he sought the girl.

"Magnus says you're sending me to Loban!" Jasper blurted, almost crashing into him in his haste. "How can I not fight by your side?"

Morgan shook his head. "If the battle goes ill, Fairymead will need a leader." His voice softened. "And I will not have you there. In Fairymead you will be a target for the Vetches—it will not be only Venom-spitters we will face—whereas in Loban you won't be as recognisable to the Goblins; their attention will be fixed upon Yenna."

Jasper tightened his armour. "Then I shall guard her."

Morgan clasped his son's arm. "As I hoped. Good man."

Jasper bit his lip as he hugged his father. "See you in victory." The traditional warrior's farewell, translated from Fäe, stuck in his throat after so many years of throwing it around in jest as a young boy with no idea what he would grow up to be.

As Morgan's arms tightened around him in response, his mother joined the embrace. "See you both no matter what," she admonished fiercely.

"I'm going to be sick—I can't breathe—" Amber pushed miserably through the suffocating crowd out into the waiting twilight, retching as the enormity of her actions overtook her.

Gasping, she pushed her hair back shakily, hollowly lifting her gaze to meet Racxen's as he reached her. *There're no words for this*, a tiny part of her whimpered as a desolate emptiness flooded her. *What have I done?*

Ashen-faced, Racxen enveloped her in his arms, tears gathering in his eyes even as he forbade them from falling, and Amber hid her face against his shoulder, gulps of air labouring brokenly through her chest as they clung to each other against the gathering, inexorable darkness.

At the Threshold

"You're going after *Thanatos?*" Horror rose vomit-like in Amber's throat.

Racxen nodded wordlessly, and she saw in his eyes that he had in his heart all this time been moving down a path that could lead to but one ending.

"But—" She couldn't say it. How could she stand in his way when he'd never stood in hers? When he had to do this, in his mind, for the same reason that she had to meet her fate amidst splintering ice and roiling fire?

Amber pushed back her fears with a staggered breath, feeling as if her soul would shatter if she couldn't control her response now. And yet how could she stay silent, when she had to watch him walk away?

"I think I understand," she murmured finally. "I just wish I could protect you from what it might entail."

Racxen shook his head. "I can't even protect myself; how can I ask it of another?"

"You wouldn't have to ask," she reminded him stubbornly.

Racxen took her hand in his. "There are things that cannot be shielded against," he reminded her softly. "Yet through all of mine, you have walked beside me."

Amber bit her lip against its sudden trembling as she strove to keep her voice measured. "But that's just it; I can't, not this time. I can't be there to walk with you through the darkness."

Racxen's melancholy smile grew warm. "No. But you will be my light at its end."

Amber blinked back prickling tears. "And when I stumble blinded from the fire caverns, you will be the darkness that hides and heals me."

"Sen," Racxen vowed. "You don't know how much I value that you haven't tried to stop me," he murmured, gently pushing her hair back from her eyes with a claw.

"There's still time," she warned sullenly. "I care more about you than your opinion of me. But," she relented, snuffling as she pressed her fingertips to the corners of her eyes to try to stop the tears from falling, "when everyone was getting all Jasper-ish and trying to forbid me from going through with the plan and everything, you stood beside me instead of in my way, so I guess I owe you the same courtesy."

"Courtesy had nothing to do with it," Racxen promised with the touch of a grin, encircling her in his arms with a sigh. "This is not good-bye," he whispered fiercely. "The same darkness shields us, the same dawn beckons us, beneath the same twilight we will be reunited—and in every minute between, my spirit walks with yours. It has been my honour to stand beside you, and very soon it will be my pleasure to do so once again."

Amber clung to him, her throat closing up with the strength of her emotion. "Curse you, Arraheng," she retorted shakily, the smallest of smiles returning to her lips as she remembered his words from so long ago now. "You're making this too difficult."

Locking the embrace into memory against whatever trials were yet to come they both stepped back, keeping their eyes resolutely to a ground now blurring through a film of tears as they each walked away alone.

Jasper stared out across the desert in silence as he walked the long path to Arkh Loban, side-by-side with Yenna in the gathering dusk. Although she had barely spoken since setting out, the Wolf Sister's manner comforted him. Back at Fairymead he would have been panicking by now, barking orders and talking so fast he'd barely be able to breathe. Out here with her, there was still space and time enough to live. In these past few hours at her side, he thought he had felt blooming between them an unspoken intimacy warmer than the desert sands, yet he feared were he to reach towards it, it would slip as inexorably through his fingers.

"In blood and toil, we'll write our fates here," Yenna intoned softly, judging his mood as intuitively as ever, Jasper couldn't help noting appreciatively, even if she could not be aware of its origin. "Remember this day, because we'll fight for it later."

As he glanced at her wonderingly, Yenna shot him a benignly smug look as though she were close to reading his mind, and in his embarrassment he dropped his gaze and settled for watching their surroundings again. The twilit air shivered against the sand's heat, red rays spilling across the flats to pierce crimson-streaked cloud-wisps as the sun sank broodingly beneath the horizon in a last blaze of gold-hued splendour. A pang of nostalgia lanced Jasper's calm. "Do the eves of battle always seem this beautiful?" he asked, grimacing.

Yenna followed his gaze. "Everything does, when you come face to face with what you might lose. Idiosyncrasy of the human condition." She paused, and Jasper realised they were nearing the Golden Griffin already. "I am glad that at least for one of us this will not change tomorrow. Until then: from here, as you are so fond of telling me, I must go alone."

The Prince stalled, attempting gallantry. "But—"

"I cannot have you here!" Yenna barked in torment. "Do you have any idea of the burden my people carry? Of what it entails: to be a soldier one moment and a citizen the next? A wolf does what is necessary to protect the pack. It is not tortured by alternatives or consequences. If I am going to accomplish what needs to be done I cannot hesitate and I cannot doubt myself. I must lock away one of my selves until this is over, and I must face undaunted the knowledge that I will return to this form with the weight of the memories of what I have done in the other. I must set aside my humanity tomorrow—and so I cannot allow myself tonight the comfort of consorting with the man who reminds me of the best of that condition."

In his stunned silence she took out her bandana, folding and unfolding it ritualistically in a pattern Jasper could not understand as he stared mutely, feeling disquietingly like a voyeur. For those moments, the Wolf Sister looked utterly vulnerable. He felt as if he were watching her wrap up her soul and hide it away with infinite care in some secret place where no one could find it and hurt her.

She tied the scrap of fabric firmly around her neck, securing the last link to her humanity through which she would retrieve her soul when this was all over. Warmth flooding back into her eyes with the action, she then adjusted her bracer, yanking the adjusting straps with unnecessary fierceness as she smiled dryly, her confidence returned. "Jasper, I never wanted to live like an animal," she reassured him. "I certainly don't plan on dying like one."

"Amber?" Yawning against her hand, Ruby squinted in bleary-eyed concern at her friend standing on the doorstep, skittish and staring amidst the night's storm. "You all right?"

As she was ushered in and waved towards the sofa, Amber tugged a hand fretfully through her hair. She couldn't think what in the Realm she was going to say. "You weren't at the briefing earlier."

Ruby shrugged, her answer muffled against a mouthful of biscuit. She waved the tin at Amber to no avail. "Didn't see the point. That was only for the soldiers, wasn't it? The rest of us are just supposed to take refuge in the Ring or go with those Arraheng blokes to that cave place, right? Didn't miss anything then, did I?"

Emotion squeezed Amber's throat tight. "No," she managed. "No, not really."

"There you go then. Stop worrying, Am—everything'll be back to normal soon." Ruby trotted back into the kitchen to put the biscuits away. "I'll knock for you first thing and we'll go together, yeah?"

But, throwing her cloak round her shoulders, Amber had already slunk back out into the rain, closing the door softly behind her before the tears slid uncontrollably.

That night, the darkness pressing claustrophobically around her, Amber couldn't even lie still. *Until I fall asleep, the next thing I do won't have to be waking up and finding this is all still real.*

She stared angst-ridden into the darkness until nightmarish visions bloomed from the blotches shifting in front of her eyes and she threw the duvet over her head, clinging to memories of better times in the pitiful cocoon of blankets.

On the lumpy, unfamiliar bed of his rented room in the Golden Griffin Jasper lay, drenched in cold sweat beneath a gathering cloud of misery, drinking in sensations he hadn't noticed properly for years: the coolness of the sheets, the pillowed softness beneath his head, the tiny chink of moonlight peeking under the fold of the curtain. Would he be afforded them tomorrow night? What about ever again?

Fitfully, he turned again, hitting the pillow and cursing savagely. *It's the eve of battle. I've got to fight tomorrow. I could die. And I can't*—he smacked the pillow again—*sleep!*

Hot tears welled in despair behind shuttered doors until, despite it all, his mind closed in protective oblivion.

Across the marshes, stalking the path that would form the start of the evacuation, Racxen mentally rehearsed the route for tomorrow.

The traditions had been upheld. The songs had been sung, the vows pledged, the meal partaken of as the Elders would have wished. He'd followed the preparations to the letter.

But it wasn't enough; it couldn't be. Restlessly, he picked up the moonshaft to sharpen it again, crouching at the entrance of the cave. *Maybe, if I can just get it right—*

Surrounded by her pack, the Wolfren slumbering in human-form tonight as was customary upon the last eve before battle, Yenna stared sleeplessly up to the moon. Yet the quiet breathing of those she had learned to trust as brothers and sisters steadied her heart back to a slower beat in defiance of the fears scudding through her pulse, and an all-enveloping warmth radiated with the closeness of their bodies to stave off the chill fears waiting to seize a lonely heart.

There are bonds not even death can break, she promised herself, a strange calm stealing over her with the words. *Fate might steal tomorrow night, but never this one. This one, like all those we've shared before, is ours whatever comes.*

The next thing Amber registered was the bugle-call piercing the pre-light of the new dawn, throwing the Realm back into the chaos of reality.

For a second she lay, bundled in a chrysalis of warmth, as the inescapable call bled into her consciousness and then, before she could summon sufficient awareness to convince herself otherwise, she heaved herself emptily out of bed, washed as if it were the start of any other day, stumbled into the most travel-worthy clothes she could find, threw her thickest cloak around her shoulders in a pitiful attempt at protection, shoved some cereal down her throat, dragged a comb pointlessly through her hair, and slammed the door shut on everything she knew to begin the long trek to the Way of Ice and Fire.

As she trudged across the dew-laden meadows, the early morning mists hanging low and thick as if attempting to shield the Realm from what was about to break upon it, a harsh cry keened to part the white-washed clouds and a disbelieving grin lifted Amber's face as Orbitor, Racxen's Zyfang, swooped to land beside her.

Mirror Lake

It could have been hours into the night, so deep into the mountain had she travelled, when the tunnel disgorged her into a wide chamber, tipping the Realm into a strange netherworld of tangled rules and insubstantial science. Amber's vision stumbled over what she beheld, for a strange light shimmered fit to turn the air to water as the cavern walls rippled with same distorting glow that flickered beneath the surface of a massive pool spilling out through the darkness before her. Clear and deep and almost gloatingly mirror-calm it lay, flooded with an ethereal light that shimmered eerily through the green translucence of the surface to dance erratically across the flowstone ceiling in distorted patterns that wavered in the damp air to scuttle into a beyond-sighted darkness as old as the Realm itself. Odd glimmers glinted from somewhere below: fish, or gems? Amber found herself questioning. Or, so far from sunlight and civilisation, something more occult?

As Amber tiptoed closer, her gaze tracked dozens of intricately twisting narrow pathways—barely a foot's breadth wide—formed of darkly glistening rock branching across the sprawling lake.

Pausing at the water's edge, Amber found her gaze drawn hypnotically to the depths below and the bright glow rippling across the surface in the otherworldly silence. The lake had to be fathoms deep, but it lay so still.

With a sense of misgiving, whether intuitive or unfounded, forbidding her from disturbing the pool's mirrored veneer, Amber's footfalls echoed softly over the lake as she padded cautiously along the first branch of the path, her toes clinging to the slippery cold as the rock's edges dug into her soles.

No further sound issued, the strangely lit water still shining glassy-still around her, and despite her initial foreboding Amber felt her confidence rise. *Not exactly the hardest quest in the Kingdom so far, was it?* she congratulated herself tentatively.

Regardless, something made her glance back towards the bank, and a chill slid along her spine to notice how far away solid ground had slipped. Surely she hadn't traversed all that already? Inching forwards, her confidence waned further as the paths grew more knotted with every step. She licked dry lips as she stared out across the watery chamber: the other side wasn't getting any nearer.

Prodding her reasoning into action before the familiar bubble of fear could wobble into her mind, Amber considered. Wouldn't it be quicker to just jump from path to path? She tensed in readiness, but her legs refused to leave the solid rock.

She grimaced. The silence was getting to her; that was all. Chiding herself impatiently, she bundled up her courage and leaped, but her flurry of elation at landing dissipated as she stumbled and sent her foot into the water. She snatched it back, inexplicably spooked, skittering hurriedly along the path as sudden echoes scudded whisperingly through the chamber, the previously reigning calm irrevocably shattered.

Unseen by the fleeing Fairy, gathering ripples bunched into a shoal to follow her.

Further along, Amber's embarrassed attempts to calm her pounding heart weren't working. What could she possibly run into here, anyway? Venom-spitter? Yeah, right. Goblin? Hardly. Vetch? She stalled. Best not think about that one. The silence pressed eerily as creeping shadows scudded the walls. She couldn't shake the feeling that something was about to go hideously wrong.

Torn from her rumination she flailed awkwardly, a cry ripping from her throat as she just managed to pull her foot back. The rock was still visible, but—

She stared in dry-throated shock at the water. There was the path; there was the rock, right in front of her. But her foot had plunged straight through, exposing it as an illusion. Yet it was all she had to follow; her only hope of reaching the other side.

Dipping a toe into the water, she spun to sweep her foot across every path branching from hers and watched with the dread of an approaching storm the mirage barely shudder as the surface smoothly yielded at her touch.

Her heart jolted into her mouth. *You just jumped,* the realisation squirmed in her gut as she cast her gaze uncomfortably across the endless rock-threaded swathes of reflection. *Onto a dead end.*

She swept her foot through again—pointlessly she knew—to check, but the surface was trembling now, as agitated as her own heartbeat, distorting the visions flicking over the water. Dread rose like a wave in Amber's chest as she witnessed it, and she wheeled round, wondering how far this one tenuous solid thread would bear her as she crept precariously back along in the direction whence she'd come.

She quickened her steps as she noticed the first ripples scud into breakers to follow her, and as she reached a fork in the rock and swept her foot again to meet with nothing but the water's greedy touch an ominous rumble gathered restlessly behind her.

She barely had time to tense before the wave burst against her rock even as a second swelled into a rolling surge towards her. Spluttering fitfully against the force of the spray battering into her, Amber gulped air as the wave subsided briefly to leave her stranded: a lone figure standing drenched and bedraggled, silhouetted against the strange light and disturbed water. She had to cross the lake—time was slipping perilously and she knew she couldn't withstand another onslaught, but how could she hope to see her way now, with the paths lost amidst the nauseous roll and crash of the ever-building waves?

The flicker of an idea bobbed and shied—maybe she didn't have to. That elusive light had to be emanating from somewhere, and it wouldn't be blocked by the visions. If she could follow the light to its source she would be guided along a clear path. Wouldn't she?

In a flurry of daring she was sure she'd soon regret, she jumped for the water. The splash shattered any spell of silence held over the chamber as the lake welcomed her in a flood of warmth, the flowing light infusing it with heat. Flinging her hair from her face with a gasp as she broke the surface, Amber struck out swimming.

Passing through images unseen without hindrance, she reached solid rock and pulled herself along it, clasping the rough, algae-glistened stone with searching fingers, willing herself not to lose contact with it as the waves slapped and buffeted around her. Gasping, she forced herself on, pushing off from the rock and kicking strongly until she reached another. *Don't think what could be below—you didn't back at the lake with Mugkafb.*

Yet the waters raged more powerfully than any predator and she struggled to stay afloat, her energy sapping fast as the swell battered incessantly around her. As she scanned desperately for the sides, unable to see above the froth and foam of the writhing combers, the rolling crash of a cresting wave broke over her, sending her powering blindly to the surface, spluttering raggedly.

Choking and coughing, helpless in the throes of the lake, Amber knew she would be soon dashed against the very rocks she had been trying to reach. Again she was sucked under. Again. Again. She flailed and rose, gasping and gulping, her breaths weakening each time. How much longer could she do this? She spat water, losing sensation of where she was. *As long as it takes.* But the depths yielded imploringly, urging her down with a whispering plea she could not much longer resist, and she knew that at any moment she could plummet like a dropped stone, further than she could ever hope through this exhaustion to rise.

WHY FIGHT THAT WHICH DOES NOT RESIST?

Whose voice was that? It felt weirdly familiar. The Nymph's? Surely even she was not so cruel. *Get out!* she screamed silently, battling panic. *I'm not scared!*

WE WILL NEVER LEAVE YOU, the voice countered. *BENEATH THE TURBULENT SURFACE, FIND CALM AT THE CENTRE . . .*

Had she actually heard anything? Was her brain so starved of oxygen? But real or not, the voice spoke truly: beneath their ploughing might at the surface, the breakers could no longer hurt her.

Too dizzy from the bludgeonings of the waves to gather coordinated breaths, Amber gulped a final mouthful of air, thrust her head under and dove, forcing herself through the thrashing surf with her eyes screwed shut against the unknown.

The booming crash of the combers resounded disorientatingly through her head, but the flooding light streamed beneath her clamped lids and instinctively she strove towards it.

Kicking frantically she forced herself down, through the churning oppositional currents, towards the rocky bed she could grasp blindly to follow. Yet relief at reaching the bottom ran out instantaneously, bleeding into the savage need for air as, rising automatically to break the surface for a breath, her back scraped something rough and in a rush of panic she opened unfocused eyes to glimpse the dark stain of gnarled rock forming the underwater tunnel now trapping her.

Amidst the light now blinding pain crushed first her chest and then her soul, her lungs turning to fire. Through a weird delirium she barely registered something slippery brush her skin and a rush of bubbles escape from a scalloped instrument her hands had been wrapped round as someone pressed the artefact to her lips and she gulped the precious mouthfuls insensibly until she could think of nothing else.

She felt the shadow of a hand pass across her eyes, and instinctively opened them, realising they were no longer stung by salt and beholding through the all-consuming light a woman with piercing ocean-green eyes and pale scarred skin, her weed-entwined hair flowing across her hips where skin mingled with scales to birth a muscular grey-green tail tapering to dusky purplish fronds stretched over silvering rays.

The Sea Maiden guided Amber's hands again, and looking down the Fairy saw a conical shell of marbling colours emitting bubble after bubble.

AS ONE CANNOT SPEAK UNDERWATER. The words danced into Amber's mind, and she stared astonished at the woman holding her gaze as calmly as she was holding the shell. *YOU HAVE THE IDEA OF TAKING SEVERAL DEEP BREATHS NOW, AS IT SEEMS TO YOU LIKELY THAT WE SHALL SOON SWIM ON FROM THIS PLACE.*

Amber found herself fastening her lips round the shell once more, gulping further breaths and wondering what in the Realm would happen next.

The woman grasped Amber's wrist, guiding the Fairy with no loss of speed as they swam together, the Maiden undulating powerfully through the illuminated passage as the water throbbed with the rhythmic beats of her tail.

It was all Amber could do to hold her breath, so swift was their pace, and yet her fears dissolved like bubbles in the presence of the Maiden, and she found herself shedding her doubts, casting them off in the wake of their speed. Glancing down as she snatched a breath from the shell, she watched the sheer rock fall away to herald fine, blanched sand that flurried up from the bottom as they passed over.

Barely discernable through the clouds of sediment, she glimpsed fallen pillars of once-towering marble resting amidst ornate dilapidated structures crumbled half-buried in the sand. Fronds of singing rippled amongst the ruins, clear voices dancing closer until Amber saw all around her Knights and Maidens swimming in convoy to accompany her guide.

As the Maiden swam on with her gathering escort the water darkened into a murky, heavy green, and Amber found herself gulping shallow breaths from the shell as her surroundings grew ever more chill. Folded curtains of slate cascaded from re-emerging rock walls as a passage closed in around them, and the Maiden slowed before the entrance of a rising tunnel leading to the surface. Looking into Amber's eyes encouragingly, she let go of her.

Glancing to the dull, shivering silver glinting above, Amber knew it was her time to break away, yet her courage slipped to guess what she would have to face alone beyond. Steeling herself, she turned in gratitude to the Maiden, and through the algal haze glimpsed the indistinct figures of her escorts waiting in a silent vigil for her to gather her strength. Buoyed by their faith, Amber turned and swam up to the surface's narrow circle glittering distortedly above.

Breaking through into the air as if returning to the Realm anew, Amber flung her hair from her eyes, whirling round to view her surroundings, breathless and gasping although no longer from fear. She had to admit that the air she sucked in through the cold dark was as sweet as the shell's gift, now that it was free and all around her, and even if the jagged shafts of slate thrusting ominously from the water to form a precarious bank threatened her confidence, they were the closest thing to land to grace the vicinity for far too long, and she found herself blessing them. A gathering chill clung to the droplets on her skin as she approached, and she wished more than ever that she could stay in the lake's sanctuary. But she had to be close to the entrance now. She had to go further.

Resignedly, Amber hauled herself out onto the slick rock. The sudden drop in temperature bit into her wet skin, sending her teeth chattering uncontrollably as, shivering violently, she looked around to try to focus on something else apart from the cloying cold. She was in yet another kind of chamber, dimly lit and coldly echoing. The urge to retreat back to the womblike warmth of the mirror lake dragged at her almost overwhelmingly.

It was the last respite before the long dark, she reminded herself, letting the words fill her consciousness, pushing away her doubt with their strength. *Take it for what it was, and be thankful.*

She turned back slowly, conscious of the shell still in her hand, and kneeling, released it. It dropped into the water with a quiet *splosh*, sweeping erratically down through the depths until it was lost from view.

Amber gazed through the ripples wistfully, wondering where the Maiden was now. Maybe she was watching. Urging her on.

Kneeling there soaked and shivering, the charmed water pooling to glisten brightly at her feet, Amber forced herself to contemplate what she must attempt next. The last link between her and the safe haven she had left as suddenly as she had entered was now severed and returned to its source, requiring her to once again continue alone.

Anticipation prickling across her skin with the chill air, the songs of the Knights and Maidens echoing through her mind to fortify her courage, Amber pushed herself breathlessly to her feet, only to stare in abject dismay at the dead-end cavern surrounding her.

Out of the corner of her eye Amber glimpsed movement against the flowstone walls, and was half tempted to leap straight back into the water again.

"One who cannot fly will always walk furthest."

Amber spun round, strangely comforted by the familiar, dispassionate voice cutting through her uncertainty as the Water Nymph stepped from the fluid shadows.

"The bubbles show all, child. Even you cannot be so naïve as to have thought I would be blind to your plan."

Amber cursed inwardly. She didn't know if she could face another round of the Nymph's particular brand of questioning.

But instead Zaralathaar paced a slow circuit around her, the Enchantress's eyes shining with the cold, strange power of the moon, her gaze both as probing as a healer's and as unsettling as a sorcerer's. "The flame of your soul flickers, yet your resolve must not waver." The Nymph's footsteps echoed her judgement on the slab-rock floor.

The scratch of tears scraped at Amber's throat at the suddenness and challenge of the disclosure. Yet something sparked in her to realise that this time, Zaralathaar was taking her seriously. "My resolve is more solid than I can express without actions," she promised steadily, her gaze taking refuge in the stone. "Give me the chance, and I will prove it to you. It's just, my strength relies on being honest with myself; and I cannot deny how empty I feel without him."

The Nymph's own gaze remained reassuringly unperturbed. "Emptiness you have coped with before, child. It cannot in itself be a source of fear for you."

Amber felt equally shocked and strangely lightened by her words. "Mayhap," she managed. "Yet there are emptinesses that cannot be filled."

"Indeed, child." The Nymph drew herself up to her full height. "And yet even they can be borne. Not everything has to be filled."

Before Amber could formulate a way to thank her for so uncommonly personal a reassurance, the Nymph pre-empted her with a warning: "The Way of Ice and Fire is closed. I will not open it."

"But I—"

"Yes, child, you have made your fool's errand perfectly clear," Zaralathaar countered irritably. "So mark you the terms, and mark them well. One, the Way is closed to all but Enchanters. Therefore, I will transport you to the entrance by magic. This term is not negotiable."

Amber bowed her head. "Thank you, my lady."

"Do not thank me, for I send you to your doom," the Nymph rebuked soundly, her voice ringing with all the power of the ocean. "Two," she continued without drawing breath, "the Way will be sealed behind you. I will not have what lies within unleashed upon the Realm. This term is also not negotiable."

Amber felt cold sweat slide from her brow. "I am ready."

"Foolish *and* unprepared!" the Nymph thundered. "Desist from such pointless exclamations, before I lose both my patience and my concern."

Amber swallowed her pride, her head spinning slightly. "Sorry, my lady. I am not ready. But I will take the Way."

"So it would seem," the Nymph acquiesced, her voice marginally less sharp as she drew forth something shimmering from the folds of her robe. "Foolish you may remain—but unprepared, I can address." Her storm-grey eyes fixed on Amber. "Once on the path, you will not be able to use the Fountain. Should you do so, it will alert the monsters, in which case you will perish as surely as the greater quest will fail."

With the stroke of each word, Amber felt her hope dimming further. Of its own accord her mind flicked protectively back to the joyous anticipation of the Presentation Eve; to the fireflies dancing in the mid-Recö night's air as the star-flecked sky stretched on forever in the company of laughter to honour the pledging of dreams.

The click of the Nymph's fingers snapped Amber back to the present, and she stared in undisguised astonishment at the softly glistening translucent orb, about a hand-span in width and with pearlescent colours gently swirling, hovering above the Enchantress's wizened, outstretched palm.

"Give me your sash, girl, quickly."

Amber did as she was bidden, itching with curiosity.

In a fluid motion Zaralathaar swept the sash over the orb, and the bubble simply melted away into the fabric as she passed it to the Fairy.

As Amber gingerly took the bundle, the Nymph gestured impatiently for her to wear it once again. "Unfurl the sash," she explained; "billow it into the air, and the bubble will reform for a solitary instant. It is far too small to carry you, of course, but it will enable you to see a scene exactly as if you were in the Fountain. Thus can you observe but once, if you choose to, whether the farther battle fares well or ill."

Amber bowed deeply, even as her mind reeled to think of what that would truly mean, and the next instant flinched violently as at the thunderclap of the Enchantress's hands the wall began to shift.

As the shudders of the rock died away and the ground sank again into dormancy, the Nymph stood back to reveal the wall conjured beyond. Its aspect towered into distant heights, traced with a thread of narrow steps so eroded by time as to be barely visible as they led up to a crooked fissure almost the mirror image, Amber realised with a chill of foreboding, of the gashed opening she had stared up to from the Fountain so long ago—the one at which this trial would soon end for good or ill.

"So be it," the Nymph intoned with finality, watching the Fairy. "Mount the stairwell, descend into the darkness, and when light returns, in whatsoever travesty it assails you, you will have stepped onto the Way of Ice and Fire. Nothing further remains to be said, or warned, or done.

"Go hence, if that is your decision, and bear the burden of that choice for the rest of your days. You have not yet lived to see what I have witnessed. Turn back, and the horrors I speak of shall remain forever to you but the darkest of imaginings. Continue, and the terrors that await you will never leave even your unwaking sight. Venture forth with caution, for there are things that cannot be erased from memory by all the sunlight of years to come."

She stood back, and Amber stepped forwards, her Realm shrinking into the uncanny passage she must traverse, fixing her gaze on it warily as she tried to stamp down the fear rising within her.

The Nymph tarried, leaving the lightest of touches cold on Amber's arm. "Come back, child." She withdrew her hand, and something approaching wistfulness and sorrow flickered across her eyes. "Do not become lost along the Way."

Nodding silently Amber advanced, ascending into a profound darkness.

Versus Thanatos

Sweat squeezed between scrunched lids to sting into his eyes as Jasper adjusted his grip on the sword again, shifting the hilt restlessly in his clammy grasp; anything to distract himself even at the smallest level from what could no longer be avoided or denied.

Feverishly, he stabbed the blade into the sand. How could the desert be so silent? How could this be taking so long? How could he already be feeling like the Realm had collapsed before he'd so much as—

Jasper's stomach heaved as his vision swam suddenly, and feeling claws dig through his shirt the Prince belatedly realised he was standing again, supported by Racxen.

"Sorry," he muttered thickly, determined to hide the truth about the sword for as long as he could from the Arraheng. "Not done this for a while. This accursed heat's just getting to me."

"We're not going to die," the Arraheng growled calmly in his ear, softly enough for no one else to overhear.

"Oh, no, cave-boy?" Jasper slurred light-headedly, wondering distractedly how long he would have to keep hold of this forsaken blade for. "Why not?"

"We haven't finished living."

Jasper tried to think of a suitably disdainful quip in response, but his throat constricted so tightly that he gave up and settled for risking a glance to his companion. "If I promise to never breathe of it again, will you please just tell me that inside you're as terrified as I am?"

Racxen gave a quiet, overwhelmed bark of what he tried to turn into laughter. "Sen."

Jasper swallowed shakily. "Oh good. I'd hate for you to come over all courageous just to spite me. That really would round off the perfect day."

Racxen tried to summon conviction into his voice. "Ah, but *tomorrow* will be perfect." He flexed his claws, trying to remove the tremor. "Tomorrow, the others will be safe."

"Yes, well," the Prince spat back testily. "I'm not quite as ready to throw my life away as you are. *Just* 'the others' doesn't quite cut it. Perish the thought I might one day have to die for my people, but in the meantime I'd rather live for them."

Racxen smiled sadly, his eyes solemn. "Sen. Just this once, I agree with you."

"Oh, you've cursed it now," Jasper dismissed mildly. "We'll be fated to die as soon as we get along reasonably with each other."

Rendering all retort forgotten, at the furthest reach of vision the Goblins swarmed into view, as tiny and deadly as an army of Gantornas at this distance, blanketing the sands with their advance.

Yenna's shuddering howl broke across the plains, and the Arkhan pack as a unit began to run, Wolf-forms flowing out across the flying sands.

Watching them numbly, Jasper struggled to keep the bile down. Everything was too soon, and too late. *I haven't been trained for this,* he thought pointlessly, awash with panic, the past proud months suddenly feeling woefully inadequate. *I only wear this accursed armour for the Ceremonies. When was the last time I fought? Actually fought when it mattered?*

"Together?" Racxen interrupted, locking eyes with him as if he could read and block those nihilistic fears.

"Together," the Prince promised hoarsely, enveloped in a tiredness more absolute than any before. This couldn't even be real any more. They couldn't all just be about to—

And yet a cry tore from his throat in the ancient tongue, throwing him forwards as if borne by imperishable wings, and Racxen was leaping after him, his battle-cry melding with the Prince's.

Even as they ran, weapons flashing in the scorching desert sun, the hordes closed in over their pitiful attempts, tearing friend from friend and wrenching apart all hope as each beating, trembling heart knew in that desperate instant its own frailty, swallowed up in the enormity of a rage surely unvanquishable.

The Way of Ice and Fire

Darkness, utter darkness, swamped the passage as Amber felt her way along, elation soaring as her searching hands touched a wall bracket and then, mercifully, a torch.

Fumbling in her pockets, she had to strike the meagre remnant of her fireflint several times before it flared into a welcome glow. Heart-thuds slowing, she gazed down the now-visible tunnel. Okay, so there wasn't a light at the end of it, she assured herself with a flood of confidence, but at least now she could stride out undaunted into the waiting darkness carrying her own.

In the flickering light, the edging primeval depths seemed to merge into savage forms, and her grip tightened nervously around the torch. Flinching at a sudden noise, she scanned the passage fitfully, her vision painfully inadequate. Were those merely eldritch echoes moaning low through the distance?

Advancing warily along the tunnel, she felt the malevolent glare of unseen eyes prickling into the back of her skull as she swung the torch hither and thither, always too slow to catch the skittering shadows shredding her nerves as the echoes of her footsteps scurried unnervingly behind. She would have given anything to have felt Racxen's calm presence as an anchor against her paranoia, or to have heard Mugkafb's chirpy voice shatter the taut silence and dispel the invading ghosts of noise clamouring inside her head, or to have seen the images of Ruby's next dressmaking design block out the imaginings flitting through her mind unchecked.

The hardest journeys are the ones made alone, the Genie's warning floated back through her memory.

"I'll never be truly alone," she promised aloud. "Because once they stood by me."

As the tunnel widened into a chamber, Amber stalled, squinting into the indistinct depths as tendrils of mist swirled wraithlike from a knotted mass floating at the centre of the chamber to drift with fluid languor against the darkness.

Amber shivered. There was no breath of wind down here, no air-current to cause their movement: evidently the tunnels once frequented by Snakelocks still held the remnants of her sorcery. The realisation turned her stomach, but with every moment she delayed the mist was spreading. Before she could think better of it, she strode into the engulfing whiteness.

A bone-reaching chill descended, cloying spectral fingers groping towards her as she waded blindly through the mists, her skin crawling with their damp, half-imagined touch. Spinning round disorientated, she glimpsed patterns in the fog, the images shifting into each other. She tried to ignore what her fraught mind interpreted them as, but on the edge of her sight a tendril snapped off to snake ambiguously through the darkness, stretching itself into a tapering bone before bunching into a savage, leering face which loomed out at her from the gloaming and distorted itself into a cavernous, fang-ridden mouth swooping down to launch itself at her.

Logic abandoning her, Amber fled for her life and collided with something, the chinkling sound of falling glass ringing through her ears as she scrambled up from the floor, heart slamming.

Realising with relief that the mist had dissipated, it took her a moment to register the visions sharpening in its absence—visions of herself.

All else faded until she was looking through an isolation room window in the rec hall, watching her reflection at a bedside pumping the chest of a casualty, alone and gripped through with terror, and Sarin entering to pull her away and call time of death.

As she saw herself crumble into shock, the vision shifted, so that instead of falling to the floor she was huddled on a doorstep—Ruby's, she realised with foreboding—and laughter floated from inside, where her friend was talking and joking with Beryl and Sardonyx and Chrysocolla; all of them, and she was hammering on the door, and Ruby didn't let her in; acted like she couldn't even hear or see her.

And now a shadow grew over her shoulder, and her mirror-self turned in relief, knowing it was Racxen—but when she opened her arms to him he froze and backed away, staring at her in bewilderment as if he didn't even know her; as if she'd got everything wrong and had ruined their friendship in one pitiful move.

And as her reflection ran, tears streaming down her face, her surroundings changed and she was running from the Samire and it was gaining, and instead of the Fountain nothing but a dead-end wall loomed.

Retching suddenly Amber stumbled backwards, overcome.

Immediately, as she crossed the threshold back into the Realm she knew, the gilded frame of a giant broken mirror revealed itself.

It's nothing but Vetch work, she tried to convince herself weakly. *You learned from Rraarl how they used mirrors as tools, and how they could manipulate stone and metal—and minds.* She shuddered uncontrollably. The idea that they had wormed into her head . . .

Breathe, she ordered herself fiercely, dragging down deep breaths in an attempt to expel the fresh tide of panic washing over her. *It's just a mirror: a mirror of might or might not be. It's not deadly; it hasn't even been original since before the Nymph was born. So for pity's sake don't let it hold sway. If that's the best they can throw at you, things are looking up.*

She let out another breath, calmer now. *There's no one in the Realm who can walk out of here for you. Keep your mind your own.* She flicked through images in her head, trying to focus on them instead of the doubts.

Ruby—think of Ruby. Didn't she look beautiful at the Ceremony? She hasn't been panicking every minute of every day like you, has she? No—she's focused on the good stuff; on the Presentation and her apprenticeship, and she's still your best friend after years and years, even though everything else is changing and falling.

Okay: her mind was starting to wander again, but maybe this was working. *What about Racxen? You wouldn't be scared if he were here now, would you? Well, fine, you would be, and so would he; but you'd get through it together like you have so many things before. And Jasper! If he ever found out you were this scared he'd never let you hear the end of it, so you'll just have to prove him wrong instead. And little Mugkafb: if he were here, you wouldn't be afforded the luxury of letting yourself be scared because you'd be too busy being brave for him so that he wouldn't get frightened.*

Chewing the thoughts carefully, she let them fill her mind until there was no room left for scurrying fears. *What did the Mirror Lake teach you?* she recalled. *That you must place your trust within, not without, in this place.*

She took a deep breath, expelled it forcefully, and turned towards the bewitched gateway again. *Face the trickery, find the truth.*

Gripping the torch like a talisman as she stepped into the mirror's frame, Amber strode heart in mouth towards the illusions, only to find them dissipating on her approach to allow her passage, reduced to the slightest wisps of ephemera. *Next!* she dared the visions silently.

But her elation fell away short-lived, for now that the mists had dispersed a stranger sight accosted her eyes. Sprawled out before her lay a darkly glittering lake, eddying mysteriously. A causeway of stepping-stones, each bobbing as if held only by sorcery, tracked the unsettled surface and, almost at the other side, the mirage of an ancient door shimmered strangely over the agitated waters. Amber felt a stab of panic. The real trial was only just beginning.

At the water's edge sat an obsidian bowl. ONE KEY ALONE GRANTS PASSAGE THROUGH THE DOOR, advised its inscription. DOOM BEFALL YOU SHOULD IT REMAIN ON THIS SHORE.

Amber's heart sank. Nestled within glinted a tangle of individual keys of all metals and sizes. How could this all hinge on choosing one—how long was this going to take?

"Look, I'm sorry not to play by your rules," Amber hissed firmly to the bowl, glaring out across the restless waters. "But this is far too important to waste time on." With that, she bundled all the keys into her sash, wrapping them up over and over so none would slip out, and swung the precious cargo across her shoulder. Before her courage could fail her, she took the steps at a run.

Buzzing with triumph, she leaped from the last steppingstone through the doorway, but as her feet touched solid ground she heard the first eldritch shrieks of the awakening Vetches.

The Briefest of Chances

Hounded by their relentless screams Amber pelted through the darkness, barely registering the row upon row of ancient doors swinging open on crumbled hinges as she fled past disorientated.

Spinning round in the hope of glimpsing empty distance as the echoes dropped back, she crashed into something, noting too late the rusted bars her hand clung around to drag herself up as an explosion of gold and char flung itself against the grate.

She threw herself back as the Griffin lunged, the terror in his hawk-eyes burning a frantic reflection of the Fairy's heart. With no one else to turn her haunted gaze to, Amber beheld with sudden clarity Slaygerin's instinctual subconscious awareness that death in a form more savage than himself was coming.

She didn't know if he thought she would rescue him, or even if he could understand the concept. Struggling for breath, knowing she was losing seconds even as she decided, Amber scrabbled for stones on the floor, smashing them against the rusted chain around the lock. Slaygerin knew of betrayal, from all those years ago—now was his time to learn of trust.

"Right," she muttered as she kicked the broken chain away, working her trembling hands over the locks and begging silently that she'd still have time. "I'll take the chance—you make the choice."

Grunting, she shoved the final bolt out of place. "I hope your last minutes are better than mine," she gasped as she heaved away the grate.

Sensing freedom the Griffin threw himself at the opening, forcing Amber to jump back against the wall as he burst past her and ran on without a backwards glance.

The scuffle of his talons on the rock died away, leaving her standing there alone, staring after him.

What, you really thought he wouldn't? she couldn't help admonishing herself bleakly, gripped through with a deathly exhaustion.

Against her rasping breath and the thundering of her heart, she had no way of hearing where the Griffin could have got to. She hoped he would find his way through these accursed wending passages to the surface, and feel daylight upon his ravaged hide once more after his long years of imprisonment.

Firing her seizing limbs painfully onwards, her pace ever slowing, she wasn't sure she ever would again.

The Queen's Pledge

On the castle ramparts Pearl kept watch, her eyes trained tirelessly down upon the meadows. Surreal it felt, to be watching for the coming of doom, now that the moment stretched imminent.

At least this might give them some small edge of time; buy them vital minutes. But no matter what she tried to tell herself, she couldn't shake the sense of shame that this was all she was doing: observing safe and removed as those on the ground awaited their fate.

The army regimented below stood stalwart, their colours bright in the innocuous predawn calm of a day soon to be torn asunder. Horse-masters Magnus and Pendril had taken their places heading the guard section flanking the White Chargers—the affectionate dubbing given to the grey horses reserved for the Medical Corps to aid recognition on the battlefield. The division's bravery was legendary, for in order to operate effectively in the field and bear casualties swiftly to safety, armour was too cumbersome a luxury to be afforded.

From her vantage point, the militia looked too insufficient a force to stand against such odds as they would soon face, and Pearl struggled to swallow back the guilt that had been rising all day through the chaos of the preparations. *You never enlisted.* The knowledge wormed toxically into her core. *They're fighting for everyone's lives, and you never even enlisted.*

Then the Queen froze, all else forgotten: through the glimmer of dawn light on the distance, although she could not pick out any discernable shapes, she could have sworn she had seen the horizon shudder. A heartbeat's pause stretched the silence, until she saw the dark movement of a far-off shadow spilling towards the meadow-green below, surging with the menace of an approaching storm.

"Guards!" Pulling on the tower bell as a warning to all below, Pearl ran down the stairwell, her skirts flying as a reckless plan sprang half-formed to her mind.

Drawing herself up regally as a man-at-arms stepped to bar her way, Pearl dismissed him soundly, indignation simmering behind her eyes. "Your loyalty to your King does you credit, Feldspar, but you cannot think so little of your Queen that you expect me to stand idly by whilst my family and people imperil their lives fighting. It is true I have no skill on the battlefield, but the talent I have I shall use, and if that is a risk, so be it; I cannot in good conscience shy from it when the times demand such things of us all. One must lead by example, and if I die today, I would have myself do so as a Queen, not a coward!"

"My lady," the Guard insisted calmly, as another soldier—Onyx—moved in to further block her. "I strongly suggest you retire to a place of safety, before I am obliged to escort you."

Clinging to her dignity by a thread, the Queen swept up her skirts and stormed back along the steps.

In the welcome privacy of the column shadows, she at last allowed her frustration to escape. "He's right," she muttered wretchedly, pressing her fingers to the corners of her eyes and trying to compose herself. "Why call them now? It would be nightfall before I got there, and no Dragon can fly in darkness."

Laksha's form lent a deeper shadow. "'Cept one, o' course," the Goblin noted obligingly under her breath as she tinkered with her armour. She fixed Pearl with the kind of penetrating stare only a Goblin could manage. "And he'll more 'n do."

Pearl's eyes gleamed, and she shivered as the idea took hold. "But the speed necessary to pull this off . . ."

"There's no point riding a Dragon if ye're going ter ride it like a horse," the Goblin reminded. "Ride it like a demon, or not at all." Glimpsing in the Queen's eyes the same determination that had borne herself through her capture before escaping with Gorfang all those years ago, a relishing grin flicked across Laksha's lips to contemplate the outrage her mistress's actions would cause.

Tears clung once more to Pearl's now-distant eyes both sparkling and sad at once. "Laksha, I could not do what you are about to," the Queen admitted in a whisper.

"Nor I what you'll accomplish, my lady," her Hand Maiden insisted in return. "We each have our roles, and they cannot all be one—or else we would not each be helping how we could best. If there are no healers, who is there ter help those who come back broken? If there are no loved ones remaining behind, who is there ter come back to? If there are no farmers, traders, teachers, everyone who makes our life what it is, who is there ter help us rebuild it after?"

Nodding fiercely, Pearl clutched her friend's hands for courage. "Go to my boy."

Laksha nodded instantly and, hearing the guards approach, Pearl sank back to the shadows in exasperation, her eyes grim and charged with the impossibility of the task ahead. "How much time is there?"

Laksha scanned towards the shadow moving swiftly against the horizon and flowing ever closer. "Time enough ter make it worth remembrance."

Stepping back, she gave the Queen a companionable shove. "Go!" the Goblin hissed. "Jus' this once, I'll pretend I couldn't stop yer."

Subterranea

Longing for the cooling darkness of before, her encounter with Slay-gerin now another Realm away, Amber gritted her teeth as she skittered through the tunnel, the infernal blackened heat scorching through the rock as if chasing her steps. Sickening realisation hounded her too, for in losing her wings she had lost more even than flight; her memory twisted cruelly to remind her that the membranes formed an efficient heat-resistance system; drawn around you like a cloak, they would reflect the battering sun like a shield. She hadn't even that defence.

Waves of nausea rising with the temperature, she rubbed sweat from her eyes as the walls twisted and turned until through the endless dark an ominous coal-red glow started throbbing somewhere up ahead.

As she crept round the corner, diabolical light slammed into her with a searing heat, gripping her in terror as she stared mesmerised through the chasmic hole gaping from the left section of the gnarled wall, an abstract panel worn away by so many years of history.

Amber stood rigid, as astonished as she was horrified, her eyes stream-ing against the vicious heat as she stared across the hellish lavascape revealed. Peering out over a volcanic core of flesh-stripping magma rivers each bearing fractured glaciers of smouldering igneous rock, she felt as if she had reached the centre of the Realm—and strayed far beyond anywhere meant for the eyes of mortal folk. Above the scalding flow, crooked rock tunnels similar to hers passed low, and Amber felt a sickening precognition of what she would have to face at the final confrontation.

Flinching back as a violent hiss rushed her Realm into blinding white, in the split-second before her eyes clamped shut Amber glimpsed a geyser spew to heights unknown as she threw herself against the wall to escape the singeing heat.

In the ringing quietness after, she scrubbed at her eyes as they smarted with vision-floaters, everything shuddering green and black until the blotches subsided and reality shifted back into solid form.

Shrinking further along, pressing herself into the pitiful pockets of darkness as the way grew evermore pocked with cavities and fissures, any uncertainty that she was on the right track tumbled fatally to the lavaflow: surely only such a monster as the Samire could make its lair here.

Still, didn't this just started off as my idea? she reminded herself, hollow with worry. *How likely is it really that I, out of all people, have come up with a plan that will actually work?* Maybe she'd find the way to the core blocked by rock-fall or something. Maybe she'd get so far, only to find there'd be nothing more she could do.

"No," she promised herself grimly, shivering at the finality held in her own voice. "Maybes are the excuses of a quavering heart and deserve no heed. Everything the others are attempting risks falling to nothing if you don't succeed in your part."

Letting the words buoy her with the dizzying hope that the unimaginable could never come to pass and that all this would fade into memory at the exultation of success, she strode on proudly.

And later, as the tunnel traced downwards into a nameless dark and sickening reality cut once again into her core, a deathly chill slipping to squirm beneath her skin until all her doubts and fears flowed like unstoppable tears through her soul, falteringly but unfailingly she pressed on through.

Centaur Aaptos

As the wind hummed across the dusty ground, Naya waved goodbye to Kantor and his parents and swung the gate closed. Strolling leisurely back across the schoolyard, she reflected on a day well spent. Everyone but Sama had been collected—Liana must be running late—and she had only to wait with her niece back in the classroom. If she were lucky, she'd get home before sunset; it shouldn't—

A moving shadow-form flicked across her vision, the weapon in his hands flaring unmistakeably.

"Stop!" The scream tore from her throat and she was running at the Goblin before logic could interfere, scratching, kicking and pummelling him with a strength born of terror. "She's still in there! Why—"

Smack—her head slammed into the dust, and her hands scrabbled instinctively at the vicelike grip that clutched at her hair, wrenching her head back to expose her throat.

"Mm," the Goblin offered. "Why am I doing this?" His grip tightened as he wriggled down next to her and laid his head on one side, so close that his fetid breath rolled hot on her face. "Maybe it's because a little pixie tells me to. Maybe it's because I got beaten every day as a kid. Maybe it's because it's the only thing I've found that works. Maybe it's all this—maybe it's nothing."

Pain lanced sharply through her neck as he shifted into a crouch, shoving her head down. "Consider that, missy, if you like—while I'm striking the first flint. Long live the King."

He sprang away, and as she scrambled fear-crazed to her feet Naya could already hear the crackle and rush as the sparks caught.

"The best thing about the desert," the Goblin mused, gazing hungrily into the flames as they spilled across the sun-scorched grass, "is that it's so dry. And the best thing about the school—being so new and close to the forest—is that someone had the foresight to use so much wood to build it. Don't do that again. Kids could get hurt. You know what some people are like."

Naya lunged in a last-ditch effort towards the door, barely seeing the Goblin's swift movement as in a sudden rush he sent her sprawling to the ground.

"Run," he mocked. "I'll keep watch. Can you guess how fast fire travels?"

Terror surging through her as she ripped her gaze away, Naya scrambled to her feet and charged towards the centre of town without another glance, begging she'd find help fast enough. It was too late to run in; she knew that with a savage certainty. Unless she could douse the flames, she'd never reach Sama. And if the school went up, the whole town could catch. At the end of the third track lay the Golden Griffin, along a path she had trodden night and day for years and could find without thinking, and the doors swung open with a whip-crack as she slammed into them, almost slipping on the tiled floor.

"Fire!" she screamed, her eyes falling wildly upon the handful of punters frozen mute at her entrance. "At the school—Sama's in there!" Her words fell over themselves as she fought to speak, her body overtaken by trembling.

Standing at the bar, the Centaur's vision shuddered as he battled the urge to wretch, his heart tattooing so violently it stole his breath. Fire: the mere word seized around his heart with a primal, solid dread. *Anything* but fire.

"I'll find her!" His pledge assailed his own ears even as his voice shook, and his restless hooves clicked loudly against the tiles in the nervous silence. "Bring water—cut through the forest!" Before his instincts could override his actions Han pushed through the doorway, leaping into a wild run and racing away towards the trees.

The townsfolk stood ashen-faced in his wake, staring out as if entranced to the billowing swathes of smoke leeching into the sky.

"Water!" Naya reminded in a yell. "You heard him!" Helplessness washing through her to behold her stricken audience, she forced her mind into clarity and in the next instant she found herself standing on the bar, legs trembling beneath her, bellowing at the top of her voice: "Look at me!"

Stupefied they turned, their faces mirroring her own terror as she dealt out tasks. "You two—down to the cellar and bring the buckets up!" she started, and the men closest to the bar jumped to it. "You five nearest the door—" she flung out another arm, "run and tell everyone you can find what's happened and meet us with buckets at the well on Second Street."

With a nod the women disappeared, and the two men clattered up the steps to fling buckets onto the floor.

Jumping down from the bar, Naya addressed the crowd with her final command. "The rest of you, grab as many as you can and follow me!"

Clinging silently to their instructions against the grim rise of panic threatening, they each rushed to their parts and, relieved to have some-one's lead to follow, as one chased after the tavern girl.

The Centaur knew the woods like no man alive, and the shouts of even the most athletic of the townsfolk fell away behind him as he galloped into the heart of the forest.

Ragged breath scorching his lungs now, Han heard the fearsome

crackle and snapping of burning branches advancing like some raven-
ous primeval monster until the air writhed with roiling smoke.

Choking and stumbling, a battering heat engulfed the Centaur and
he reared up with a braying yell to stare terror-stricken through the
shuddering air at the spewing fire spitting and roaring and thrashing
like a mass of serpents spilling across the ground beneath smothering
putrid smoke. And there was no other way through—

Coughing wracked his body, and he fell to his knees. Yelping as a
tongue of fire licked at his fetlock, he lurched into standing and danced
sideways, the taken grass crumbling to ash beneath his hooves as he
stared through smarting eyes along the smouldering path that despite
all things still held him immobile.

You will cross this path, he yelled in his head, the heat too overpower-
ing to countenance risking doing so aloud. *And whatever happens you
will not stop. You will find the girl and save her. All will be well and all
will be over. Say it! Mean it! Do it!*

Weakening panic threatening to smother him faster than the heat,
Han skipped back to where the smoke had less of a hold and, bellowing at himself in his mind to hold his ground, willed his heart to slow
right down. His eyes closed as he brought himself back to the soul of
the forest. There was just him now; him and the trees, for he was back
amongst the youngest saplings, when the forest was at its newest and
brightest. Those flames at his feet were but the orange leaves of Requë
dancing along the path he must run, the roar of the fire merely the
rushing wind blowing them high to a far free sky.

Retreating further inside his mind, the Centaur felt the instinctive
fire-fear of his ancestry fade as the cool, shaded forest welcomed him.
At one with his thoughts he snorted, eyes glazing over and hooves paw-
ing the ground in rhythm with his heaving breath. Han tossed back
his head and a wild cry erupted from deep inside him as he reared up
invincible and seeing only with his mind's eye, barely registering the

flames licking up from the ground that would later lead to sleepless nights and full-nursed wounds, he charged forward untouchable, hearing as if from elsewhere the coal-hot stones leaping to chink and split as his hooves connected with the path hissing beneath his feet.

Running, running, running, dimly through the crackling roar of the forest and his trance-held state he heard the scream of the child arch shrill with terror and he veered suddenly—

Eyes streaming as she fled through the choking heat with the sound of the school collapsing lodged into her fractured memory, Sama shrieked in horror and whirled round at the sound of stones cracking behind her closer than the fire.

"If you go down to the woods today," a Goblin voice mocked, the queer light gleaming in his eyes more terrifying than that of the flames, "you're sure of a big surprise."

"Get away from me!" Sama spat as fiercely as she could, her voice trembling into a squeak. "Help!" she sobbed desperately, as the fire and the Goblin danced closer. "*Heeeeelp!*"

"Haven't you heard, sweet thing?" the Goblin mused in a travesty of concern as he pushed close enough to whisper. "No one answers anymore."

The branches around them crashed in a splintering explosion as through the trees burst a half-equine man, flanks heaving and hair flying, eyes wild against the smoke as he skidded to a halt amidst a scatter of stones.

"Maybe not in your Realm," the Centaur gasped, grinning roguishly. "Welcome to mine."

He spun to Sama. "On my back—now!" As her arms wrapped tight around his waist, Han turned back to the Goblin. "This is my forest!" he couldn't help adding, keeping their assailant's attention whilst scanning restlessly for the safest path through the blazing trees. "These shadows are for sanctuary seekers, not skulking stalkers; these roots are for dreams, not fears—and these leaves whisper my words, not yours!"

Clinging to Han, Sama yelled out in warning as the Goblin lunged and a groaning protest ripped through the air as with a hideous tearing crash the tree toppled and fell before them, pinning their attacker beneath its burning weight.

Sparks flinging up amidst the shuddering impact, Han's vision surged with roaring heat as the flames ravaged across the timber. "Hold on!" he yelled hoarsely, leaping over the consuming fire and its charred remains. With Sama's arms still tight around him, the Centaur threw his weight forward as he landed, gasping in bellows through the scratching air, his muscles screaming unbearably as he powered sure-footedly through the draining heat. His hooves kicking ash as he charged across the scorched ground, Han raced through the fire-taken forest as the flames closed in, the child heavy on his back as he ran for both their lives.

From the Ashes

Their rotten stench twisting through the stagnant air even before she saw them, as Amber inched on her belly along the dank, low tunnel, she knew the passageway must now be taking her directly over the Vetches' stronghold. She found herself perversely grateful for their soul-draining hissing screeches, for without them they would surely have heard her by now.

Just a short way further, she instructed her skittering mind, almost relieved to cling to this new challenge—to the gasping heat and the sharp stone peeling the skin from her limbs—for it staved off for a few minutes that which must inevitably come after.

She stopped dead, her previous thought glaring obscenely frivolous and quelled forever as she stared at the rift broken unbreachable across the tunnel, severing her from any hope of crossing as her tunnel fell fractured away to the Vetch-haunted cavern below.

It couldn't be negotiated; it just couldn't. At least, not safely: crawling right to the edge, Amber felt her resolve liquefy and slide trembling to lodge itself between the rock crevices as she stared down, appalled.

What did it matter, the length of time that passed then, when she knew it would be the last she spent in this Realm?

Five-score Vetches, the tiny part of her mind that was already detaching itself noted. *There are five-score Vetches below, with no way forward but down; and you have to continue, or all is lost.*

And so, while the deeper part of her that could be neither distanced nor comforted railed and cried, her outer self clung grimfaced to the rocks scuffing into her ribs and wriggled forward.

You can't die, she ordered herself. Piteous hopes weren't going to keep her alive though, were they? She might as well try to get authoritative. *You have to get through it, so you will. Isn't that how it's supposed to go?*

No answer came of its own accord. No auspicious echoings; no sign at all. Just the rasp of her own fragile breath, and the slavering hisses of the Vetches down there.

Fine, she growled in her head. It would have been simpler before, when there had been laughter in the sunlight and talk of heroes around the fire, but she'd be cursed if she couldn't maintain the delusion that had stoked her courage thus far for just a little while longer.

There is only fear where there is uncertainty. Here, she countered, *there is no choice to worry about: there is simply what must be, and what must follow.*

Absurdly, her body kept inching along, dragging her mind with it. A timorous thought squirmed protectively that—because it had to be, didn't it?—if this was her predestined duty, then her survival had to be somehow preordained, too. She'd soon be home again, crying and terrified and alive, because no matter how bad things had got before, that was the only outcome she'd ever encountered. It wouldn't be real until she was safe and looking back on it.

Yet weakening fear stabbed through her defences and jumbled into a tumultuous mantra: *I don't want to die, I don't want to die*—and no matter how desperate the plea she couldn't pretend it would stave off the inevitable. *Don't think of your death*, she ordered herself as she descended. *Think of their lives.*

Fumbling for the first protrusion to block out all further thought, she clung to it as if stuck, achingly aware of each roughened curve of the rock against her skin; of every nuance of subtly shifting air, knowing it was all about to be snuffed out.

Vibrations pounded through the rock overhead and she heard stones skid and crack as a massive tawny blur pelted round the corner and ran straight towards the edge. Hanging partway down the sheer face, she was powerless to stop the creature even as his identity registered.

"No!" she screamed, forgetting herself and the danger. "Slaygerin!"

Staring in horror, she saw him launch from the edge above her with a keening cry that was half lion, half eagle—saw those golden wings stretch wide with archangel majesty, framed against the darkness—and then a wing-beat snapped the air amidst a blinding flash.

Her grip loosening in shock, every scrap of Amber's orientation fell away into the panic of curling tightly as the rocks savaged her tumbling body, aware only of the searing light squeezing through her scrunched lids and the scalding heat of the ground that assailed her as all around her rose a dervish of hissing screams.

Amongst the last fading eldritch shrieks, Amber dazedly uncurled and staggered to her feet. As she coughed the remnants of smoke from her lungs, the wracking echoes died, obscenely out of place, as her vision slowly returned to assault her with the devastating enormity of what had come to pass.

Ash and silence coated everything, and the acrid reek of burning clung to the air in a stench she knew she would never be rid of, branding itself into her memory in a signature of horrific sacrifice. Of the Vetches, there was no sign, but a tiny bereft sound escaped her as her gaze fell upon the scorched leonine form slumped now in a travesty of slumber.

His body lay, awkward and immobile, its bulk somehow rendered larger by the utter stillness it now inhabited—with not the slightest movement to reassure the eye, his remains seemed beneath her gaze to grow more solid; heavier, as if formed of stone or some such other substance too indelible to remove from either the situation or her memory of it.

Collapsing numbly beside him, Amber stroked the Griffin's ravaged coat, tears brimming as the residual heat seeped into her fingers in a cruel mockery of the warmth of a life the soulless fire had stolen from him. Blinking fiercely, she carefully preened the proud remnants of gold shafting through the pitiful blackened mess of his fur and feathers.

"He redeemed himself!" she pleaded angrily, flinging her challenge to the empty cavern. "He's not supposed to die for it! It's not supposed to end like this!"

Letting out a ragged, steadying breath, Amber gazed into the blank stare that had once fixed on her with such terrible intensity. Now neither savage threat nor haunted fear gleamed in those empty eyes.

"I'll tell Roanen," she whispered, as the hot grip of emotion tightened unbearably around her throat. "You saved me—maybe all of us—and I have no way to thank you; no way to honour you save for keeping your memory in my heart and telling the others of your sacrifice." *And what use will that be?* she found herself thinking bitterly, suddenly exhausted. *What good did it do Rraarl?*

She shook the thought from her head. "Slaygerin, Lord of the Mountain Realm," she continued gently instead. "May you find peace and soar unhindered far above us, cursed no longer by the sufferings of this Realm. Fly . . ." she gulped, and steadied herself resolutely, although her voice quavered, "free."

As her voice died away the quiet darkness closed in, leaving Amber crouched uncertainly beside the body of the Griffin. She had to go; she knew it, but she couldn't just get up and leave him here without a backwards glance. Yet for now all was preserved in reverent silence, so neither did it feel right to say anything else and break it.

He never craved your touch in life, she reminded herself severely, berating herself for her sentimentality. *He needed his distance. He still needed so much longer to heal. He wasn't Rraarl.*

Unsure, Amber stood to leave. On impulse, stepping back to a respectful distance, she quietly kissed her fingers and blew, before turning and tiptoeing from the cavern.

Dislodged by her breath, a single untarnished golden pinion feather floated down unseen to rest amongst the ashes.

The Final Chamber

Sweat sliding into her eyes unchecked as with trembling hands she clung to the rocks to claw her way up as her cramping feet scrabbled for purchase, Amber dragged herself unceremoniously onto the other side as the path flattened again. *You will endure this*, she demanded of herself, forbidding more tears and wiping her face with the back of her hand as she glimpsed the deeper shadow-ink signifying the entrance of the next cavern. *He died to give you this chance, and you will fail neither him nor the others.*

Her eyes slowly adjusting, Amber crept inside, not sure what to expect. After the traumas of the other chambers, she wasn't sure if she could cope with anything else.

But, from what she could see, peering into the gloom, this one seemed almost normal. Shadowed corners, cobwebs and silence: after the blinding light and ravaging heat she had earlier endured, the chill darkness enveloped her like a blanket against the hurts of the Realm. She could almost feel the relief seeping from her pores.

She tiptoed further, her hand trailing across the cavern wall as she investigated, finding herself loathe to abandon its semblance of security as she frowned at the shadowed shapes that seemed to rise from the ground-mist as her eyes settled in the darkness. What were they—furniture? Down here?

A shudder coursed down her spine: they'd better not be anything else. Actually, with a little imagination, it did look like a room, she reassured herself as the shapes acquired familiarly angular forms beneath her relieved gaze. High-ceilinged, dank and austere; not at all like the King's workshop she'd stumbled into—how long ago did that now seem? She allowed herself to grin in the darkness, letting the memory rise to momentarily sooth the fears of the past hours as she absorbed her peculiar surroundings.

These chambers, she reasoned, could have been frequented by an underground people: maybe the Dwarves Professor Cobalt had discussed during History lessons. This cavern was as big as the rec hall at least, Amber judged as she strayed into the centre, her gaze trailing into deeper darkness before she could glimpse the far side.

Something brushed past her face and she shrieked, hands flying to her face only for her fingers to clutch at mere cloth. Her laughter bubbled out in relief now that she could see it: just some old drape or something, threadbare velvet worn through in a reddish shade, and she ran it through her fingers to calm her nerves. So, this was what Dwarven royalty had lived like. The decadence! This must have cost uncountable golds. She shrugged. The Dwarves were the ones who had mined it—why shouldn't they be the ones to enjoy it? Confidence growing, she wandered more freely.

Her vision shuddered suddenly in the half-light and she stumbled on nothing. Her mind was playing tricks on her now; the walls of the room almost looked like they were sliding. *Serves you right for travelling so long*, she admonished herself, rubbing her head tiredly. As she watched the uneven ground more carefully, she noticed that sections had been rubbed smooth, worn down as if water had flown fast and deep to carve a passage years ago. Judging by the hollows pocking the ground even now, there must have been a lot of it left for the inhabitants.

Her musings catching her in a welcome distraction from the fears she had just fled, Amber didn't notice until she had almost stumbled upon the throne, studded with dulled gems and wrought from dark stone as if rising from the bowels of the Realm itself. Circling it in solemn majesty were a dozen and one seats, surrounding a huge slab of stone like a banquet table. Resplendent in mottled, swirling marble, it drew the eye hypnotically: tarnished gilt curling around the legs and leading her gaze to a chest beneath with its hinges broken and its contents strewn enticingly, glittering like jewels.

Amber's breath caught in her throat. Would the Dwarves willingly have abandoned anything of such worth? She squinted deeper into the gloom. All this had been here the whole time, hidden in the dark. Hadn't it? She could have sworn the cavern had looked empty before—strange that she'd missed anything, even in this low light. *You've been travelling so long down these accursed tunnels it's narrowing your senses*, she rebuked herself absently. *Five minutes ago you even managed to trip over the floor. Take a moment to gather your strength, then move on from this respite.*

Submitting to her own advice, she slumped down onto a stone lump that must have functioned as a seat beside the low table and allowed herself to catch her breath. She shivered. It was weirdly cold in here; considering she no longer had the ice formations to contend with. She glanced down at the table. It was stone, as you'd imagine Dwarven antiquities to be, yet something made her brush away the dust of the ages to peer more closely at the carvings etched into it, faded now by wear and time. Professor Cobalt would be proud of her—she could tell it formed some sort of historical record.

Yet as the images shifted into clarity she almost fell from the seat in her haste to distance herself, her hands flying to her mouth as she stared in shock. These were scenes of suffering from the Sea Battle: Vetches were everywhere, hunting, torturing, murdering. Men and women of all peoples ran and cowered and struggled and died, frozen in the stone with their faces screaming endlessly through the silence.

Amber shuddered uncontrollably: these depictions of atrocities weren't from the perspectives of the victims, replicated by a shattered people to beg future generations to prevent its reoccurrence; instead they glorified an event so horrific the survivors had dared not mention it for seasons. *This was Vetch work.*

She spun round, overcome by revulsion. The Dwarves hadn't lived here—it had been the stronghold of Snakelocks. This was where it had all started: whence her poisonous mind had seeped out with plots and plans and terror—this was where the Maidens and Knights who dared stand against her had been branded and tortured before exile and the promise of death. This was the room they said could drive you mad; where amongst the opulence the Vetches had resided whilst outside people starved and froze. Where sorcery seeped into your mind, where men looked on gilded treasure and gouged their eyes, and where you could not hear your own voice for the haunted whispers of Snakelocks's name.

Heart thudding, Amber scrunched shut her eyes and plugged her fingers against her ears. Stumbling back until she collided with the wall, she reached her hands to the rock to steady herself. Her mind flailing in abject terror, she felt her hand plunge into oozing Vetch-slime, the putrescence drawing her in, seeping through her hair, over her face and into her lungs, until she was falling and choking.

Yelling and spluttering she lurched forwards, flinging the tendrils from her and frantically smearing them onto the floor, but they kept coming.

"Stop!" Her own voice this time spliced through towards her, parting the fog. *You can breathe!* She heard herself wheezing, and focused on the gasps. *There's nothing else*, she promised herself. *You're safe. Your friends would tell you, were they here, but as they're not you're going to have to trust yourself instead.*

To slow her breathing, she traced her name onto the ground as Rraarl used to, drawing each breath out to the length of the stroke.

In her mind she sensed the Gargoyle behind her, watching her back; felt Racxen cut through the swathes of slime with his claws until it fell away, felt Ruby pick the last remnants gently from her hair, felt Mugkafb hold the hand she'd been scared would never be clean, smelled Yenna's warm exotic scent as the Wolf Sister leant to fasten her bandana around her neck for strength, and heard Jasper calmly berate her for letting her imagination get the better of her.

Giving silent thanks for her friends, Amber stood shakily, and automatically lifted her gaze to glimpse skeletal forms sitting before her in readiness for an ancient feast, and on the table—

She shrieked and stumbled back, forcing herself to screw her eyes shut, although that meant that the skeletons could get her.

Goblin cackling exploded within her head; ringing out so loud it had to be real, and she flinched violently. "Get out!" she bellowed, screaming until her voice drowned theirs and she was too hoarse to continue. Sobbing brokenly, she flung her gaze about the room, searching desperately for the exit as blood seeped through the walls and surged towards her.

It's not real, her thoughts clamoured pitifully against her senses. *Block it out!*

The shell of the Maiden flashed fleetingly through her mind and she grabbed onto the image, letting it flood her senses until the demons couldn't get in: the pearlescent gleam, the wavelike curves echoing the Sea Folk's domain, the fragile egg-shell contours.

Focussed entirely on her efforts, in her mind's fevered eye she thought she could see Sprites; glimpsed the tiny glowing figures of elemental spirits flitting beside her, shifting from her vision every time her gaze sought them properly. Glinting as if carved from ice they hovered around her, their chill touch dulling the pain and numbing her despair. Oblivion stole over with their needle-like fingers, and freedom from hurt.

Trying to fix her gaze on these ethereal allies was like attempting to sustain conjured memories of Rraarl: glimpses might hover on the edge of vision, just close enough to reassure her of their presence—but the moment she turned directly towards them they would dissipate, like a half-finished painting abandoned by a spooked artist before a premature and impatient audience, leaving the remembrance smudged like his name beneath her tears in the ice cave.

Yet the living wraiths wouldn't let her rest. Hands were on her again, this time kindling a warmth that sunk into her very soul, rousing her, stoking her spirit and reconnecting her with every driving emotion—each source of indignation and honour, every injustice needing to be righted and promise needing to be upheld—every burning desire she needed to get back on her feet and fight, urging her on until she dragged herself off the floor with a vague memory of sparks and snowflakes dancing in her head when she opened her eyes and rubbed them uncertainly.

The figures vanished. She was alone. Her thoughts were under her control and had no power to hurt her, the voices chased away and impotent. Her mind was her own, and the walls to her soul, although battered, remained unbreached, and stronger for the test.

The exit opening towards her sight-returned eyes, Amber offered a silent *thank you* as she staggered towards it.

The Nymph had been right. This had been the Way of Ice and Fire indeed.

The Prince and the Goblin

There was a crazed shout behind him and Racxen spun round to see Jasper fall to his knees, clutching at his sword arm, oblivious to the combat around him and bellowing as if the Realm was ending.

Immediately, the surrounding Goblins seized upon the sound, stalking towards him.

His moonshaft cutting warning swoops through the taut air, Racxen shoved a dried root into Jasper's hand as he reached him. "Chew this," he barked above the noise of battle exploding around them. "It'll help the pain."

Frantically, the Prince did as he was bidden. He began to feel dizzy; his arm growing heavy, tingling instead of hurting. He swayed, feeling hands and needles on him as the ground lurched.

Hauling the Prince off the floor, Racxen stared wildly in all directions, knowing they were wide open to attack.

Jasper yelled out in pain when Racxen pushed in front of him as a shadow forced bodily towards them—the first Goblin.

"All *right!*" their would-be assailant protested, wild-eyed with exertion, "the sun shines brightest in Recö—or Requë—or I don't flamin' know, good *grief*—"

"Laksha!" The Prince stared at her open-mouthed as his eyes refocused.

His mother's Handmaiden flashed him a sharp-toothed grin, hiding her concern at the sight of his arm. "Thought I might be useful 'round here." She slapped Racxen on the shoulder in hearty gratitude as she exchanged places with him, wrapping her sinewy arms around Jasper. "I got yer, mate," she growled soothingly.

The Prince let his weight sag onto her as the sands shuddered in front of his eyes. "I don't know if I can fight another Goblin after this," he murmured indistinctly.

"They're tryin' ter kill the only family I know," Laksha answered shortly, her eyes trained on the sky for the warning shadow of arrows. "If you don't, I will."

Jasper scowled in pain as he tried to keep his footing, stumbling alongside her with his good arm wrapped round her rough-skinned shoulders. "Have you any idea what you're risking being out here?" he admonished weakly. "Our side could kill you by mistake." His words blurred as he tried to focus on her again. "You're a diamond, though," he added belatedly, realising thick-headedly that he hadn't thanked her yet.

She grinned, as only Goblins could. "Yeah, I know—in the rough. Look lively, we ain't come this far for you to fall now. We're headed for the castle, so yer better get there in one piece, bein' royalty an' all. If they see me with yer, I'm gonna have to growl murder, an' frankly I got a splittin' headache so I could do without that pref'rably. Shift yerself."

Grumbling away in a voice so gravelled that only four people in the whole Realm could have possibly heard the warm note mixed up in the growl, Laksha barraged away almost carrying the Prince, snarling death and thunder to their aggressors as Racxen did his best to follow and protect them.

"And ignoring his wounds, beneath the heat of the desert sun Gorfang plunged his sword into the sands that sing still of his glory, bowing to his people. And as the great blade sank beyond all saving the warrior was bathed in a light so pure it burned into the prisoners' shackles to release them; and when it faded, they saw that his powers had too, but he had given them to save them, and remained ever a hero in their eyes, and not even the Goblins dared stand in his way as he helped them to—"

Jasper shifted groggily. "If I hear one more word of that pitiful excuse for a story . . ." His eyelids drifted up slightly, and he managed to focus on the Arraheng with a grudging smile.

"You're awake!" Mugkafb shouted gleefully, flinging his arms round the Prince's neck as Jasper clutched his good hand dolefully to his head.

"Sarin fixed up your arm," the Arraheng updated, his eyes following the Matron as she strode in. "I helped," he added proudly, waving an ice-pack.

Sarin smiled, her features softening. "We need all the help we can get around here, don't we?"

Mugkafb nodded importantly, peering over her shoulder with interest at the X-ray the Matron was holding up to the light. "Wow, Jasper—your bones are hollow!"

The Prince grunted, rubbing his eyes, almost forgetting the state of his other arm until a lance of pain stopped him short. "How else d'you think we'd be able to fly? Magic?"

Mugkafb frowned in concern. "But are your wings going to be okay for a while?"

Jasper nodded, surprised. "I should think so, thank you. They shut down if you're really ill, you see. Nonessential system. I'll explain it to you one day, when there aren't three of you lurching about."

"You're in luck, it was a reasonably clean break," Sarin reassured him as Jasper's eyes closed against nausea. "We've stabilised the arm; the bones are back in their correct position. Don't interfere with the splint, and ice it for fifteen minutes in another hour—Mugkafb's helped you out with that whilst you were sleeping." She gave a confident smile and hurried out to the next patient.

Jasper shifted groggily. "If it's just broken, why do I feel like this?"

"Anaesthetic. And Goblins," Mugkafb muttered shortly. "We're lucky none of their poison got into you."

Jasper wanted to question him further, if only the words would stay on his tongue, but the young Arraheng's face was tight and closed, so he changed the subject. "Quite the apprentice, aren't you, kid?" he approved lightly, his vision lurching as he tried to focus on the boy. "I thought Racxen warned you to stay in Arra . . ." his mind fumbled for the word, "where's it . . ."

Mugkafb eyed him severely. "Yeah, well, if you had a brother, you wouldn't listen to him all the time either," he pronounced.

Commotion and shouting assailed them from the far entrance, and Mugkafb shoved the ice-pack into the Prince's good hand. "Look, I better go see if I can help," he said hurriedly. "Do what she said with this and if the pain gets really bad or anything shout. Try and get some sleep, if you can. That's what Sarin's telling everyone." The Arraheng raced off.

The only time I'm not expected to take charge, Jasper thought wryly. Left alone, he half-lay, propped up with pillows and loathe to move for risk of disturbing his arm, and drowsed in the synthetic dusk.

Moment of Reckoning

As her voice died away into the distance to be answered by none but the plain-winds, Pearl blinked fiercely, trying to quash the rising flood of inadequacy that threatened to rob her of any further attempt.

You're an archer, she heard her mentor prompt in her head, and she was back all those years ago practising with him in the desert heat. *If you don't hit the target, what do you do?*

She felt herself automatically adjust her posture. "Aim higher, shoot harder," she murmured to the memory. Closing her eyes, she reached into her soul: letting her love for those she stood to lose wash over her, letting the courage that had brought her thus far alone into the wastelands rise above the fear of what would happen if it didn't work, letting all the times that had shaped her into who she was surface from her mind until the forgotten and the never-to-be-lost reforged themselves as one.

When she lifted her face to the skies again tears glistened on her skin in the glaring sun, and her voice rose like a wolf's howl, tremulous and yearning and powerful, in a plea of wordless promise.

Her call faded into the desert, leaving memories floating in the parched air in its wake; of love and loss, and of those she refused to countenance losing. Surrounding her so clearly, they tingled along her spine to conjure images of her past: of those she had walked with long ago before she had become Queen; before all this responsibility, before she had met the man she loved with every fibre of her being and before she had ever found the courage to trust she could rise to such a challenge as this.

Magic shivered around one particular memory—of finding a mentor who would change who she was forever: Roanen. Tears squeezed into her eyes at the thought of him having to have made this step alone.

Her hand strayed to her belt, gifted to her by the Nomad in parting, and her fingers found the knotted insignia woven at the clasp: the intricate, unending pattern hidden within the primary circular design. Pearl smiled as she traced the symbol of the Ragnor, or Unfading Race, the clan-name adopted by those who after his departure continued to champion Gorfang's code of honour, despite, or perhaps due to, the opposition of the corrupt Authorities and their quest to see the Emperor's law returned. In all Ragnorian articles was hidden this symbol-within-a-symbol, in recognition that although the Authorities could forbid the movement, they could no easier vanquish it than they could snatch a subtle breeze slipping through a field of savage thorn before it built to rise as powerful and uncatchable as the highest storm.

The Queen nodded, her eyes warm and proud. *Unfading, unforgotten—and unforsaken.*

While the lonely wind rose across the sands in a mournful, ethereal song of its own, Pearl stared to the horizon. No frustration glittered in her eyes now, only anticipation.

Against the pressing heat, the Queen realised she was shaking. As if holding her heart in her hands before the whole Realm, she sang of its contents until she was nothing but the song, her soul soaring majestic and magic-touched into the domain of the Sky Serpents.

This is your final test, she reminded herself, the magnitude of her endeavour roaring through her memory as the melody flowed. *To call a Dragon is to conjure words of magic from a Realm some say no longer holds any. Neither with a spell, nor a curse, nor any sorcery no matter what the Authorities might try to twist it into, but instead with something they could never cast: a vow of intention and transformation. A peaceful thing, a powerful thing, which can neither be captured nor killed, not amidst all the wars of the Realm, and which will bring hope incarnate as surely as a Phoenix brings light unfading . . .*

Her thoughts finding the hands of her husband, son, mentor, handmaiden and friends, the Queen breathed more steadily as she gathered them around her in her mind.

"I call you amidst the direst battle our people have faced to my knowledge," Pearl informed the emptiness amidst the fading echoes of her song, speaking as calmly now as if she were seeking an audience with an esteemed friend. "I ask humbly, Ancient One, in the spirit of he with whom you flew before: if you will aid us, come to me now."

The wind seemed to drop at her words as the Queen waited, with nothing to disturb the potent silence until—

A pulse like a second heartbeat caught in her chest, too low to hear it properly. As the night air hushed in expectation Pearl straightened, her eyes straining in the shimmering heat. Waiting. Waiting.

Trembling with disappointment, she let out a shuddering breath into the perfect, wretched silence that greeted her as callously as it had so many years ago after every attempt at calling them had failed. What had she been thinking? What place did a Queen have out here in the desert? What did she know of such ancient ways?

The beat slammed again, growing stronger and steadier, slipping inside her consciousness until it thrummed with the rhythm in her veins. Pearl stared to the sky, tears welling suddenly in her eyes as she dared to hope. *Oh, please . . .*

The unmistakeable cry exploded through the distance, as another pulse slammed through the air and made her ears pop.

A hulking shadow blocked the blazing sky with its descent, and as the majestic form prepared to alight she glimpsed the wing membranes stretched full in transparent white fire against the sun, the Dragon's identity clearing beyond all doubt.

Sand billowing amidst the dulled tattoo of his landing, Pearl waited noiselessly for the flurry to fall to earth, finding she was holding her breath, battling the urge to jump back. *You've waited your whole life for this. This is for your people. You know you can trust Dragons—now learn to trust yourself.*

As the air cleared, Pearl felt for all the Realm like that young girl waiting at the window those long seasons ago. She knew, with a strange awakening beating in her heart, that the vision of the serpentine curve of the Dragon's battle-scarred neck framed ethereal against the deepness of the desert sands was a memory that could never be replaced. She stared with the astonishment of her younger self as the Dragon stepped forwards and snorted, the massive, armour-scaled head snaking down to the level of the Queen's—so close that she could see into his clouded eyes as a tongue the length of her arm flickered out to taste the air and build a picture of her presence.

The Queen bowed deeply. "Akutan," she breathed, her voice breaking into sobs as the ground trembled beneath her feet. "Akutan!"

Through the Looking Globe

So far away, crouched at the entrance of what had to be the final tunnel, Amber, terrified and alone, in what she feared would soon prove to be her last moments in the Realm, unfolded the bubble-orb gifted to her by the Water Nymph, and gazed through the distance to the plains of Loban, searching for her friends . . .

The Goblins were massing, under a darkening sky.

Struggling to keep orientated with the air growing thick with bewitching herbs as the horde advanced, Racxen glimpsed the nightmarish figure of Thanatos rise phantasmal through the wraithlike gloom. The Arraheng choked and retched, fear closing his throat quicker than any curse as flashbacks threatened to overpower him.

Close by, he could hear the growls and snarls and yelps of the Wolfren continuing their assault; being closer to the ground the smoke had not affected them. He heard Han bellowing orders, and felt the first touch of fear in his voice. If they caught the Centaur—

Your fight is with me, he warned the Goblin King in his mind as he slunk through the chaos, locking his eyes onto Thanatos.

The closer Racxen prowled the more heavily the sorcery pressed into his exhausted mind. All confidence drained from him; he wanted nothing more than to throw down his weapon and run while he still had the chance. Instead, he gritted his teeth and clung to his mind. *Rraarl got through worse.*

As the smoke scratched into his parched lungs the herb-haze stung into his eyes, making the ground before him shimmer as the Goblins seemed to float closer and further in the deception of enchantment as if they were already shape-shifting and shadow-summoning.

But years of night-tracking had honed Racxen's senses. Closing his eyes, he quietened his mind and lunged.

The next instant he was sprawled on his back, fighting for his life as Thanatos's teeth snapped for his face in a ferociously animal-like retribution. Seized in a terror so engulfing it threatened to consume him as the Goblin King's cloak still clinging with the rotten stench of the fate of his previous victims billowed around him as if to snuff out all hope, the Arraheng's retaliations faded, pitifully ineffectual.

Feeling him weaken, Thanatos in his excitement shifted slightly.

It was all Racxen needed. Bucking frantically, somehow he squirmed out of the hold, and wrapping his legs around the thrashing Goblin grabbed wildly for the throat.

Thanatos's claws raked across his face as he writhed desperately, and Racxen scrabbled for a better hold, feeling himself slipping and knowing he was fast losing any advantage he'd had.

Hardly able to breathe let alone register what was going on around them as he clung on grimly, Racxen belatedly realised that the sand kicked up around them was settling and that the air had cleared. That the Goblin's struggles were weakening and that he still had the edge—or at least, hadn't died yet.

And that there was an audience.

Realising the same, Thanatos lay suddenly still beneath him, appraising the situation. His troops had encircled the two combatants as if unable to comprehend what they were seeing whilst Yenna, back in human-form, stood at the head of her pack with her bow trained unflinchingly on the once-unconquerable tyrant.

Muscles cramping from the hold, Racxen didn't dare shift; didn't dare make the same mistake Thanatos had moments ago. In the silence, he felt the itch of liquid sliding down his face and, unable to risk moving, he saw the blood drip from his cheek. The Goblin's blackened tongue snaked out appreciatively to catch it, flashing his deadly grin as the Arraheng grimaced.

Racxen fought the tremors that fell upon his clenched limbs. *What now?* he found himself asking the fraught silence. He hadn't dared think before that he would actually find himself in this situation. *What do I do now?*

There could only be one answer. The head of the serpent lay within his grasp, after all.

Breathing mechanically, Racxen steeled himself. Surreal it felt that this man, this monster, this plague of nations now cringing in his grasp was, without the illusion of his bewitching herbs and the terror of his reputation, *mortal*: strong but not supernatural, fierce but not unbeatable. He was nothing more than what he was—and soon would be no longer.

The effort bleeding into an agonised cry, with one hand Racxen jerked the Goblin's head back to expose the neck, as his other hand closed around the moonshaft.

"Healers!" the cry sprung up from the crowd in a sudden commotion. "They're dying; the arrows are poisoned."

Sending the blade flailing harmlessly into the sand, Racxen instinctively glanced to his soulroot pouch, his attention wavering, helplessly torn as the cries and chaos rose from the crowd. And yet—

Thanatos sputtered weakly with laughter. "Give in, boy. Either way, you cannot win: while I still live you can never reclaim your soul, and if you resort to murder your victory will be sweeter yet for me, for I will see in that moment the soul you guarded so jealously reforge itself after all your efforts into my image—and you'll never want it back after that."

"Darkseeker?" the Genie's voice floated, strident through the chaos. "You know healing herbs better than most!" On the wisp of the desert wind, without the protection of his lamp, he looked as fragile as a dream.

"But there is only one way to end this!" the Arraheng gasped brokenly.

"And you know which!" the Genie insisted. "Taking a life cannot change the past. Saving one will change the future. Haste, friend— there is but time for one action!"

Racxen's eyes watered. "For so long I've sought my chance for revenge." His grip wavered on the hilt.

"Revenge, or redemption?" the Genie hollered back. "Do not confuse them—only one can bring you peace!"

"I've fought for so long to keep my soul," Racxen growled as he flung the Goblin down. "You're not taking it now. I will have a life, not a death, on my conscience." Springing away he raced after the Genie, drawing the soulroot from his pouch as he ran.

"Not so fast," Han's strong voice rang out to Thanatos, and behind him he heard the creak of Yenna's bow.

"No General can ask of their troops what they would not risk themselves!" Han bellowed as he dragged the Goblin King into the centre of the shocked, hushed ring of watchers now formed around them. The Centaur snorted in contempt, barely able to keep still. "Death before dishonour, your leader asked of you!" he shouted, his gaze never leaving Thanatos as the tyrant sprawled cringing in the dirt, his eyes widening with terror. "What say you now?"

"No!" the Goblin whined, the single word splintering irretrievably into the loaded silence.

A weight lifted from the Centaur's neck, although his expression never changed. "Don't tell me," he growled quietly, leaning in closer. "Tell *them*."

A ripple of dissent snaked through the watching horde. From one side there was a lunge and a doglike snarl as two Goblins broke line and rushed forwards, and unstoppably the mob surged.

Vindication

"Magnus!"

Through the chaos of battle, the horse-master spun to the cry, swinging out strongly as the Venom-spitter lunged. Staggering back in a frantic attempt to regain his balance amidst the ferocity of its counterattack, he was forced to resort to increasingly clumsy manoeuvres as the distance closed irreparably. Panic overtaking him, as the monster's fangs flashed and snapped all he could think of was what would happen if so much as a drop of that venom were to enter his wounds.

Desperation lending him strength, the next instant those jaws snapped he changed tactics and thrust the axe with all his might into the maw, the haft connecting solidly with a resounding crack to an explosion of snarling. Seizing his moment the horse-master hefted the blade in a final downward blow, hacking into the exposed neck, severing nerves and joint and leaving the monster thrashing mechanically as he wrenched the blade free before another could charge in its place.

Finally he could nod his thanks to the King pulling his own blade from the ribs of a massive, limp-eyed carcass. "Sire!"

"The northern defences are holding," Morgan gasped, scanning through the fading light for his next target.

"As good as ours?" the horse-master spat hollowly as he did likewise, frantically kneading life back into his battered hands as he shifted his grip on the axe. "We're beating back the wolves one-handed."

His companion's words faded as the King swung his sword with a wild cry into the nape of a springing Venom-spitter, ripping his blade free to send the monster reeling part-cleaved and convulsing on the churned ground.

Although he had to force it into a lower register to disguise the shudder that still gripped him as he lifted his sword to them, the King's strong voice rang out determined and reassuring into the hearts of the fighters. "Aye! We're beating them back!"

Rhisk thundered towards them in the lull, and even the tireless reptilian toll guard's flanks were heaving as she ran up to report. "Ssire, the ssoldiers are flagging; unlike ours your armour is not part of you, and desspite their courage your casualties are many. The rec hall is working beyond capacity; it's at the verge of collapse."

Morgan nodded grimly. "Take the most vulnerable to the Ring."

Magnus turned, ashen-faced, to the King. "Sire, we cannot save them all!"

Morgan looked aged by his answer: haggard and wearied by an impossible burden. "We will save all we can," he insisted, as Pendril nodded and ran to relay the information to the Captains.

Magnus's face froze as a figure shifted into view against the darkening horizon, alone and far but moving closer, incongruent against the chaos reigning around the soldiers. "My lord—"

Pearl! Morgan mouthed, silently for fear of alerting the enemy. Relief flowed from his gaze out to her, striding tiredly into view as the valley reached the plateau just beyond the battle.

"Sire, she comes alone," Magnus warned hollowly.

The King's heart refused to sink. "She tried. And she is safe."

"The Queen failed?" someone nearby echoed, all strength draining from their voice. "Then hope is lost!"

"Courage, man," urged Pendril. "We're still standing."

But other soldiers had heard now, and the horse-master could find no words to dispute their fearful mutterings:

"Shouldn't have sent her—never even stood on a battlefield before."

"—left to pick up the pieces."

"—over-run—over-powered."

"Just the time for these, then!" Tanzan yelled suddenly, although no one knew quite how he'd got there. His horse was nowhere to be seen, but he wore a tunic of the White Chargers, ripped as it was in an attempt to provide anything for a bandage and the remainder so dirty and bloodstained it was almost unrecognisable. Staggering under their weight, he dumped an armful of equally filthy blades and arrows before the soldiers. "These're from the rec tent; I thought—"

The King nodded swift gratitude as the men and women who had broken or lost their own grabbed more ammunition and weapons. Morgan clapped a hand on the boy's shoulder, gesturing to the Captains as he bellowed an address to his troops: "Take courage, for we must follow Pearl's example and attempt the impossible now. I'll gather the soldiers on the left flank, we'll—"

"*Hashtaka ki'aaaaaaaaaaaan!*" a woman's voice whipped across the distance, as majestic and far-reaching as the plainwinds.

Morgan stared. "But that's—"

Trekking across the desert to join the battle at Loban, stumbling in his haste over the sand he'd traversed more times than anyone else left in the Realm, the Nomad's eyes flew to the darkening skies in wonder. The Dragon's roar he never thought he'd hear again exploding in his ears, Roanen punched the air in triumph. "That's my student!" he bellowed hoarsely to the sky in delight. "That's my Queen!"

Eucatastrophe

Staggered across the battlefield, as one soldier the platoon stared to the sky as swooping up from the valley with a mighty bellowing cry soared a beast consigned by the Authorities to legend, screaming a cry the monsters had heard before.

Through the Dragon-blazed night, flanked by a convoy of Zyfang and their Arraheng riders, the Fairy Queen strode from the gathering darkness, burning a bright silhouette against the lashing storm.

"Pearl!" whooped the King, the battle forgotten in that moment. "*Pearl!*"

"Akutan!" blurted Tanzan, forgetting himself and grabbing hold of the King in his realisation. "He can't do this without us!"

"To me!" the King yelled, knowing their very lives depended on it. Charging straight towards the fray as Fairies, Arraheng and Basilisks raced to meet him, Morgan bellowed orders to the section leaders— Laksha, Magnus, Pendril, and Rhisk—as they drew abreast of him with the Zyfang warriors circling above. Together they drew their fighters into a herding formation, readying weapons as they spread like a ring of fire ever closing.

Driven tighter together, the Venom-spitters raged and riled, snarling and backtracking like trapped Gantornas as the troops descended, the Dragon wheeling closer.

But as the troops closed in, a soldier stalled in fear, breaking the circle—and at once the Venom-spitters sensed the weakness and lunged. Magnus flung his axe, but it was a wild, weak throw and caught the monster only a glancing blow, sending it blundering, pain-crazed, towards the regiment and awakening the blood-lust in the rest of the pack.

"Ya-sen kash nay!" Tanzan shouted weakly, the only Dragontongue phrase he knew, useless as it was as their plan splintered into terror. As a Venom-spitter locked its deadly gaze on Laksha he loosed all his arrows into it only to watch helpless as it maintained its limping pursuit of the Handmaiden, who drawing both daggers turned and charged to mete her vengeance.

A majestic eldritch cry pierced the chaos, the snap of wings pulsing the air as the Dragon plummeted from the sky, trapping the monster within the scaled prison of his wings with the ease of a Zyfang pouncing on an insect, before snapping its neck in a single bite. Without pausing even to roar, as the regiment gathered their wits and reformed amidst barked orders to ring-fence the enemy, Akutan thrashed like a serpentine colossus of legend through a broiling living sea as he lay about the monsters: shaking one as a wolf does a rat, trampling one underfoot, sending one running terrified into the waiting swords of the soldiers; until the ground tattooed with the Dragon's pounding attacks and the yowls of dying Venom-spitters drowned the cries of wounded soldiers.

For Tanzan, as good as weapon-less with his quiver empty, the battle seemed to last forever in one drawn-out nightmarish blur of running amongst the combat scrounging arrows from the sodden turf and releasing them with as much accuracy as he could muster whilst the adrenalin fumbled his grip and narrowed his aim, in a vain attempt to stop the further monsters reaching the soldiers trapped in closer combat. Unused to the distance, his first efforts fell pitifully short, skimming the grass or bouncing off flanks—but his next shot embedded itself in a black-furred throat, its monstrous target stumbling with a gurgling snarl, and the following found its mark between savage red eyes, the fletchings dancing wildly as the brute collapsed.

Yet, reaching round for another arrow, his hand clutched empty air and his desperate gaze fell upon the Dragon pausing wide open to attacks to devour a carcass instead of keeping its guard.

Too late he ran to rouse it, flapping his arms in a ridiculous echo of scaring the scavenger birds away from his mother's farm.

"Son!" Pendril ran to him, his gait strangely drained compared to seconds ago. "It's over."

"But—" Tanzan stared, stunned. A fractured stillness held the ravaged land in a vision so alien to his eyes that he couldn't at first register it: the monsters were dead. Now that the ground was strewn with the corpses of the Venom-spitters he could see just how far the battle had sprawled, and he couldn't help shuddering.

A weak cry sputtered from the torn ground, and Tanzan was already running towards the sound. Cursing himself for his delay, he scanned wildly for someone to aid him, but Pendril was threading between the hulks of the dead monsters, checking for the silent fallen who might yet be alive.

With a pang of guilt for having not thought of that, Tanzan turned his attention back to finding his casualty. The soldier lay quietly now, clutching his leg, his face greying as his eyes slipped their focus from his face as Tanzan split his Gem and daubed the smeared liquid onto the man's lips.

"It'll be okay, mate," he murmured, seeing a bloodied tongue lick out slightly at the sticky, bluish fluid. "I need help!" he bellowed at anyone who could hear, scanning nameless faces hurrying to and fro across the churned field as he struggled to lift the limp body.

As powerlessness threatened to overwhelm him, a sweet-strong voice cut through his despair and as his own vision faltered he saw the Queen and Laksha run bearing a stretcher towards him, and he stumbled to assist them in their battle now; the one far from over that would play out fraught and frantic in the field tents and rec hall.

Reaching the battlement, the distance unregistered against the horror that drove him, Morgan leapt the stone steps apace with an empty search behind him and a thousand fears invading his mind with every fruitless moment. His presence was barely noticed amongst the mass of physicians, nurses, healers—anyone who could help—rushing back and forth dealing with wounded military and civilians, with every floor-space taken up and every capable survivor assisting.

"Jasper!" the King pushed through in panic, trying in vain to find someone to ask, with for once no one answering to his authority as they swept past caught in the urgency of their work. "Where's my son?"

"Side room!" Mugkafb shouted, skidding out to meet him. "Laksha got him, he's with Sarin now—engo ro fash!"

Relief blossomed weakeningly through every fibre of Morgan's being. "Thank you," he murmured heavily, his eyes closing in gratitude. Then he clapped a rousing hand to the Arraheng's shoulder. "Amber's fight is not yet finished. We ride for Dread Mountain!"

At his piercing whistle Mugkafb pelted after him, running out to the familiar answering whinny. Leaping onto Bright Shadow's back behind the Fairy King, he clung on tightly as with a shrill whinny the Bicorn sprang to the sky, speeding through the clouds towards the far lonely structure where fate had yet to be decided.

Change of Plan

Jasper woke not knowing where he was, his mind and the light equally subdued. Registering distractedly the far-off noise of battle, he noted hazily that it must have been day, and the same one at that. A fuzzy placard on the wall advised him that he was under the care of the Fairymead Guild of Physicians and Healers, and he realised with a bewildering flood of relief and dismay that he was still encased in the pseudo-darkness of the rec hall.

With nothing in particular to orientate himself to, the strong torch-light outside soothed by beige linen curtains permanently drawn to ease burnt minds and shattered forms and encourage sleep, the Prince struggled to gather his thoughts. *You,* he admonished himself, *have spent enough time lying here. Your people are out there. Get up.*

"Well, your Highness, your strength must have returned, even if your sense has not." A calloused hand planted itself in firm warning against Jasper's shoulder and he realised that Sarin must have been standing there tending him all this time, awaiting his return to consciousness and observing his rather pitiful attempts at movement.

The Matron nodded in approval when Jasper sank back, and he squinted against the blazing light as she parted the curtains.

"What is that, your Highness?" Sarin asked curiously, gesturing to the scrap of cloth now clutched bloodied and sand-streaked in the Prince's hand, smartly turning the sheets as Jasper leaned carefully this way and that. "Couldn't get it off you for safe-keeping when you came in."

"It fell when Yenna—the Goblin tried to—I need to give it back," Jasper slurred urgently, struggling to sit up again. "I couldn't leave it in the dirt, but I couldn't find her, but; I thought if I kept it safe maybe it'd keep her safe."

Sarin pointed an admonishing finger. "Far be it for me to disregard a direct order from royalty," she retorted briskly. "But within these walls, my word is law, and you will disregard me at your peril."

Sluggishly acknowledging defeat, Jasper subsided again. Watching the Matron hasten out, he disjointedly wondered where she got the energy to deal with so many injured and still give the impression that, in the midst of a bloody battle that no one had any hope of knowing the end of, everything in here was under complete control. Then the Realm swam before his eyes, and his lids drooped into sleep.

"Psst!"

Jasper jolted into waking, blearily staring towards the noise. The curtain was talking to him.

"Jasper, come on. You told me earlier, if you got injured I had to get you back out there," Mugkafb hissed, materialising beside him. "The Zyfang brought you back to Fairymead, but there's just as much fighting here."

Jasper tried to focus on the indistinct blur hovering by his bedside. "That was before I failed," he muttered thickly. "Before I became . . . even more of a failure."

"Shut up," Mugkafb reasoned. "You've had a smack on the head or something so you're bound to talk rubbish for a bit. What you're forgetting is that you ventured into the Lobanian stronghold and retrieved a weapon that struck fear into even the craven heart of the Goblin King, for the sake of your people and because you wanted to give your friends a chance."

"Did you swallow that accursed book?" Jasper grumped shakily, trying to open his eyes again. Maybe the kid was right. It seemed like a dreamtime away, but he had done it. Looking back, he couldn't think how, but . . .

"Oh, if you insist," he muttered, mostly to himself, but there was an enthusiastic squeak from somewhere in Mugkafb's direction, and Jasper decided he had better put on a decent effort. Grimacing cautiously, he braced himself to shift onto his side. *Get up. For pity's sake, man, get up.*

Inching his legs out of the bed, his mind crawling with frustration at how much energy that measly manoeuvre had cost him, Jasper finally with his good arm heaved himself upright. His chest and abdomen spasmed screamingly in protest against the assault on his muscles, but he swallowed against the pain and reached out to grasp Mugkafb's shoulder in thanks.

His aim faltered, his hand instead brushing the little Arraheng's cheek and meeting damp skin.

"Jus' 'cause I'm helping you, doesn't mean I want you to go out there and get hurt or anything," Mugkafb sniffed defensively.

For once, no retort came to Jasper. "Engo ro fash?" he offered gently, hoping he'd got the words right.

"Sen," Mugkafb grinned. "I'll distract Sarin so you can sneak outside."

Stealthy footfalls pattered, and then Jasper was alone again. Clutching his plastered sling-arm gingerly to his chest the Prince heaved himself upright, unbalanced and cursing virulently, although he tried to force into mind the recollection that it could all be a lot worse. Testing his standing strength and finding it mightily insufficient, gasping at the exertion he managed nonetheless to totter towards the door, clinging to the wall like a winglet would to a branch when first learning to fly.

The rec hall staff were bustling about tending to the massive influx of patients at well-practised speed, and they had no time to pay heed to the figure shuffling towards the outside world, his movements becoming surer gradual step by careful step.

The roar and crash of combat assailed Jasper's ears as he stumbled squinting and disorientated into the hall's moonlit courtyard, where White Chargers stood foaming whilst their riders hurried figures slumped and silent or screaming and contorted with pain into waiting arms for ready treatment.

It felt an age had gone by to Jasper by the time he had painfully manoeuvred the steps to meet the field.

At the base, grim-countenanced guards stood in his way, and the Prince waved them aside bad-temperedly. "I demand that you let me pass, I must fight with my people."

They stood their ground. "Your Highness, the injured are not permitted to rejoin the battle. This is for the good of all the troops." The woman who spoke had the air of one who had been trying to as kindly as she could break this news to her comrades all day.

Jasper hovered wretchedly. "But—"

"If those who are injured want to help, your Highness, we require them to stay where our men and women do not have to risk their lives to protect them, and thus positioned use their talents to look after the wounded," she responded meaningfully. "We need everyone we can get for that task, and you can satisfy your honour by trying to save lives rather than aiming to snuff them out."

Jasper cursed savagely to himself and stalked back. He knew the guard was right. He'd endanger the life of anyone who tried to protect him. Still, he kicked at the ramparts in a fit of fury at his own helplessness until the pain sobered him and the futility of his actions glared into him.

He dragged the night air slowly in and out of his lungs, forcing himself to calm down. But how could he as Prince stand by and watch his people fight? If he'd had the chance to join them, he'd have been terrified, he tried to remind himself. He'd probably have wanted anything rather than to have to fight. Yet he'd be proving himself, standing with his people, whereas now all his authority bled useless into the ground, for the choice could not be his and he struggled to still the anger roiling in his gut at the injustice of it all.

"You ready?" Mugkafb darted out from the building's shadow to Jasper's side.

The Prince wondered groggily how Arraheng always seemed able to avoid detection when it suited them. "It's no use," he muttered thickly.

The Arraheng's face fell. "But I got you a Bicorn and everything!"

Mugkafb let out a barely discernable, dog-pitch whistle, and Jasper heard the steady clopping hooves of a Bicorn attempting to be inconspicuous. Later he would wonder how in the Realm Mugkafb had managed to summon it, but right now standing upright was causing him enough difficulties.

"Send it away," the Prince countered light-headedly, the words floating reproachfully through his mind as he struggled to capture them. He clutched weakly at the closest turret as exhaustion swept nauseatingly over him.

"Yeah well," the boy dismissed, "you're not my Prince, so I'm not listening." He stroked the nose of the Bicorn, who was standing patiently next to him. "C'mon, Jasper, she wouldn't be here if she didn't think she'd help."

There was a call from Sarin, and the Arraheng ran back inside before the Prince could say otherwise.

Laboriously, Jasper mounted the Bicorn, his movements slowed and his hands clumsily tentative as they stroked the glistening velvet marble of her neck and entwined through her silvering mane. Watching the fates play out between distant figures rendered tiny and too remote for him to do anything to assist, he felt miserably voyeuristic. His father was down there, as were his friends; in some deep forsaken corner of the Realm Amber was facing alone a foe just as terrifying, and Mother had strode off by herself into the desert for help. Everyone he knew; everyone he loved, was down there somewhere, doing what they could whether it would work out or not, while he was standing here so far removed. In a daze, he led the Bicorn down the castle steps.

The equine snorted as a panting figure careened into view, skidding to a halt in front of them.

"Ruby!" Jasper stared aghast at Amber's best friend. "What are you doing here? Why aren't you in the Ring, or with the Arraheng in the caves?"

She ignored him, staring around disconnectedly in stained-eyed shock at the war exploding below them.

"Ruby, I can't help it," he started miserably, wishing he could believe it too instead of feeling so wrenchingly guilty. "I can't help anyone—"

"You can help me!" Ruby shrieked pleadingly, her eyes welling with tears. "There's fighting everywhere I look and I haven't seen my best friend since yesterday and I've been looking all day and I don't know what to do."

She fixed the Prince with such a look of helplessness that the Bicorn stopped of its own accord and he could have sworn that even it was waiting for him to act.

Jasper stumbled out the words, taken aback that she didn't know. "Amber—she'll be in the Dread Mountain passage by now. To lure the Samire."

Ruby's face froze in horror. Then she looked at the Bicorn, determination glinting in her eyes. "You know how to get there, right? To that Fountain thing?"

Jasper swallowed. "What are you going to do?"

Before he'd realised what was happening, Ruby had run up and jumped onto the Bicorn behind him, reaching around him for the reins.

"Not I, handsome," she corrected. "We."

She flicked the reins with a wild shout and the Bicorn leapt to the sky, racing through the night at breath-taking speed.

Lair of the Samire

This was it—the Samire.

Creeping forward, her heart froze as she beheld it. Slumped in a travesty of peace it slumbered, its massive bulk sprawled directly across the winding, ruinous path she must take leading up into the mountain and over the lava lakes until all would end at the Fountain.

C'mon, she tried to convince herself, dragging a sweat-clung hand across her brow. *You haven't fought through scorching heat and glacial cold, inmost fears and visceral horrors, to slope back broken now to sob with guilt in the darkness later. It's not that much bigger than the others; you've faced worse.*

Even as she psyched herself up to make her move and wake the monster, shadows shifted behind her into a nightmarish apparition of far more leviathan proportions.

Turning numbly to stare up into its gaping jaws as the cavern exploded into a bellowing challenge robbing her of all hope or thought, she felt everything rush into mortal focus and just ran, vaulting over the dormant juvenile before it could recover its senses, the Samire crashing after her.

Adrenalin slamming through her so strongly she barely knew what she was doing, she could hardly keep track of where the twists and turns of the tunnel were leading. The volcanic stone warped as gnarled and precarious as candle wax, and through the melted gaps she snatched a hellish glimpse of the broiling lava lake below flanked by hissing geysers spewing almost to the height of her platform.

As she fled deeper into the mountain the passage abruptly branched. With no time to consider she threw herself for the left fork, scrabbling frantically as she lost her footing and gashing her hands badly on the hot stone as she scrambled up.

A guttural roar shuddered from the right, and despair lanced through Amber as she realised the monster had taken the other passage. She couldn't afford to lose it—couldn't allow it to overtake.

Volcanic light flared as a tunnel section gaped wall-less, spilling out onto an uneven platform with nothing between Amber and the sputtering magma below if she should fall. Flinging herself raggedly up the last few steps she skidded to a halt as a new roar, that of raging water, accosted her ears.

Sobbing with exhaustion, she gasped for breath and stared—it hadn't been some trick of the mountain: before her stretched the narrow, perilous causeway below which rose the Fountain. Whether for good or ill, an end was approaching. Her limbs seized by violent tremblings now that she'd stopped running, in the sickening knowledge that at any moment the Samire would be upon her again Amber forced herself to wait, her fraught eyes straining at the tunnel. Any second now, but when—

A rancorous snarl answered from above, festering lips writhing spasmodically across the rows of daggered fangs as heavy ropes of venomous saliva dripped from the cavernous maw to scorch the rock below.

Riveted in horror, Amber could only stare as with a roar of primal savagery the Samire leapt onto the platform.

The impact threw her off her feet and sent her sprawling to the ground, and as her head smacked against the rock her vision rolled on a wave of nausea into nothingness.

Reality flickered through distorted as Amber drifted back into consciousness. Her head pounded sickeningly, vicious pain lancing through her neck as she tried to move. Through concussion-glazed eyes she half-saw the Samire lower its head as its roar of triumph crashed over her beleaguered immobile shell, barely able to focus her swimming vision on its monstrous form as it turned with a snort and began pounding its way back to the stairwell.

You've failed. The words floated, ineffectual, as all sense of urgency leaked with her blood onto the precipice. She didn't even have the strength left to weep. Now that nothing remained that could be done, everything faded. Even the pain felt detached, slipping as distant as the faint rushing surge of fire below as her memory blurred any recollection of why she had ever thought she could have succeeded. And yet . . .

One—her hand twitched—*last*—she grasped the rock—*try.*

With every instinct in her body screaming against it, she pushed herself onto her knees and staggered half senseless to her feet.

Body heaving, eyes hard, Amber stood defiant. "Who said you could leave?" she managed weakly, spitting blood.

As if in slow motion, the monster turned back, bellowing its wrath and tensing to charge.

Not yet—not yet—not yet—the words tattooed through her heart as she gulped a last breath.

Her terror futile now, instinctively she knew she had left it too late into the charge even as her mind narrowed into one last chance and she ran for the edge. The monster was coming too fast and too close, and as the edge loomed she slowed automatically and the Samire gained, crouching to spring.

As it leapt for her, she threw herself from the precipice with a wild yell, hearing its jaws crack shut on empty air as they both plummeted.

She hit a bubble from above and, as she felt its oily surface yield to encase her, the sights and sounds of the horrific reality outside now comfortingly distorted, her first instinct was overwhelming relief. As she was swept into its glorious path, her soul lifted in almost painful ecstasy in recognition of that lurch so close to the surge of flight.

But something was wrong, deathly wrong, for she was still falling ever faster: it wasn't going to stop.

Sickening fear clutching her heart, it took her a second to register exactly what had gone so irreparably wrong. Ripped from its orbit by the force of her descent, the bubble was hurtling straight towards the central abyss, trailed by the other orbs torn into its path of destruction, as trapped powerless inside, she—

But the abyss rushed to engulf her and the blurring visions swamped to black.

Aftermath

At the Fountain chamber, on the ledge the watchers stared in horror as the bubble containing Amber plummeted into the sucking void below and the other globes, dragged in its wake, broke their orbit to follow it into the maelstrom with a horrible gurgling rush.

With a thunderous roar the plunging water rebounded in a towering column spewing so high it nearly reached their precipice, the sheer force of the surge flinging a hulking indistinct form from the Fountain's rush. As the once-terrifying Samire crashed limply onto the rocks beside them, Ruby screamed, Yenna snarled, and Jasper drew his sword clumsily with a shout, but as they stared at it numbly their fear was finally snuffed out. Locked into the unrelenting grasp of the surging throes below, it had been dashed against the rocks until all life had been beaten out of it. Mugkafb prodded it gingerly with his foot and the black head lolled back lifelessly, staring eyes fixed on him in an unseeing gaze.

Yenna's lips contorted over her teeth as she fought to stay in human-form and contain her anger.

Racxen shuddered and looked away, bile rising in his throat as he struggled to force away the torturous images squirming into his agonised mind. *If the plummet had destroyed such hulking malevolence as the Samire, what piteous hope had*—he shook his head furiously as if it could dislodge the thought, forbidding himself from finishing it.

An empty moment passed as the water-column fell crashing into the chasm below and the last terrible echoes of the draining rush rang tumbling through the chamber into a suffocating vacuum of silence.

Amidst the deathly hush, the friends stood frozen. Mugkafb sought his brother's clawed hand silently and clutched it tightly. Racxen stared down, his eyes dry and unseeing, throat hot, breathing shallow, begging himself not to believe what he had just witnessed. Ruby's Realm shrunk into tears and silent pleas. His thoughts thickened by his injury, Jasper refused himself the relief of looking away. His hand gripping Racxen's shoulder, the King's eyes darted over the glisteningly ominous rocks laid bare by the dredging of the inferno, his taut face drawn and haggard. Yenna closed her eyes, and listened, searching the internal map of her senses.

Minutes stretched into eternity with nothing to free their Realm from this curse.

Then Racxen shouted in alarm and Mugkafb jumped back as the rock beneath them began to shiver and a terrible howling grew from deep below. Glancing grim-faced to each other as the shrieks reached Vetch-pitch in their magnitude, against the screaming urge to flee the friends lined together, gripping hands to stand their ground in unspoken unity.

A tornado-like wind tore from the basin, dragging the bubbles out in a dervish and streaming in the watchers' eyes as they desperately scanned the orbs for any sign of their friend.

Squinting against the battering winds, gritting his teeth Racxen watched helplessly as the bubbles swept through the chamber to slip beyond reach forever, rushing away unchecked to impossible heights as if the whole Fountain were breaking beneath the ravaged sky.

Against crushing despair, he realised distractedly that the din was still growing—and changing, rumbling through distant tunnels with the menace of a gathering tempest.

The chamber exploded into a deafening roar as a spiralling mael-strom burst forth from the centre of the basin, rising thunderously as the Fountain spewed out its final bubble and sent it rushing amongst ever-growing waves.

Mugkafb shrieked and as one they all ran to the side, yelling exul-tantly as they saw riding on the crest of the wave flung highest of them all: Amber in the bubble, tiny against the rushing swell, whilst to their triumphant shouts the force of the surge flung the orb towards the bank. As her friends broke her fall the bubble burst from around her and Amber sprawled gasping, drenched, and shivering.

"We knew you'd do it!" Mugkafb yelled right in her ear, jumping about excitedly.

Racxen pulled her into an embrace, trying to stop her from trem-bling. "Engo ro fash, Amber; you did it. It's dead; it's over. You're safe— we all are."

She clung to him and laughed shakily, unable to speak as the tears tumbled unstoppably down her cheeks.

The King swept his cloak around her as Jasper helped her to her feet. "Lean on me," Racxen offered, sliding his arm round to support her as she stumbled dizzily.

"Always have," she murmured hoarsely as she clung to his shoul-der. When she'd got her breath back, she stole a glance at him. "I saw you with Thanatos," she divulged as her voice choked with pride. "The Nymph gave me this tiny bubble orb. I saw what you did."

Beside them, Jasper shook his head teasingly. "Haven't you had enough run-ins with magic to last you three lifetimes without dragging the Nymph into this?" he chided.

Amber snorted. "You can talk. Remind me: who retrieved the 'Cursed Blade'?"

The Prince waved a hand, embarrassed. "Yes, well. Royal duties, and all that."

"Maybe." But she was serious as she turned to him. "But, still."

He allowed himself a smile, stepping back as Ruby pressed forwards. "Likewise."

The moment Ruby threw her arms around her, Amber felt like they'd never left Fairymead. "How exactly were you planning on making yourself presentable in time for the necessary celebrations?" Ruby scolded fondly, stroking her fingers through her tangled hair. Amber burst out laughing as she flung her arms around her friend. "I guess I knew you'd turn up in time."

Yenna touched Amber's arm. "You want us to get rid of it?" she asked meaningfully, her golden eyes blazing consuming fire at the monster. "What remains of it?"

Convulsed with shivers, Amber nodded.

Insisting grumblingly on assisting even as the exertion swayed his vision and earned him growling admonishments from the Wolf Sister, Jasper helped Yenna drag the Venom-spitter's body to the edge and together they heaved the cadaver from the precipice. Needing to witness the moment, the friends watched the Samire plummet, silhouetted against the bleak rocks until it disappeared into the black hole at the centre. They couldn't be sure whether it fell to eternity or whether Mugkafb was right and there was the faintest thud as it hit unseen ground miles and miles below. But either way, there was no doubt anymore. It was dead; never again to return, never more to terrorise the Realm's inhabitants.

Staring into the void amidst their own reflections the friends stood, gathering their thoughts until they could turn back to one another.

All but Amber.

The King caught her avoidant gaze. "No more sadness," he urged. "You've saved so many."

"But not enough," Amber grimaced guiltily. Grief lay heavy in her voice as she struggled with the inexpressible. "I guess, despite everything, I managed to make myself believe that in the end everything would be okay."

To her surprise, when she dared lift her eyes again his gaze held not sympathy, but the twinkling of a smile. "Mayhap it wasn't quite the end. Look to the basin, Amber."

Questioningly, she did so. It was just the same as it had been moments ago: empty, barren, and unnatural, a shocking testament to the magnitude of the events having so recently taken place here. She was about to turn away again with a shiver, wishing the King would let her try and forget, when Mugkafb shouted in amazement and Racxen pointed to the centre of the basin with shining eyes.

Amber stared in awe as from the pitiless void bubbles began once more to silently emerge. Tentatively they glided forth, glistening as if newborn, transforming the air into trails of shimmering colour as the globes began their orbit, each bringing a different shade to the sky until Amber saw in astonishment the hue of her Fairy Gem, the marsh-green of Arraterr, the lighter shade of Jasper's Gem, the red of Ruby's, the stone-grey of Rraarl, the blue of the Sea Folk, the silver of the Water Nymph, the brown sheen of Finsbury's scales. All those who had helped, every single one of them, were represented here in a translucent patchwork of rays that spread from the Fountain to form the most glorious rainbow sky.

Flooding out joyously to the horizon, it stretched across the entire Realm to be witnessed not only by the watchers here but also by the Leaflings in their Golden Fields, the Sea Folk who cavorted amidst the sparkling azure calm of their swelling ocean, the Fairies dancing in celebration through the meadows, the Arraheng who sprang from the safety of their caves to rush laughing to the swamps, the Nymph far below whose eyes filled with tears of thanks, the Karp in his Great Lake leaping high in delight, Han who reared and bucked like a colt half his age, the Wolfren who as one threw back their heads and howled their conquest, the Genie who looped and dove and looped again, the soldiers who whooped and saluted, Sarin and her staff who threw back the shutters so their patients could share in it, Naya who threw the tips bowl in the air with a yell and Roanen who swept her into his embrace, Seb who raced the children outside to look, Bright Shadow who set the sky ablaze with the pounding of her hooves, and Akutan who keened out as only a Dragon can across fields upon fields with a cry that shivered across the horizon to lodge into collective memory for another hundred years as all those who heard him stopped in their tracks to gaze wonderingly to the sky.

Finally, far away in the desert as rheumy eyes fixed on the light, a wizened steel hand froze around the last uneaten insect. The Goblin felt its wings flick and buzz against his fingers as it squirmed in his grasp, writhing with the desire to live between the crushing press about to be applied as the last moments of its life rushed through his fist.

Transfixed by the sky, he stared until his eyes watered, clouded with memories evoked surely too far gone to now be reclaimed. His fist uncurled and the insect darted out from his devastating grasp, scurrying away across the parched ground. Watching it go, he fought the temptation to snake out his hand.

Now that the insect had gone so had the urge, and beneath the bathing light he felt, unfamiliarly and strangely, slightly stronger.

Absentmindedly his gaze tracked its path as it scuttled away. It was heading in the direction of Fairymead, he realised dispassionately: two days' trek even for a Goblin, yet this puny creature, which might well die before it got there, had decided to try for it anyway.

Fairymead. Something stirred in his memory.

Laksha. His sibling. She had always been . . . different. They had taunted her, targeted her, when she had left for that Kingdom. For the first time, he found himself wondering how her life had turned out.

Awkwardly he untied his knapsack and removed the jars—all but the water—unscrewing their caps to watch their contents release into the sandy ground with a hissing sigh. His pack lighter now, he shouldered it and stood unsteadily, his lips cracking as they pulled into the unfamiliar grimace others dubbed a smile. If he met a fate little better than the insect's along the way, what of it? His senses told him this could be a road worth taking, and he'd never found one of those before.

Staring after the tiny speck skittering far ahead, he took a faltering step forwards.

The basin flushed with light, now that the bubbles were once more floating serenely in their original orbit, Amber risked watching them more closely.

Bewildered, she stared transfixed. The bubbles still depicted the Realm-wide occurrences they always had—and yet against all odds the scenes had changed: where once was suffering, lives were now being lived out in peace and safety once more.

Open-mouthed in wonder, Amber walked along the platform. An unseen observer, through the glassy sheen of the spheres she saw the young Fairies whose silent clamouring for food had haunted her day and night now seated around tables eating their fill, their silent laughter shimmering through the orb. She watched Arraheng children, whose staring eyes as they crouched terror-stricken in the darkest shadows of ransacked caves had never left her, now splashing and playing in the marshes, those haunted eyes glittering renewed as the swamp-water scattered into rainbow-infused droplets.

They were all there, she realised as an impossible weight lifted: all the nightmarish scenes she had been unable to erase from her mind in the deepest reaches of the night were now being transformed into visions of hope. There were no longer Venom-spitters to hound and harry those of the earth, no longer Goblins to imprison and oppress those of the sands, and no longer Vetches to mutilate and curse those of the sea.

Crops were being resown, homes rebuilt, friends and families reunited, and dreams reclaimed. The chapters on the horror-filled past were closing, and life was beginning anew as if surging forth from a newly remembered song now able to be taken up without fear by each soul.

Amber let out a shaky breath she hadn't realised she had been holding and found she was half crying, half laughing.

Hearing her sob, Racxen slid an arm round her shoulders. "This is thanks to you," he reminded her with a smile.

"Thanks to everyone," she corrected, embarrassed, as she grinned back.

The ghost of a voice drifted on the air. "Don't dismiss the magnitude of your actions, Amber. They might not have seen it all, but I did."

"Genie!" Amber greeted him in confused delight. "You mean you were there?"

"I might be but a smoke-entity," the Genie acknowledged sagely, "but I could flit amongst the mists curling through the caverns, and soar upon the steam racing from the geysers—just to make sure you weren't alone." His insubstantial chest swelled with pride as he wafted serenely before the companions. "And now, in the interest of illuminating things you already know, it gives me great pleasure to inform you that the Way of Ice and Fire will no longer hold anything of fear for you. Having traversed and thus conquered it, you have dissipated any power it held over you. Just so you know—as you already did," he promised, timing his dramatic fading so he could throw a smugly knowing glance in Jasper's direction before he disappeared.

"I knew about your so-called enchantment all along," the Prince protested quickly to the air, although his smile was warm. "I suppose I should thank you for *nothing*, then."

Morgan rested a comradely hand on his son's shoulder, and his gaze passed over each of the friends in their contemplative silence. "Homewards?" The King's voice was steady once more, as if an age had rolled back to reveal a warrior in his prime once more—no, not a warrior, but instead a man at peace able now to hang up his shield and return home.

They nodded as one, striding forth both tired and renewed. The Genie had been right: now that evil had been defeated and fears had been faced the channel held no sway, and the passage once named Ice and Fire now lay empty and uneventful. Ruby led the way on the Prince's Bicorn once more, Bright Shadow arching her neck regally until the Fairy felt for all the Realm that she was a Princess of legend, at least for today—and far more so than Beryl and that lot would ever be, anyway.

As the tunnel birthed them back into daylight and onto green fields, the friends gathered at the edge of darkness and stepped into the light together; finally free in person if not yet in memory from the horrors they had faced.

"Now you don't need it, can I carry your sword?" Mugkafb prompted winsomely into the silence, interrupting Jasper's introspection.

"No," the Prince admonished automatically, then checked himself. "Oh, go on, then," he relented. "Keep it in the—"

Interrupted by a metallic *ching* and an amazed "whoah!" he sighed heavily and changed the subject, turning to Amber. "Not that I'm doubting your abilities," the Prince appeased hastily, "but how did you get past the Vetches in the end?"

"I have to tell Roanen," Amber warned flatly with a pained grimace at the appalling recollection. "I owe it to Slaygerin."

"The Griffin?" Jasper echoed, not looking at her.

"He was there," she confirmed, her voice tight with emotion. "When it mattered."

"No, Amber, seriously," the Prince interrupted, his voice touched with wonder. "Look to the sky!"

Shielding her eyes, she beheld a vision of burnished gold wreathed in transforming light, the feathers of his formerly ragged charred coat now gleaming in all the shades of fire as his unfettered wingspan stretched majestic in flight, his familiar haunted eyes now shining as he glimpsed the companions below and his once-chained gait flowing loose and free in a ripple of tawny strength as he alighted to greet them.

"Slaygerin is now a Phoenix," the Genie confirmed with deep satisfaction as the friends stared mutely in awe. "He has risen from his ashes and will fly unbound forevermore. The Sprites, you see," he explained as the stunned silence stretched, "the energy beings that inhabit the Way of Ice and Fire and gifted it its name, witnessed the redemptive action of his ultimate sacrifice. They knew it would only take one feather, and they were pretty sure a certain someone would take care of that."

Shooting an embarrassed grin to the Genie, Amber knelt before Slaygerin as her friends bowed their heads also. So close, she felt the Griffin's radiating warmth emanating from him. "Now I have the opportunity," she whispered, her gaze meeting those blazing hawk eyes, "I need to thank you for saving us all."

The Phoenix opened his hooked beak in a fierce smile.

"Slaygerin, wait!" she blurted, noticing the clusters of gold and bluish hues beginning to surround him. "I wanted to give you life . . ."

"Hush, young one," he urged in a soft growl, and after everything that had happened somehow it felt right and not at all surprising that he had acquired speech.

"The Sprites will guide me and I shall take the path across the sun now. None could give me life after all I've been through, but you gave me something better that I never dared hope I'd feel again—for you gave me peace."

Amber's throat squeezed too tightly for her to answer as the Phoenix sprang to beat his wings once more without shame or fear in the most glorious symphony of golden shades. Surrounded by the aura of dozens of Ice and Fire Sprites he rose through the brightest of skies, spiralling higher and higher until he was indistinguishable from the dazzling rays of sun streaming down upon the land.

"Although he has entered another Realm," the Genie reassured Amber with the lightest of touches at her shoulder, "this one will never be closed to him. Whenever the sun pierces shadow and stars burst through the night, we will hear the rustle of wings and glimpse an arc of light across the darkest of skies—and we will see Slaygerin."

Snuffling and trying to rub tearstains from her face with the corner of her sash, Amber nodded diligently. "Will you ever leave?"

"Nah," the Genie prophesised brightly, twirling as he scudded the clear blue. "Not while clouds still curl into skytop Realms, or dreams are still whispered amidst the smoke of birthday candles, or mists still soothe the night's worries with dew at each new dawn—so till that all stops," he winked, "well—you'd best be careful what you wish for."

With a cheerful wave, the Genie dissipated into a curl of cloud, only to reappear beside her a moment later, making her jump. "You won't throw away the lamp now, will you, though?" he checked anxiously.

Amber nodded, before realising she was once again gesturing to empty air. "I won't," she assured the sky with a smile.

"Good stuff! Last time, I promise—oh, look," the Genie materialised again, laying a conspiratorial finger aside his spectral nose. "How did that happen? The sun's come out! Cheerio for now!"

Before she could ask what he meant, hoof-steps thudded ecstatically across the turf towards them. "Han!" Amber shouted as the Centaur cantered over, his hair whipping back and his grin splitting his strong face.

"Welcome back!" He swung Amber off her feet into a hug. "Sorry for the delay; not all of us equine-folk can just fly off to the mountain,

I regret to admit." He threw a teasing glance to the Bicorn, but Amber could glimpse in the tightness of his jaw the guilt he was carrying.

"Not all equine-folk have your boundless energy and spirit to run so many of the wounded to safety alongside the White Chargers," Amber countered him warmly. "I'm surprised even you have the energy to come galloping after us."

"Wouldn't have missed it for the Realm," the Centaur declared. "And it hasn't all been dread and anguish, I'll have you know. I've been fulfilling essential duties regarding celebrations, too."

Amber shook her head in wonder. "You were that sure there actually would be anything *to* celebrate?" she asked ruefully.

A look of panic flashed across Jasper's face at Han's words. "Would anyone mind terribly then making haste to Fairymead? I, for one, do not wish to return triumphant to the Kingdom to find that the castle kitchens have been razed to the ground; and Racxen if you would be so kind as to explain to me what kind of foods constitute the finest delicacy of your people hopefully I can prevent well-meaning but incompetent individuals from serving you beetle soup or something equally cringe-worthy."

Han drew himself up importantly. "Sounds like a task for our company's fastest runner!" Bowing low with his forelegs, he sprang away as lithely as a fawn.

About to follow the irrepressible Centaur, Jasper first awkwardly turned to Yenna. "I kept this for you," he mumbled, drawing from his breast pocket a bloodstained, dust-clung scrap of crumpled cloth. His hands shook as he held it out to her. "I hope you don't think it a dreadful impropriety; it's just I know how important it is to you—it's a bit messy I'm afraid, I got hurt . . ." Trailing off as his courage almost failed him, he steadied himself beneath the warmth of her eyes as her gaze flooded into him.

"There was a moment when I fell," Yenna murmured, her brow

creasing in astonishment. "I was injured and tried to shift from my Wolf-form, but I was seized by a coldness such as has never gripped me before and I feared, for the first time in my life, that I would never be able to change back. And then—it felt as though someone had picked my heart up before it could get kicked through the dust—with the warmth of sunrays piercing a chill mist my strength returned; as did I into this form."

As the Wolf Sister bowed her head to allow him to tie the bandana around her neck once more Jasper, his hands lingering as they brushed across her hair, found himself standing so close now that he could catch her scent—sweat and dust and open plains and something so comforting and intoxicating all at the same time. He couldn't think what to say: he'd imagined this moment so many times, and yet now he felt wretchedly unprepared. "You were never as alone as you felt," he offered simply, the closest truth he could dare to reveal as he stepped back, the knot tied.

Yenna's eyes swam with wonder. "It was you who picked it up. In the midst of battle, when all hope and humanity was falling away, you salvaged my soul, tucked it away safely, and kept it next to your own."

Her expression flickered with an aspect he never expected to see, and one he felt honoured to be gifted with, for she looked—just for a moment—almost shy. And then those blazing eyes flared as strongly as ever, their glance hinting, just to him, of a risk worth taking; and the Wolf Sister of Arkh Loban without lowering her gaze from his answered: "Prince, hold me as close to your heart as you did then, and you will never be alone again."

Jasper's own heart slammed, the hold around his throat falling away at the precious knowledge that her feelings mirrored his own as he watched her stride away to her pack and her people. Eyes overflowing as he gazed after her, at her grinning backwards glance he ran, face split with pure happiness, to join her.

Watching them, King Morgan nodded gently, then turned to Mugkafb and pointed to a shimmering form in the distance. "Shall we catch up with Bright Shadow?"

Mugkafb considered. "What about Racxen and Amber? They'll—"

Beside Amber, Racxen smiled. "They'll catch you up."

Mugkafb regarded him questioningly for a moment and then nodded, dashing after the others and calling excitedly for them to wait for him.

Alone, the two friends stared out towards the horizon, drinking in the green meadows rolling out beneath them, the glittering silver of the river twisting away to the Great Lake, and the Golden Fields swaying in the distance beneath the softest Recö breeze. The time of darkness was over and something new would begin: something peaceful, something good.

Racxen's dark eyes shone as if beneath the moon, now that the shadows of the past no longer haunted his steps. "Did you ever wonder about this?" he asked her, almost shyly. "What it would be like when it was over?"

Amber smiled shakily, struggling to express what she meant as she watched the grass shiver joyously in the breeze. "I didn't really let myself," she admitted. "I just tried to focus on believing that it would be."

Seeing her shudder as fragments of the past rushed back, Racxen slipped a comforting arm around her shoulder. "In time they will fade, to be replaced by new times and better memories."

She nodded, not trusting herself to speak. Yet after all they had been through no words were necessary as they stood side by side, gazing at the scene playing out below them. Trying to capture every detail of the landscape they had both feared they would never see again, Amber belatedly realised she was squinting. Watching the sun stream out from between the clouds, Amber felt her heart scud as she finally grasped what the Genie had referred to: it was over, and she was standing beside Racxen, and—

"I'd hoped for sunlight," she blurted with a lop-sided smile. It had been so long ago; he'd probably thought she couldn't hear him, and more likely than not he'd been unconscious when she'd said it, too, but just to stand here with him, safe now, was the most beautiful thing.

Tenderly, the Arraheng took her hands in his. "Didn't we agree we would?" he whispered, the warmth of his smile calming the sudden skitter of her pulse.

Tentatively, Amber closed her fingers around his claws. "Your voice reached me that night when nothing else could, and I tucked your words away to remember always. You got me through, Racxen. There were times I felt like the darkness would never lift—but to you, and through you to hope, I could cling when everything else fell away."

He smiled a wordless question, his eyes holding her as safe as they always had.

Breathing deeply, she nodded.

And so hand in hand, having journeyed beside each other through so many nights of pain and Realms of darkness, Amber Amazonite and Racxen Darkseeker once more, in the most companionable of silences as the Recö warmth washed beneficently over them and the gleaming watcher in the sky sent her last rays splashing low across the fields to anoint everything with golden splendour, walked together in sunlight again.

Reunion

As they neared the castle, Amber felt herself slowing to lag behind, a cold weight squeezing into her chest and dragging at her heels. She felt as if a shard of ice from that fateful cave had lodged itself irreparably into her heart. She couldn't go up there. Not to where he'd always waited. It would make it finally and inescapably real. "I'll follow, honest," she reassured Racxen as he stopped to wait for her.

"You don't have to bear this alone," he promised with an understanding glance.

She nodded. "It's the only thing that helps," she murmured in thanks. As Racxen bowed his head and followed the others, she stepped back to let Ruby, who was eagerly following in the Prince's footsteps as he strode up the castle steps, push past her.

Now though, she'd run out of reasons to not join the others. Painfully, she mounted the stairwell, each step an age, a finality. By the time she reached the first turret window, she had to stop and grasp its edge to steady herself, gulping down great draughts of the air breezing through. This was just too hard. Her joints ached feverishly; she could barely stand.

She had to grip the harsh stone to steady herself. *Oh, fingers,* she couldn't help berating miserably. *If you'd known it would be your last chance to memorise the contours of his hands; or eyes, your last moments to sear his imprint onto inner vision, on that last day you would have paid no heed to the warmth of the sun, no heed to the clean hue of the sky, and been entirely satisfied in your focus, instead of unknowingly frittering your attention on such wretched permanence then, only to be left found wanting now.*

She gazed out between the parapets to distract herself, watching the wind play across the rippling green fields far below. She would have given anything to have seen Rraarl again; to have met the unwavering gaze of those gleaming jet eyes or felt his silent presence beside her again just one last time. The heavy sting of tears prickled into her eyes with a weight far greater than stone; threatening to drag her under as surely as the Vetches had Rraarl. *Enough*, she admonished herself severely. *He wanted to save you. Let him. Don't dishonour his memory by allowing anything attached to it to condemn you. You have to let this become a sorrow, not a sentence. He'd want you to keep going. He'd want you to live, not just survive.*

Releasing a heavy breath, Amber dragged all her energy into setting her features into a carefully neutral expression and prodding her feet numbly onto step after step.

Hearing Ruby stop ahead of her, she realised in trepidation that she was nearly at the top.

"That's strange." Ruby's voice floated back to her, full of innocent surprise.

Amber dragged her mind back to the present. "What is?" she muttered flatly.

"I never knew we had statues up here."

Amber's heart sputtered erratically, stealing the breath from her lungs. She stared up at Ruby, barely daring to trust the hope that surged as her Realm bloomed with possibility once more and she ran.

Her life turned into those steps as she pounded up the stairwell. After all this time, could it be? Breathless and terrified, her heart threatening to freeze and overflow at the same time, she stumbled to the top.

And she saw him: saw him crouched there on the ramparts as if he had never left; still and strong and silent, an indelible solid shadow framed against a blazing sun.

The Sea Folk! she realised, euphoric. Against all things they must have reached him in time; there could be no other explanation—and such earthly things as reason faded into ephemera as those jet-black eyes fixed on her once more, his gaze resting so deep within her it felt as though he were coaxing her soul out of hiding; as if the shards and burns of what had happened in the ice caves and lava tunnels were melting and cooling, and she felt warm and shivering all at once.

Surrounded by the multitudes she could do nothing: if Rraarl had chosen not to reveal his true self to the crowd, she could hardly risk betraying his trust. Yet to be held in his gaze was enough—was every-thing—and she just stood there, letting the waves of belonging wash away the gnawing grief and bathing in the comfort of his closeness.

As the Fairies milled around, gazing down at the now-cleared mead-ows where such a short time ago the monsters had lain siege to their lives and where finally the flowers were free again to grow, Amber qui-etly threaded through the jostling crowd to sit unnoticed on the wall beside the Gargoyle.

Staring out across the fields as her eyes swelled with tears at the familiar comfort of leaning against the formidable icy bulk of his shoulder, Amber laid her hand on his arm; tentatively, wonderingly, allowing herself to relearn the contours of those feature she had ach-ingly consigned to memory.

And slowly, undetectable to any save for the one whose touch was infusing warmth through his stone body and into the very core of his being, the Gargoyle's snarling visage shifted into a fierce smile, the black eyes glittering as his hand turned painstakingly slowly to grasp her arm in the warrior's greeting, and in the reassuring touch of a friend.

With the others starting to leave the ramparts, Amber turned her head to press her lips lightly to his stone skin in a kiss of thanks and everything else that could not be voiced here and now. Her touch lingering just slightly before she straightened, ignoring the bemused expressions of those present with her head held high and feeling Rraarl's softest gaze at her back she strode right past the crowds and back to the stairwell.

Muttering amongst themselves briefly, the Fairies dismissed the silly girl from their minds and drifted down the steps until, his gaze resting wonderingly on the statue for a long moment, the King inclined his head in a respectful bow before turning with a smile and a sweep of his cloak to follow his subjects.

Kingly Gifts

Exhaustion bettering exuberance as the backwash of adrenalin began to leach from them in shuddering waves, Amber, Racxen, and Mug-kafb sprawled along the sea cliffs, squinting out to the ocean beneath the blinding sun and listening to its triumphant roar. By unspoken agreement, they had journeyed to the furthest, most isolated and exposed corner of the Realm together. This journey had started so long ago with the three of them; and so instinctively the first thing they each wished to do, before their respective clans could pounce with exhaustive questions and endless celebrations the rationale for which they suddenly felt uncomfortably ill-equipped to process, was to steal away together one last time; to snatch what moments they could to simply let everything sink in; to reflect in the presence of friends upon what could not yet be put into words now that something so vast was over. Swapping gazes with the two Arraheng, Amber knew they had made the right choice. *Now* it felt completed. *Now* she knew what they had done was real—had genuinely worked—and that they had truly not only survived but triumphed. Utterly content she lay next to them and watched the dancing ocean, and it wasn't until late in the afternoon that they acquired further company from an unexpected source.

Amber looked up enquiringly as the King approached, but the guardian of Fairymead said not one word. Instead, as he stopped before the trio, he fished into a pocket of his robe and retrieved something Amber couldn't quite see.

"My apologies for the interruption." The flash of sunlight catching glinting liquid colour drained all doubt as King Morgan opened his palm. "This belongs to you, Miss Amazonite."

Amber's widening gaze fixed anxiously on him as she awaited his acknowledgement of his mistake. No one had ever received a second one before; she knew that.

"Nor deserved it more than one who proved willing to relinquish it for another," Morgan noted, seeming to read her mind as she bowed her head and he placed the amulet pendent around her neck in electric silence.

She lifted her face once more, her eyes shining with an elation she could barely contain as a wide grin broke across her face, able now it was over to finally realise truly how much they had all survived, achieved—and become.

Mentorly, he encircled her in his arms. "Be proud of yourself, my child."

As she stepped back, grinning her thanks, the King beckoned to Racxen, another Fairy Gem revealed in his hand. "It is but a trinket," Morgan acknowledged with a smile. "But it means what you want it to mean, and is the most beloved accolade of our people."

Courteously, Racxen knelt before him and bowed his head as Amber had done.

Tying the pendant around his neck, the King regarded him for a second. Then, wordlessly, he dropped to one knee, punching his right fist into the moist earth.

Grinning concedingly, Racxen looked up to meet his gaze, and mutual understanding flowed between the pair as the King cupped the side of the Arraheng's face and calmly smeared a crescent-line along his cheek.

As she bore proud witness to her friend's moment, Amber's heart lodged painfully in her throat to realise that since the disintegration of the tribes this must have been the first time in so long that Racxen had been granted such an honour by an elder in recognition of his efforts instead of, barely into adulthood himself, taking it upon himself to keep such traditions alive as the oldest tracker of his people to have survived the first onslaughts seasons ago.

Rising smoothly, Racxen's eyes followed Morgan's as the Fairy King shifted his gaze to where Mugkafb stood quietly fidgeting, happy of course for his friends and yet feeling slightly out of place and sad.

In their shadows again. The boy scratched mud off his claws industriously to hide his disappointment. *C'mon, don't be such a baby*, he tried to tell himself. *You helped them. Just 'cause no one knows; I mean, Gorfang never got praised for his heroic stuff—*

"Mugkafb? Come on, hero."

Mugkafb jumped. The King—the King of Fairymead who rode Bicorns and spoke with Sea Folk—was smiling, but there was no sarcasm in his ringing tone; and he was beckoning him, flanked by his beaming brother and Amber gesturing both surreptitiously and encouragingly, a wise smile twinkling in his shrewd eyes.

Mugkafb grinned from ear to ear, swamped in excitement as he dashed up to take his place.

Once more, the King dropped to one knee and plunged his fist into the earth, smearing the mud onto Mugkafb's cheek.

As the boy turned back to his friends, shining with pride, Amber nudged him in the ribs. "You didn't think we'd forget you, did you?"

Mugkafb grinned, wriggling between her and Racxen to link arms. "Can we go to the party now? Please?"

A fierce smile stole onto Racxen's lips, his expression distant. "Almost."

Nimbly, he darted across the tumbled rocks of the hill where Amber had so long ago taken her first flight. Reaching its apex, with the Fairy Gem clutched tightly to his chest the Arraheng stood in silhouetted relief against the radiant sunlight, staring down to the flowing canvas of lives playing out in peace once more.

In one fluid movement, Racxen unlooped the Gem from around his neck and flung it as far as he could. With a glittering flash against the skyline as the jewelled facets caught the light it fell, swallowed up by the fathomless green rippling below.

"When the time comes, may it give hope to the one who finds it," Racxen explained, dropping lightly down beside the companions and catching the question in Morgan's approving smile. His gaze rested upon his brother and Amber. "I have all the hope I need right here."

Following his gaze to where the Gem had settled, with a sigh of contentment Amber nodded to herself. To whomsoever chanced to find it, the Gem would be a very special gift indeed.

A smile crept to her own lips as a secret thought struck. "Racxen," she asked, her eyes agleam. "Can you call a Zyfang?"

Seconds later Orbitor exploded through the sunlit sky, shattering the silence with his harsh cry of greeting as he swooped to alight before them.

Quickly, Amber scratched diminutive words onto the back of her Fairy Gem with her fire-flint. Then, stroking his huge unshorn muzzle, with a whispered request she offered her amulet to the Zyfang, who clamped the cord delicately between his teeth, and she watched him launch into the air with a flurry of powerful wing-beats, the precariously swaying treasure sparkling from his jaws until he was lost from view.

Nymph's Journey

Far away at the Enchantress's Fountain, in the ancient chamber that could not be reached save for by air or through the terrible passage traversed and now conquered by one who could not fly, a gargantuan memory long faded from the Sea Battle alighted on an age-old arch of towering calcite. Bowing his great head the Zyfang opened his jaws carefully, letting a glinting treasure fall twinkling through the permanent twilight of the basin.

The Water Nymph snaked out her gnarled hands to catch the trinket. Curling her limbs protectively to her chest she waited, watching with guarded curiosity as the creature flung itself into the air with slapping wing-beats to soar on the updraft and rise, spiralling swiftly until he was lost amongst the vast Realm above that she could remember only dimly.

Alone once more Zaralathaar hesitantly unfurled her fingers, and the Gem glinted on her palm as a solitary shard of pale light pierced shiveringly through the stillness to charge the jewel with the last ray of the day's sun. The ghost of a smile flickering across her face, the old Nymph peered through misty eyes at the scratched inscription:

YOU GAVE ME YOUR BELIEF. I GIVE YOU MY PROOF.

Recognition filtered with a solemn gravity. It had come to pass: that naïve, outspoken girl who awoke legends and befriended monsters had, together with her friends—the fates only knew how—restored peace.

One who cannot fly will walk furthest, indeed: the words rose through the ages, conjuring memories of the enigmatic spectral figure who had appeared amidst the night of all nights and guided her study to the words required to banish the Vetches when it had seemed light would never again return to the Realm.

Even as dusk laid a soft cloak to dampen the light, the act of looking skyward for the first time in so many seasons caused the Nymph's eyes to well against the unaccustomed brightness. Yet the tears did not fall, nor did her gaze yield beneath the slow-climbing moon.

Bowing her head, she settled the Gem's cord around her neck. As she lifted her gaze once more, the years weighing her countenance fell back, and her deepening smile crinkled her haggard face into an expression not unlike that which she had worn so long ago on that first journey to the Southern Sands as a young Sea Maiden swimming proudly amongst her friends and elders. Within her clouded eyes grew a fiercer aspect and slowly, with great care and dignity, the Nymph walked over to the basin wall and muttered ancient words in a tongue forgotten by all but the singers of ballads and the weavers of tales.

As in times of old the stone conceded once more to her authority, revealing shimmering in the moonlight previously unseen steps wrought so many seasons ago that she had blocked them from her mind all these years hence.

Placing a hand for support on the flowstone cascades draping the walls, the Nymph lifted one foot to the stair. Step by step, gaining in poise and purpose she conducted the long, spiralling ascent to the rest of the Realm.

Never hurrying, never slowing, she reached the top of the stairwell and stepped out onto a soft green sea of verdant grass perfumed by a breeze that played across her skin as warmly as any René tide-wind. Shielding her as yet unaccustomed eyes from the wan gaze of the moon, she clutched the Fairy Gem tightly to her breast and gazed out across an unblemished scene stretching further than the deepest oceans she had yet swum and holding as many possibilities as there were sands on the shore.

The tapestry of life was flowing out unfettered once more, filling its inhabitants' minds anew. It was right that they would not miss her too much. After all, she had time enough for but one more . . . what would the Fairy child have called it? Adventure.

Aware of how fast her medium was fading, ice and fire surged within the Realm's oldest magic-wielder and through the mortal heart of a strong and ageing woman as Lady Zaralathaar, the only Water Nymph True Realm would ever have to grace and hold and protect both its shores and seas, began to walk. Amidst singing grasses rustling with the familiar voices of the waves she strode, into a distance swirling with the gathering darkness of the oceans she forsook seasons ago, until the sky deepened into night to envelop her in an embrace as welcoming as the sea she had longed to return to for so long now.

A New Adventure

As the air exploded into fireworks, Amber leant back against the beam of the marquee and stared absently into the sky, trying to work out why she felt quite so, well, weird.

You got used to the adrenalin, that's all it was, she told herself with a fractious sigh. *And now it's leaving you. You'll find your life again. Everything is different, now that it's back as it once was. You can't very well bemoan the fact you're looking back now and feeling lost when it's a privilege to even be here to do so. What price a gift if you refuse to recognise its worth?*

She breathed more calmly now. This would be a night as they used to be: a night of revelry and high spirits, but also a night where Ruby would flirt outrageously with every guy present, point out various would-be suitors and think Amber crazy for not considering them, and leave her dancing by herself for a good portion of the evening. Amber grinned begrudgingly. *Then life really would be getting back to normal.*

As she watched the Prince wander self-consciously through the crowds in an awkward attempt at mingling, his gaze caught hers for a moment and lingered in a gentle, knowing smile. What he was looking at her like that for, she had no idea. She smiled back, though. They had been through a lot. Maybe he could tell how she felt, and wanted to remind her that the bonds forged in those fateful times would not be broken; that some things would change now, of course they would, but that what might henceforth come to pass could never lessen what had once been shared.

Her smile broadened into a grin as Jasper fled embarrassedly from Ruby's advances. Left standing there alone, she took a breath and threw her head back, laughing to the stars. Let the future come and bring what it may—everyone she loved was safe, and she was home again. No one had to dance with her for her to know how graced she was. The food was good, the stars were bright, the night was warm, and laughter floated into the star-flecked sky to entwine with the intoxicating rhythms of the percussive Centaur music catching in her chest as she watched Han dance in the flickering glow of the dancing spiralling, the sparks flying away into a night deeper and clearer than she could ever remember having seen. *You'll find your life again*, she promised herself more firmly. *Everything will be as it should. If you can't make it now, fates help you.*

Grabbing a couple of ribbon-poi, she started swinging. The rhythm calmed her, helped her to breathe again, the movements loosening muscles that had felt like they'd never be able to relax till next Restë, the lights whirling hypnotically until everything else but the moment was driven from her. It had been so long. *See*, a small voice promised. *You can still feel whole again. It'll sink in, if you let it.*

She felt eyes on her now, and she swooped the poi clumsily to the floor as she saw Racxen watching, the firelight dancing in his eyes.

For a moment, neither spoke; it was like they didn't have to anymore. Then, glancing towards the others dancing at the centre of the circle, Racxen held out a hand. "Shall we?" he asked softly.

Her heart slammed. "Okay." It slipped out before she could check it. But the smile that sprang to her lips pained her, for she dared not show how this tugged at her heart; to come so close to what she knew would never be. Yet she would rather bear this pain and see him happy than confess and reveal feelings that so different to his own would cause him hurt; would rather dance with him as a friend than with all of Ruby's suitors put together as anything else.

I can't dance, I can't dance—But as the music ebbed and flowed, and her body moved closer to his, willing, tentative, cautious, he didn't laugh. He didn't pull away. He held her, and they danced.

As the moments flowed, precious and fragile as gossamer, Amber dared not risk to dream ahead, willing herself instead to store each second into memory for the greyer times of the future. *Enjoy it for what it is*, she warned herself. *You've been through a lot together, and now it's over. This is just a friends thing. Ruby dances with all the guys like this; it doesn't mean*—

"Amber." Racxen's voice was soft at her ear now. "Turn around."

Oh, help, she thought desperately, more distraught than she knew she should be. *I've ruined it all and overstepped the mark.* Wretchedly, she turned to apologise.

But Racxen's face was close to hers, and he was gazing into her eyes with a look that made her forget all her worries. A look she'd never seen before from him, and had never wanted to see in anyone else. A look she loved. A look she returned.

And as his arms encircled her tenderly, holding her as safe as his spirit always had, her lips parted to meet his, and their worlds joined, lost and found in each other.

Seconds later, time must have returned, because he was leading her to the side of the dance-floor and in her mind the night was glowing as if flecked with stardust. Not daring to hope of what his touch had fired in her heart, terrified he would at any moment decide it had been some stupid mistake, Amber followed him with her pulse hammering, knowing the whole Realm had just changed for both of them and only dimly registering the night continuing oblivious around them.

Give me back the Vetch Queen's chamber, the wayward thought flitted through her mind irrationally. *At least that had a map. Curses, Amber!*

There's no way back from this. This is Racxen. Racxen! You'll fall apart if it goes wrong!

And die happy if it goes right, the Genie's voice echoed as if in her mind. *You've faced death and despair. Life and love can hold no fear for you now.*

Reaching the edge of the dance floor where the music was quieter and the night breeze drifted with the chatter and laughter of friends milling happily, sipping flutes of dewberry cordial or swigging flagons of dragonfire punch wrapped in their own small and wonderful Realms rendered safe once more, Racxen turned to Amber, taking her hands gently in his. She couldn't stop the thought flitting across her mind that his claws and her fingers fitted together perfectly.

"I thought I'd left such fear behind after the monsters, but I've felt so sick this evening," Racxen admitted with a crooked grin when he could trust himself to speak. "I was terrified I'd misled myself; that if I said anything it would jeopardise what we have. Your friendship means too much to allow myself to do that, it's just—I told myself in the deepest reaches of the unending dark that if we managed to get through this, would speak my heart to you; it kept me going. The chance to try to make you happy," he pledged quietly, "is worth any fear of ridicule on my part: my regard for you is not dependent upon your decision, and whatever your choice I will count our friendship amongst my dearest treasures until I lie under the earth that now sustains me."

Amber struggled to speak against the knot of emotion growing in her throat, frightened that she would shatter this new magic as her vision swept to a future unknown and uncharted—realising that nothing had ever felt so compelling; so safe and so exciting entwined into one. With Racxen: the man who had stayed with her through the longest nights and fiercest storms, who had seen her at her weakest and never lost faith in her courage, who had fought beside her and not forsaken her, and who when nothing else could be done had followed her into the depths to walk beside her, who had dragged her to her feet when she no longer had strength enough to stand, and who had lifted her face to the stars when she had lost all hope of seeing them again. With the man to whom she could now attempt haltingly to express what she had so long denied herself to feel.

"I can't believe you feel the same way," she managed, cursing herself in embarrassment as she felt herself well up, her grin mirroring his. "It's perfect."

Gently, Racxen brushed her tears away with a hand, ever mindful of his claws.

They both jumped as the tower bell rang, clanging through the music and laughter and unchecked loudness of freedom with the reminder of reality when it had felt for all the Realm as if tonight had brought its own time instead, immeasurable by mere hours and minutes.

Amber sighed reluctantly, not wanting the night to end. "Only one hour left till dawn."

Racxen grinned roguishly. "That gives us one whole hour still of darkness."

Leaving their laughter echoing under the marquee, hand in hand they ran with dancing hearts and soaring spirits, slipping away from the crowds to seek refuge in the waiting night together.

Outside in the cool, clear air they found the Genie rippling in the breeze, the colours of the fireworks scattering far above reflected across his insubstantial form. Somehow it didn't surprise either Amber or Racxen that he beheld them both with a proud benevolence thoroughly devoid of astonishment.

Amber couldn't wipe the grin off her face. "Happy endings, huh?"

"Not this time," the Genie prophesised.

Amber stared in protest. "But—"

The Genie grinned, catlike, as he faded. "Some things never end . . ."

Alone once more, under the soft caress of moonlight, shyly their lips met again, and instinctively she let her mouth drift open; this was Racxen who had faded all previous doubts, to whom she had already learned she could entrust her heart and life and of whom no part could feel a threat, and she let her tongue—

She felt him pull back, and stopped immediately, ashamed. "I'm so sorry, we don't have to—"

"Amber, it's not that," he promised wretchedly, with a look of such tenderness she knew she had found forever in those eyes. "It's just—in Arraheng culture, it is believed the soul resides in the mouth; in the tongue. I just—I can't ask you to take this Goblin-tainted soul into your own."

"Racxen," Amber whispered, stepping closer, her smile rising. "Afford me the honour of making my own accursed mistakes."

He laughed quietly, understanding. "Sen . . ."

Softly, oh so softly, their lips met, kissing twice, thrice, and as his breath came harder Racxen stepped in closer; so close that Amber melted into his embrace, her arms sliding to entwine round his neck. Her eyes closed of their own accord, the feeling blooming too intense to cope with more than one sense at a time as his hands strayed lower. Ruby talked about drowning in kisses, but this was like—like coming back to life; and as she opened her mouth to let his tongue meet with hers she felt their connection catch through her whole body. Clinging to him she gasped and stumbled, his scent filling her lungs as they tumbled to the ground. "Why doesn't this feel like surrender?" Amber murmured, her voice hoarse with emotion as his softest touches brushed electric across her body.

"Because it never will be," he promised, his voice meltingly warm in her ear as he brushed back her hair with a claw as he had in more frightening times now an age away. Taking her hand in his, keeping his eyes locked deeply into hers he pressed his lips against her fingers in a soft, sealing kiss.

　　　　　　　　　　　　　　　　　　　Earth-Bound

"That's," she gasped, grinning ridiculously at the memory, her whole body tingling beneath him, "how close I feel to you even when we're not touching."

"Soul to soul," Racxen murmured, his eyes glittering in the darkness.

"Always have been," Amber promised. "Always will be."

Above them, fireworks soared and burst, showering the Realm with new-claimed hope.

"Tell me," he pre-empted, his eyes soft and encouraging as Amber's courage stalled, a question hanging unformed on her indrawn breath.

"Sorry, I've got used to having to stop myself thinking like this," Amber admitted with an embarrassed grin. "It's so wonderful to be able to now. I was just thinking about that night . . . that maybe we could . . . now that the fears of that time have faded, you know, like . . ."

An amazed smile spread slowly across Racxen's face. "What we shared then will be inscribed forever in my memory," he admitted in a whisper. "It felt deeper than anything I ever let myself dream was possible, and to return to it in better circumstances is a precious gift I never dared hope to be possible for all the magic still left in the Realm. But Amber, I need you to know that I love you whatever we do or do not; if we never went further—"

She nodded. "I know. It's what makes me know anything we share will feel just as special, because it's us." Her heart overflowed as she stroked her hands across the contours of his body, marvelling at the soul within. She bit her lip, suddenly shy. "How can this be; to find a best friend and lover all in one?"

Laughing softly, Racxen rolled her playfully into a tighter hug. "I was going to ask you the same question."

Wrapped in his arms, held so close and safe, she had to laugh back out of pure happiness: it felt indescribable to be able to do so after the nightmares of recent times, and as his kisses and his touch welcomed her and she wriggled closer, nestling her cheek against his chest and feeling the strong pounding of his heart as if it beat only for her, it was as if nothing had changed between them; could ever change in the way that Ruby said happened when you took this step. This newly allowed desire could never usurp the utter reassurance and comfort of his presence, nothing they might share in the future could make joint memories from their past less cherished, and neither 'lover' nor 'friend' could come close to describing half of what he would always mean to her.

As if reading her thoughts, holding her tightly like he'd never let her go again, Racxen breathed a deep, contented sigh, as if the weight of the past had lifted in this moment and everything had finally become right again.

"Engo ro fash," Amber murmured appreciatively, drinking in the moments with every fibre of her being, not wanting to risk losing the preciousness of these new memories after the long, long arduous perils they had been through together, as overhead fireworks burst again into a myriad of stars to bathe the night sky with golden warmth.

A young voice floated to them on the air, and with a start Amber scrambled to her feet, laughing self-consciously at her own embarrassment.

"Engo ro fash," Racxen whispered, squeezing her hand in reassurance. "I would love you to the ends of both our lands—and the whole of True Realm—even should we never have another moment alone. But wish it, and there will be other nights." He grinned. "All other nights."

Amber grinned back. "Sounds like a promise," she murmured.

Racxen's smile widened. "I've got a feeling it's going to be binding."

Striding up suspiciously, Mugkafb glanced appraisingly at the pair of them, and rolled his eyes dismissively. Then it was as if nothing had changed, as he tried in vain to hide a yawn, and shot a disapproving look at the Prince who was now just visible against the rising dawn's pink-streaked sky amidst the darker hues of night yet unshed. "Jasper says the beds are made up at the castle and that I have to go to sleep. I don't, do I? No one else is going to! It's not fair."

Amber grinned. "C'mon, you want your appetite back for the celebration feast tomorrow—well, later today—right? I'll read you a story to help you sleep, how about some of the Legends? Find your book and I'll meet you there in a second."

Mugkafb screwed his face up in indecision, and then acquiesced with a grin, racing back to tell Jasper.

Amber sighed deeply, every sense attuned to the hand gently resting at the small of her back; the soft breath by her ear; the unfailing, strengthening presence beside her who had guided her through the darkness even when he was not there in body. "I don't want to move," she confessed, half-turning. "It feels so strange that I'm allowed to tell you."

Racxen stepped closer; so close she—

"I'm sorry," he whispered, turning his head slightly, but holding her gaze as she looked into those deep, dark, compassionate eyes that reflected now the feelings he had for so long dutifully silenced. "I should let you go," he finished guiltily. "I just—I keep fearing that this is a dream brought on by the delirium of what we have faced, and I don't want to wake up, and find that I'm right . . ."

Amber stopped him then, with a kiss of her own. "We proved perfect companions through the worst of nightmares," she reminded him softly, gaining the courage to trace her hands across his body in an echo of his actions. "I think we're perfectly entitled to share the best of dreams."

She felt Racxen's breath as if it were her own, as he rested his brow against hers, his hands trembling with emotion as his claws gently brushed her face, as if he couldn't quite believe she—and this—were real. "Curse you, Fairy, you're making this too difficult," he teased, his laughter as soft as his touch, his lips so close as he spoke that Amber realised she had moistened her own with her tongue in anticipation, her own breathing even more unsteady now. Amber grinned embarrassedly. "Sorr—"

But the rest of her reply sank away into his kiss as his lips found hers again and their souls entwined, soaring to the stars to the combined rhythm of two hearts irrevocably joined for so long, now finally beating as one.

Beginning

"And they all . . ." Somewhat later than she'd intended, Amber turned the last page to whisper the final words, smiling in the darkness at the young Arraheng already fast asleep, worn out by his adventures. ". . . lived happily ever after."

She closed the book quietly and slipped out, carefully pushing the door to before padding outside to stand hand in hand with Racxen as fireflies danced and hopes mingled with stars as the future stretched out joyously without fear.

Together with the King and Jasper, Yenna beside him, Tanzan chatting animatedly with a delighted Ruby, Han and the Genie, Rraarl watching fierce and proud and calm above, they watched the sun rise in triumphal golden splendour, emblazoning across the optimistic purple hues of pre-dawn to herald the beginning of a new era of peace for all peoples.

Yes, Amber thought, contentment spreading through her. *They all lived happily ever after.*

And so will you.

Far, far away and yet somehow not so, somewhere between tomorrow and a long time ago: against a once-again peaceful shore, a Gem scudded the ridges of the shallows, tumbling amidst playful lapping waves and gleaming with the iridescent hues of the fireworks bursting high above.

A seal-like shape smoothly parted the star-scattered reflections of the deep, glittering phosphorescence streaming in its wake as it nosed towards the sparkling treasure. Probing whiskers brushed it lightly, in an exploration as gentle as a thought.

Vestiges of an old power lingered at the surface—the seal-like one sensed it as clearly as if the Water Nymph were still holding it—but it was the younger spirit thrumming embedded within which drew this sea-born soul. Plucking the Gem reverently from the shallows, the figure sank out of sight, as swift and mysterious as a dream—a dream readying itself to be re-conjured.

Acknowledgments

As the culmination of *Air-Born*, *Earth-Bound* has been part of my heart for even longer, so it means even more to me to be able to share it with you. Releasing these stories into the world has been an unforgettable adventure, and I will always be immeasurably thankful to everyone who has been part of that—particularly those of you who bought those first editions and who I met at those first conventions—and most especially those of you who have shared with me what *Air-Born* has meant to you; I am truly honoured and humbled and I hope *Earth-Bound* has done justice to the chance you took when you picked up *Air-Born*.

I really hope you will join Amber, Racxen, and all your favourites in the next instalment of their continuing adventures: *Sea-Drawn*. It'll be their best yet . . .

Fly free!

About the Author

As a qualified Occupational Therapist with a Master of Arts in Psychoanalysis and experience working in a variety of psychiatric settings, Laura is especially passionate about using writing and other creative pursuits therapeutically to help children, teens, and adults cope with and recover from mental illness and trauma. A steadfast believer in the value of fantasy as a nurturing space and safe escape, she draws inspiration from everywhere wild and magical and seeks to both celebrate and inspire the indomitable nature of the human spirit through her writing.

Lightning Source UK Ltd.
Milton Keynes UK
UKOW01f0857300616

277390UK00002B/54/P